The Road To Riches

Suzanne Schreder

May God Bless You!

The Road To Riches

Suzanne Schroeder

Columbus, Ohio

The Road to Riches
Published by Gatekeeper Press
2167 Stringtown Rd, Suite 109
Columbus, OH 43123-2989
www.GatekeeperPress.com

Library of Congress Control Number:

ISBN (paperback): 9781662905865

Foreword

Bob Huggens walked through his fledgling pecan orchard studying the saplings; planning and dreaming of the time when his investment in these trees would finally begin to pay off. He had cleared the land the year he lost his job as the gardener at the Lile estate. He tried various agricultural endeavors with little to no success. Finally, he bought the pecan trees. He didn't realize at the time how long the process was...he just knew he would need something to carry him through retirement.

On impulse Bob sank to his knees next to one of the trees. He prayed for the trees to flourish, to produce, to give him and Mae a prosperous future. When he rose to his feet a good 15 minutes later, he thought how uncharacteristic that eloquent prayer was for a simple man like himself.

Bob would always remember those moments in the quiet spring sunshine. He was always careful to give God the glory for the success of his orchard and credited that year's spectacular weather conditions and the beginning of his trees producing nuts to that time on his knees. But with all that happened before the next spring, Bob wondered if he had somehow made a pact with the devil.

Contents

Contents   vii

Chapter One

George Jacob Ray had been unable to settle down in one location for any length of time since he graduated from high school; now he was ready for a new adventure. Actually, George was always up for adventure as long as there was money involved. He needed money and lots of it to keep him happy — money was his security and the altar at which he worshipped. And he had an idea that just might pan out — but he needed the perfect place and he wanted it warm.

As he drove through Alabama he paid little attention to the scenery though he had never been in this part of the south before. He was currently engrossed with going over yet again what it would take to establish his new identity when he arrived at the place, wherever it was, where he would settle. George had always considered himself lucky to have been given three interchangeable names, and he figured this time he would use Ray Jacobs as his identity. Jacobs seemed like it had a nice "Southern" sound to it. It didn't really matter to him as he was used to being called by his surname anyway. Drill sergeants and prison wardens had a way of doing that.

He remembered how much he had hated being called Georgie as a boy. One foster mama would call him in for supper with the biggest yell any woman had ever had! The sound of that lilting

"GEEEEOOORGIEEEEE," was audible anywhere in the Texas town where he was living. Sometimes he thought the whole county could hear her. Then the boys would pick up the chant, "Georgie Porgie, puddin' and pie..." Oh yes, he would be glad not to be George any more!

That memory brought back others from his childhood. He remembered the time in grade school when he took a box of his foster daddy's pens, the ones with the logo for his insurance company on them. They were pretty cool and he sold them at school for a quarter each. That ended when a rival insurance salesman saw his son using the pen....come to think of it, that was probably the beginning of the end of that foster home, too. In junior high he had a foster brother about his same age. They hatched a plan to steal high-end bicycles, repaint them, then sell them. They convinced Mama that they had a business giving makeovers to kids' bikes. It was a successful operation — until some kid saw them taking a bike and tattled! That earned George his first Juvie appearance. It was the end of another foster home, too. Seemed like most of the trouble he got into was because he always wanted more money than he legitimately had. He still considered that the best home ever though — because of the brother, Weasel.

The one constant in his young life had seemed to be church. Living in the heart of Bible-thumping country, all his foster parents were addicted to church. George went along mainly because he found it fascinating to think about what would make a whole mess of people follow one preacher. He always wondered what it would be like to have that kind of influence.

The only fly in the ointment that George could see was that he had to leave Weasel behind. Weasel had come to Minnesota when George called him, and it was good to know someone always had his back. He knew Weasel was aware that he might plan to change his name; after all, Weasel had crafted the new ID. Although people would say that they were *only* foster brothers, and that *only* for about 4 years, neither of them took that into consideration. In the way they thought they were closer than brothers had any right to be. He was confident that when he was successful, he and Weasel would get back together.

Chapter Two

Early most mornings in the downtown area of Pecan Grove, Alabama, people could count on several things happening. The first occurrence was the rhythmic thump of the morning newspapers hitting doorsteps as the paperboys bicycled through town. So far, most people in Pecan Grove liked getting their news on paper rather than on the computer. Mark Griffiths was one of the paperboys for the Southern Gazette. Though he was only twelve, he was shaping up to be one of the best yet at hitting every porch step dead-on without hardly so much as touching his handlebars.

Mark had become accustomed to getting up early for his paper route, although at first it was difficult to get out of bed at 4 am, a time his dad referred to as "o-dark-thirty." But by the time he had pedaled through the dimly lit streets to pick up his papers, he was fully awake and found that there were interesting things to see and learn in the quiet streets. The rattle of a trash can usually meant he could catch sight of a raccoon, or even a family of raccoons, raiding someone's garbage. Sometimes a possum would slink across the street too. He kept a close eye out for skunks though, that was one animal he sure didn't want to run into!

And, if sometimes he saw someone who didn't want to be seen, well, it wasn't any of his business, was it? Like the gal who regularly climbed the rose trellis behind her home at about 4:45 am. Being fairly new to town, it wasn't as if he recognized many people anyway.

The next reliable morning occurrence in downtown Pecan Grove was that at 5:30 am the constable on duty, who was usually young Jimmy Fletcher, would stroll leisurely down Main Street peering into the windows of the yet-to-be-opened shops. He thought he looked smart in his well-pressed khaki pants and uniform shirt -- and he did, if you like short skinny guys with big noses! Ostensibly, Jimmy was making sure everything was shipshape before the start of another business day. Not too many residents were fooled. They knew Jimmy's stroll was a way of getting from the police station on the east end of Main Street to the Garden Cafe on the west end of Main while still on department time. He needed his morning coffee and gossip fix.

Ruby Carter's brisk jaunt through town was the third event that people could set their watches by. At the same time every morning Ruby could be seen walking from her small frame house just south of downtown to her job waitressing at the Garden Cafe. She needed to be there when the cafe opened for breakfast at 6:00 and she was never late. Every morning she left home at exactly 5:40 and arrived at exactly 5:55. Walking to work was one of the ways Ruby saved money. Her old Chevy would still take her to the city if she needed to go, but she saw no reason to waste gas driving across Pecan Grove. Her legs were still good enough whatever the weather — she hadn't melted in any rainstorm yet.

This morning was no different, but since early February mornings could be a bit chilly, Jimmy Fletcher was wearing his official lined khaki jacket. He liked the way the black fleece lining emphasized the style of the jacket. He was oblivious to the fact that his professional appearance took a hit when he walked with his hands in his pockets.

Mark was enjoying the cooler mornings because tossing papers could be hot work, although he looked so nonchalant. He was meticulous in his own way and he wasn't going to miss a beat as he biked, rolled papers and tossed just because it was a little frosty.

A careful observer might notice that Ruby wasn't just walking briskly this morning (her usual style) as much as marching. That is, if a grandmother with the beginning of arthritis in her knees could be said to march. Ruby was worried and it showed in her military and precise footfalls. It seemed as if she felt that if her steps were ordered, her life would be ordered as well. As she walked her thoughts were centered on Zeke, her much beloved but undisciplined grandson. He had landed on her doorstep yet again last night. Although Ruby loved him with all her heart, she knew he was heading for trouble with a capital T. She wondered how much it would cost her this time before he shuffled off on another harebrained scheme. Ruby's march ended at the door to the Garden Cafe, but her thoughts were no more ordered than when she started from home. There was no help for it; she would have to put on her smiley face, cloak her worry with chat and charm, and rake in some good tips today. She knew Zeke was going to cost her, one way or another, and she'd better be ready.

———

The bustling town of Pecan Grove was immediately appealing as one drove down Main Street. Storefronts were well kept and doing a thriving business with cars parked on both sides of the wide streets. If a town could be called sleepy and bustling at the same time, that would be the impression Pecan Grove gave to a visitor: sleepy because it seemed a little shabby and outdated; bustling because people were out and about tending to business.

It had been a long and frustrating journey through several southern states for George, who was beginning to get used to going by Ray Jacobs. He had taken side roads, back roads and winding roads, looking for that perfect town, which he thought should have a combination of down-home friendliness as well as an element of wealth and prosperity. He felt that any town he settled on needed to have a variety of churches, employment opportunities and professional services, all without being too big. Driving toward Mobile through more forested country interspersed with cotton fields and groves of well-tended trees, it began to seem that that perfect town didn't exist.

When the highway he was following intersected with another main route, Ray found himself in Pecan Grove. Situated near enough to both Mobile and Montgomery to attract commuters, the town had an area of new construction; he noted the high end homes with approval. As he neared the downtown area there was a section of beautiful old homes with spacious, well tended lawns and gardens. Main Street had beautiful historic buildings which had been repurposed into a variety of different shops. At the end of Main Street he came to the Garden Cafe and, impressed with what he had seen so far, Ray stopped for coffee and breakfast.

In the mornings, the Garden Cafe did a thriving business as the locals swarmed in when they opened for their breakfast. Seemed all those who were headed off to work needed their morning coffee, a bit of gossip and maybe a donut or two. After the first rush of commuters came a slight lull until the shopkeepers from town came in for breakfast before opening their stores for the day. By ten o'clock things had settled down before the lunch rush with just the old timers lingering over coffee and a good long chat.

Sarah Jane, the buxom blonde hostess, seated Ray at a small table near the center of the restaurant. "You must be new to these parts," she said, and Ray got the distinct impression that she was flirting with him.

"Well," he replied in the same light tone, "if I had known *you* were here, I would certainly have come sooner!" It was lame, even to his ears, but he was out of practice.

Sarah Jane didn't seem to care. "You have yourself a great meal then, and maybe our cooking will keep you in town awhile," she said, laying her hand on his shoulder and bending close to his ear. Ray got a good whiff of her rose-scented perfume and a glimpse of ample cleavage. "Hmm," he thought, "maybe there are more benefits to Pecan Grove than I expected."

Just then Ruby bustled over with the coffee pot. "Looks like y'all could use a little liquid energy." At Ray's nod, she deftly turned over his cup and poured steaming hot coffee, all while reciting the breakfast specials. Ray felt right at home with the southern drawl — he could almost feel the patterns of speech that his Texas upbringing had imprinted on his brain land on his tongue again. He never had blended with those dang Swedes up in Minnesota.

"Yeeeeahhhh," he drawled, "That there Joe hits the spot alrighty."

As Ray ate his meal he managed to listen to the conversations around him. Much of what he heard was local gossip that didn't mean much to him, but he memorized the names and stories just the same. It was an old habit and one that had stood him in good stead many a time. He noticed Sarah Jane's friendly banter with the customers, but saw her big blue eyes frequently stray in his direction. Each time, he gave her a grin or a quick wink. Yes, this town just might be allll right.

When Ruby stopped by to refill his coffee cup, Ray asked about places to stay in town. "I'm plumb tuckered out from driving for three days to get away from Minnesota," he said. "Where can I get a room? Preferably one where I could stay a day or two — or more — and be comfortable?"

Actually, Ray had stayed a day or two in several towns across the south since he left Minnesota, but that was beside the point. None of those towns had suited him for one reason or another. Pecan Grove gave the most promising first impression, but there were many factors he needed to consider before he settled down.

"Well, there's that new chain hotel out on the highway," Ruby mused. "But if you're staying more than a few days, my friend Bella has a few rooms for rent that are really nice. I think she has a vacancy right now too. I can give her a call and check if you'd like."

"I could just drive over and see, so I don't put you to any trouble..." Ray was secretly delighted at Ruby's offer.

"Oh, no trouble at all!" Ruby was already punching in numbers on her cell phone. After a brief conversation it was all set. Ray could move into the front corner bedroom on the third floor of Bella's large home as soon as he liked.

———

As Ray left the cafe, Ruby thought about what a nice man he was. He was so polite, attentive, and personable. She sure hoped he found Bella's room comfortable and that he would stay awhile, maybe find a job and settle in. Pecan Grove needed younger blood because too many of the next generation had moved to Mobile or Montgomery. There was no place like Pecan Grove to raise a family, though. It was Ruby's personal opinion, and one she expressed loudly and often, that the trouble with her grandson, Zeke, could have been avoided if his mom hadn't been so uppity and determined to move her family to "the city" where "the kids would have all the advantages." Pecan Grove might not have art museums and arboretums, but the people had down-home values, and that was much more important as far as Ruby could see!

But it seemed the younger generation didn't care much about values and that had caused many families to leave. Now the town could use an influx of cash from a few new families buying homes, shopping for groceries — AND spending money at the Garden Cafe, especially if they tipped as well as Ray Jacobs. Didn't appear that Sarah Jane would be adverse to Ray sticking around either. But that girl never met a man she didn't flirt with. Not many were as good looking as Ray though. And he seemed to be more clean cut than most of the guys she'd taken to hanging out with. Ruby couldn't exactly fault the girl. There just weren't that many fellas around to pick from once you came close to your thirtieth birthday.

Sarah Jane's thoughts paralleled Ruby's, although she wasn't about to let the older woman know. But she couldn't stop thinking about Ray; the way he wore his dark brown hair a little long so it curled on his shoulders. What she wouldn't give to be able to run her hands through that silky looking mop! And when he grinned and winked at her, those adorable dimples....well!

Ever since her junior year in high school, Sarah Jane had suffered a reputation around town as a loose woman. "That stupid party," she thought. "Will I ever live it down?" Overall, it hadn't really mattered. She had enjoyed dating and flirting with a variety of men, and if she had to fight them off after the first date, oh well. But lately she had been noticing that almost all the guys who asked her out were divorced, with a whiny ex-wife and a couple bratty kids. It seemed they never wanted to take her anywhere fun — they just wanted to sit on the couch, drink beer and watch television. Probably why they were someone's ex.

Sarah Jane was ready for a serious romance with someone who wasn't on the biggest loser list. She wondered if this new guy was involved with someone back wherever he came from. He certainly was intriguing and she wondered how he got to Pecan Grove. It wouldn't hurt to find out more about Ray. She liked what she saw so far!

Sarah Jane "overheard" that Ray was going to rent one of Bella's rooms, and she determined that she would just have to be in the vicinity of Bella's house a little more often. She wondered if it would be too old fashioned to take Ray a welcome-to-town gift of some home-baked cookies. She figured if she ever wanted to date someone respectable again she would have to take the initiative.

———

Ray didn't rush on his way to Bella's. He took a little time to meander the streets. He noted that the homes were well kept, the streets broad and tree-lined, the cars mostly newer models and clean. He passed a Methodist Church, a large Baptist Church and a Catholic Church that were all within a few blocks of the town square, which also boasted the county courthouse. From the conversations he had overheard at the cafe, he knew there must be a seedier part of town, but it hadn't crept into the area he saw. He noted that there were small signs that the town needed a boost: the Little League park had grass growing in the basepaths, the sign on the city hall needed repainting (or upgrading to digital), and the public library announced reduced hours.

He saw the neatly lettered sign announcing Bella's Bed and Board before he could read the house numbers. Bella's place was a three story Victorian with all the gingerbread trim one could hope for. The garden looked well cared for and he could imagine the colorful display of flowers in the spring and summer. The house itself would need repainting soon, but it still gave off a genteel air. He rapped smartly on the door.

The third floor corner bedroom at Bella's Bed and Board had been occupied for the past five years by Rupert Hammond. It was one of Bella's most expensive rooms, so she had been dismayed when Rupert decided to move nearer to his son in Arizona. She had been fretting over the loss of income ever since he left five months ago. There just wasn't as much call for a boarding house anymore. That apartment building they'd built on the south side of town was taking her business! People said she should turn the Bed and Board into a Bed and Breakfast but that would take a major remodel and redecorating. At nearly seventy years of age, Bella wasn't feeling up to the work or the expense. Truth was, she wished she could move closer to her children too. They only lived as far away as New Orleans, but she wouldn't mind having someone she could count on if her health failed.

Today Bella was waiting on the new gentleman lodger that Ruby was sending over and she couldn't quite figure out what was taking him so long to get from the cafe to her place. After all, one only needed to traverse about eight blocks of Main Street, turn left on 6th Street and go up the hill for a few blocks. While she waited, Bella dusted the parlor. Not because it needed dusting, of course she had done it yesterday afternoon as she always did, but because she wasn't one to sit idle for long. She liked to think she was following the admonition in the Bible: "Redeeming the time, because the days are evil."

That was another thing about Bella: she prided herself on her ability to see evil in the folks around her. Some people were known to whisper about Bella, calling her 'Batty Bella' when they thought she couldn't hear, but it didn't bother her much. Just another example of the evil around her. Where was that lodger, anyway? Ah, that must be him at the door now. She hoped he wouldn't balk at the price of Rupert's room.

The large room with a view of the town in two directions pleased Ray immensely. He could see all the way to Main Street from the one window, and from the other he could see east to where the highway entered town. It was perfect for his purposes. He figured he could live with the list of rules and regulations Bella had recited with *emphasis* – for the time being, anyway. Quietly he mimicked Bella's high-pitched nasal whine, "Gentlemen are on the third floor, ladies are on the second floor. The doors on each landing leading to the bedrooms are *locked* and only accessible with the *proper* key. The rooms on the first floor are common rooms for mingling and dinner. Dinner is served *precisely* at 5:30 pm. If you wish to partake of the evening meal it will be $5.00 a day extra, and you *must* pay for the entire week in advance... " Oh, shoot (Ray had to remember to keep his oaths mild), the rules were even posted on the bathroom door! No TV in the bedroom, but at least the place had WiFi. Ray sat down at the desk, opened his laptop and began to record his impressions of Pecan Grove....

Chapter Three

O thers might say that justice had been served, and that George Jacob Ray had done his time. But he would not forget— could not forget— and he had no desire to forgive. To his way of thinking, George Jacob Ray had cheated him out of his inheritance. The lawyer said there was no proof that his father was not of sound mind when he signed over his house, his securities and his bank account to the man who had been his companion. And when George was finally prosecuted, it was for a different matter. That's not what he called justice.

Yeah, so he hadn't been to see the old man for ten years and they hadn't parted on very good terms either. Who could have known the parsimonious old bugger was worth that much? That money, the cool half million, should have been his. He'd get it back from George — with interest, if possible!

Almost all of the citizens of Pecan Grove were on the rolls of ONE of the many churches in town. If they didn't attend regularly, they weren't about to advertise that to their friends and neighbors. Although the owners of the Garden Cafe were among the minority who didn't claim a religion, they had soon bowed to the general will of the residents and closed on Sundays. For one thing, they kept losing staff who refused to work on Sunday morning. Second, no one came for breakfast or, for that matter, for lunch either. Apparently a home cooked Sunday dinner was a *requirement* for "Grovers."

Sunday morning found Ruby on foot again. She was one of those who believed that regular attendance at the worship service of your choice was part of being a good citizen, a good example to your children and neighbors — and it was also a good source of gossip, if not gospel. Although it looked like it might rain later, Ruby was prepared with her water resistant jacket and umbrella. At least the temperatures were a touch above average today.

As she entered the front doors of the First United Methodist Church, she was surprised and pleased to see that Ray Jacobs was already there talking to Reverend Findley. On one of Ray's visits to the cafe during the past week she had mentioned that the Methodist church was full of friendly people and he could network for a job there, if indeed he was serious about settling in Pecan Grove. Looked like he was following her advice.

As Ruby went to hang up her jacket and umbrella, she noted that Ray was now talking to the head usher. And if she wasn't mistaken, there was Sarah Jane hovering nearby. Well, if Ray could get Sarah Jane to come to church, that was reason enough to convince him to stay in town! Before Ruby could even get to her usual spot, which was in the fourth pew from the front, aisle seat, Ray spotted her and made a bee-line over to her. "Thank you Ruby!" he gushed. "I've been talking to some of the folk here, and they sure are as welcoming as you promised. I even have a line on a couple jobs that I might be interested in," Ray chuckled a little self-consciously.

Ruby was spared a reply when Sarah Jane and her mother interrupted to ask Ray to sit with them on the other side of the church. She almost laughed out loud as she watched Sarah Jane and her mother, the indomitable Cora Windham, try to outdo each other in introducing Ray to their friends (and enemies) as they made their way to their usual pew. Ah, well, Ray WOULD get a taste of Southern hospitality now.

When Ruby's friend Jeanine slipped into the pew just as the organ started to play, she whispered, "Who IS that young man the Windhams are so intent on showing off?" Ruby barely had time to reply that Ray was new in town when the song leader stood up to open the service. She knew the subject wasn't closed and that the usual gang would be twittering about Ray later. At least it would be a break from the usual tired gossip and would keep her friends from probing too deeply about what Zeke was doing now that he was back in town. That was another reason Ruby was glad Ray had come to church.

———

Ray was making good use of his first weekend in town. Saturday night he had attended the mass at St. Stephen's. Although he didn't find any "kindred spirits" there, he made a point of being noticed, at least by a few eligible ladies (and their mamas). After the early service here at the Methodist church, he planned to take in the service at the large Grove City Baptist Church. It was a Southern Baptist church and it was nice that they had two Sunday morning services. Ray figured it was in his best interests to be known about town as a devout Christian. He was aware of how church people tended to associate mostly with others of their own religious persuasion so he didn't figure there would be much overlap in the afternoon gossip groups. Probably no one would notice that he was bestowing the honor of his presence so widely.

Ray was pleased that the Methodist service was more contemporary than the Methodist church he had visited in

Minnesota. He liked the lively songs and choruses they sang with a piano accompaniment better than the slow, ponderous hymns and organ music that were so common in northern churches. Ultimately, he hoped to find a pastor with a personality he could get along with. He needed someone respectable and with some influence around town to befriend him so he could ride his coattails into the kind of society he wished to associate with. It might take a little time, but so far, everything was moving in the right direction. And Ray had a little time, thanks to a legacy from his previous *generous* employers.

Chapter Four

Business was booming at Sim's Computer Repair. When John Wayne Simonson started the business in Roseville, Minnesota, he thought he would be like a doctor for ailing computers. However, as time went on, he found that it also gave him insight into a variety of illicit operations going on around him. It was amazing what people thought was hidden on their computers when in reality, a third class hacker could easily access all their private information. And Wayne Simonson was much better than third class. If he did say so himself.

Never in his life had John Wayne been called by his proper name. His parents had always called him Wayne. His brother gave him the nickname Weasel because he could usually weasel his way out of punishments. The nickname stuck, because by high school he had perfected an innate understanding of technology, and could weasel information from any device.

Usually, Weasel ignored any incriminating information he came across. Oh, he might let a hint of what he had seen slip out if a customer was late paying or otherwise reluctant about the fees he charged. That usually got them to open their wallets quickly. Occasionally though, there was enough evidence on the machine that Weasel felt compelled to warn his customer of possible repercussions. Then he would introduce them to his sideline - a false ID. George had suggested that kind of work to him, and it was really lucrative, but one he didn't care to undertake too often. Too dangerous!

Somehow, George had convinced Weasel to make a couple fake ID's for him. He'd gone on about the new security measures they were building into Minnesota driver's licenses and how Weasel really needed to practice duplicating them. It was a valid point, and despite Weasel's initial reluctance, George made it seem so *logical*, so *fun*, so *harmless*, that Weasel had eventually complied. As usual. They worked together until the technique was mastered, and it was only later that Weasel started thinking about the repercussions of giving George access to quality alternative identities. Then Weasel began to worry. What might George be planning now, armed with two or three different names?

The pool hall in Pecan Grove was an eyesore as far as the self-righteous, upstanding members of the city council were concerned. The building itself was in poor shape and the clientele was comprised mainly of younger folk at loose ends; unemployed, uneducated and unmotivated. However, the owners paid their taxes, the location was on a backstreet on the edge of downtown and there was nothing to be done about it except to have the local constabulary keep a close eye on the business.

Zeke didn't really feel as if he fit in with the crowd at the pool hall. But coming back to stay with Grandmaw Ruby, he found there wasn't much place for a college dropout like him to hang out in Pecan Grove. So oftentimes he could be found midday meandering aimlessly toward the pool hall. He didn't really have the money for playing pool. He didn't have the money for a movie either. Shucks, he didn't even have the money to buy himself a coke. Maybe he could go by the Garden Cafe.... Grandmaw Ruby had said no more handouts, but a couple times he'd run into that Ray Jacobs guy there and Ray would spring for a donut or two. Ray was a really decent guy; never minded talking to a younger man and never made him feel like a loser.

Deep down Zeke knew he had messed up, but he wasn't going to come out and say that to Ruby. He loved his grandmaw, but he didn't need another self-improvement course from her. He *should* have found a way to finish technical school. He had only a couple credits left before he would have had a degree in web design and computer graphics. Now no one would want to hire him — although he was as good as anyone else out there! 'Course he could maybe get freelance work, but that would involve scrounging around, asking, advertising himself... Zeke just wasn't that motivated.

If only one of the enterprises he'd been involved in had taken off the way it was supposed to! Yeah, looking back he could see a couple of them were harebrained schemes. Like that website he bought back in high school to sell miracle vitamins. The website was only 35 bucks! And they promised he'd make thousands every month. So far, so good, right? But then, when he didn't get any business in a couple months, he spent a few thousand of the college fund Ruby had scraped up for him on "marketing help." That's where he really got sucker punched. There had been a few more of those schemes. Ruby was on his case about his "impulsive behavior," but the real trouble was that Zeke wanted money and he didn't like hard work.

Computers now — that was a different story. Zeke could work at a graphic or web design for hours and it was more like play than work. That's why he should have finished his degree. That's why he got as close as he did, but the latest opportunity was *such* a great idea. And they had to move fast. And he couldn't do all that his buddy Brad wanted and study, too! So he quit.

Thing was, he still hoped the business would make money, but it was taking way longer to catch on than he and Brad had anticipated. Brad's cousin was a former Atlanta Falcons player and he'd put Brad in contact with a mess of other former stars. They figured people would pay for a subscription to a site where they could get live game-day commentary from former players, with background information and even chats with former stars. Zeke had built a killer website and Brad had started to get the players on board, but the customers were too suspicious. They thought there must be an NFL rule against what the site was offering and that if they got involved they'd be sued. The pittance he and Brad were making didn't begin to cover rent and groceries. So he left Brad in Louisiana and moved back to Pecan Grove to live with Grandmaw. And here he was — contemplating his disreputable past, his distressing present and his dismal prospects.

Elise and Jason (Jase to his friends) Griffiths had moved to Pecan Grove ten months ago when the Bethel Bible Church called Jason to become the youth and music pastor. It was a step of faith because with six kids the salary was only going to cover the basics. They were able to buy a big, old house that had enough space and was solidly built. Yeah, it needed some fixing up and wasn't in the best part of town, but it worked for them. Jason supplemented their income by doing some carpentry around town and he helped the boys run a mowing business — that brought in quite a lot of money, both for the boys' college funds, and for the family grocery bill. Mark, their oldest boy, had landed a paper route, too. Of course, with two teenage girls and four growing boys the grocery bill alone was astronomical!

This morning, after the kids helped themselves to breakfast, which was usually just cold cereal or toast, Elise rushed them into getting their chores done before Bible time, which was always the beginning of their homeschooling day. "Megan, get the floor swept pronto! Morgan, those dishes aren't going to jump into the dishwasher by themselves!" she admonished as she dashed through the kitchen on her way to check on the boys. As usual, Matt and Mark had their beds made (sort of) and were arguing over whose turn it was to walk Jethro. Elise wished there were some way of turning back time so she could say an unequivocal NO to getting a "watchdog." Yeah, Jethro would watch any burglar walk off with the jewels, as if they had any. "Matt, get out there and run with Jethro! Mark, run the vacuum through the schoolroom." Elise was still searching for the perfect system where the kids were motivated to get their chores done decently and in a timely manner.

The little boys were wrestling on their bedroom floor. Elise giggled a little as she watched them quietly for a moment. They were still so cute but she marveled that by 5 and 7 years of age they had so quickly outgrown the baby stage. "Micah, Miles, did you get your chores done?"

"What are they again, Mom? I forget," Micah, the master manipulator, replied.

"Well, did you check the bathrooms for toilet paper? Did you put out water for Tinkerbell? Have you cleaned the bathroom sinks? Get on it now!" She knew none of those things were done. "Hurry up! Today is library day."

Chapter Five

∽

He knew when George left Minnesota, but didn't understand how he had missed knowing about his plan to leave. Although he tried to act like he knew what he was doing, he was new at this surveillance business. He casually asked his acquaintances - he liked to think of them as his informants, - but no one knew anything. What if he dared to ask the one they called Weasel? He'd heard they were close like brothers... No, that would tip his hand, and Weasel might warn George. He would just switch to watching Weasel. That wouldn't attract attention and Weasel might eventually lead him to his brother...

The month of February had been warmer than average in Alabama, although still cool by southern standards. Folks were jawing about "global warming" and "disappearing polar ice caps." Bob Huggens had lived in Alabama long enough — shoot, he had lived long enough, period — to know that the weather was variable and he figured global warming had little or nothing to do with it! He had been busy working in his grove of pecan trees, fertilizing, mulching, tilling and aerating the soil. He was hoping they didn't bud too soon and get clipped by a late frost. He loved his small farm, but trying to make a go of it was difficult. The pecan trees were a lot of work to get started; hopefully it would be work that would eventually pay off. At least they weren't going to escape and get into his neighbor's gardens like the goats he had been raising had!

Ray found the cooler weather tolerable. He figured he had built up a little immunity to cold while he was in Minnesota. Although the February mornings could be frosty, Ray was glad to be out of the bitter cold. When he lived in Minnesota, he felt as if he had been living on the Siberian tundra. Even in the summers, when everyone complained about the heat, he had been cold. And the people, man, they were colder yet! There was none of what he considered Christian warmth in the suspicious Scandinavians that populated Minnesota. Ray thought that was probably why they were attracted to the frozen north: the cold weather resonated with their cold hearts.

Ray had taken to spending his mornings walking through town and chatting with the shopkeepers and charming the ladies. Nearly every day found him at the Garden Cafe for a late breakfast. He enjoyed watching Sarah Jane flit around the restaurant, stopped by almost all of the guys with some pick-up line or another. "Hey Sarah Jane, why don't we ever see you down at the Fish Hook anymore," or "Sarah Jane, I'd love to have you be my *permanent* hostess." Sarah Jane deflected all passes with a friendly but evasive manner. He wondered a bit why all the girls were so cool to her.

Both Sarah Jane and Ruby looked forward to the morning visit from Ray as a welcome distraction from the tedium that was February. After all, Ray was so much the opposite of their usual clientele, being handsome, interesting *and* funny; he could make the day sparkle with just a wink. Often during slow times he would stop to chat — an added bonus for the women.

As Ruby watched Ray leave the cafe with a jaunty wave, she was still chuckling over his last joke. "Oh but he's a smooth talker all right," she thought. "And Ruby-girl, you've always been a sucker for a smooth talker. Just like your late husband." At least Ray seemed more successful than her husband had ever been.

By afternoon the weather had warmed a bit and Ray had taken to golfing at the local country club. He had paid for a year's membership the week after he arrived in town and he was finding it a good place to meet the well-to-do members of the community. At first Ray had golfed alone, but after a few weeks he was pleased to find that he often ran into Pastor Will Stewart from Grove City Baptist and was asked on more than one occasion to join their group. It seemed one of their regular golf foursome had moved away and there was a gap that they were happy to have Ray fill.

After nearly a month in Pecan Grove, Ray finally asked Sarah Jane out for a movie and pizza. They had a good time whispering during the show, holding hands, even sneaking kisses and generally acting like a couple of high schoolers. At Mario's Pizza Parlor the conversation got a little more serious. Sarah Jane was determined that she was not going to waste her time on another guy who just wanted to find out if she was as easy as everyone said. "So, Ray, I notice you haven't got a job, and don't appear to be looking for one," Sarah Jane stated. "I've been involved with my fair share of losers, and I'd like to know something about you before I spend more time with you. What brought you to Pecan Grove and what kind of work do you plan to look for now that you're here?"

"Well, I haven't really wanted to make this too public, but I guess I can trust you to keep my secrets," Ray replied, speaking in a near whisper. "Thing is, when I was in Minnesota I finished my degree in Bible. But what really held my interest was some classes I took from the Online Trading College. It's where you learn to trade stocks and futures on the stock exchange," he explained at her blank expression. "I think I have a knack for knowing what the next big thing is, especially in tech gear and software. So, with a little inheritance money from a grandma I never met, I'm able to cover my living expenses and focus on investing. Fact is," and Ray's voice sank to just a breath of sound, "I've already more than *tripled* what she left me. And I think I'm onto something *really* big coming up soon."

Sarah Jane listened with wide-eyed attention, leaning forward to catch every word. She breathed an excited "wow" or "I see" at all the right places. This was more like it! Ray might be a wealthy man - not just a good looking and respectable date!

As for Ray, he figured he had about 24 hours before the fact that he was making money on Wall Street was well known all around town. He couldn't envision a better result.

Ruby spent her evening at her desk, calculating how far she could stretch her income from waiting tables at the cafe and the miniscule amount of social security from her late husband. The number of days he'd worked during their marriage was so small, she wasn't entitled to much. Honestly, Zeke was a lot like him. They both expected that the train to wealth was coming around the bend and would surely stop for them! Her husband's funeral expenses had drained nearly all of the little bit she had saved up for her own future and Zeke had squandered the money she'd saved for his education. Ruby knew her knees weren't going to hold up to waitressing forever. The arthritis was getting gradually worse and she figured she'd be "one of those women" who needed a knee replacement, possibly two. What was she going to do for income then? It took awhile to recover from those operations. She had kind of been hoping that Zeke would be able to get a good job after he finished school and maybe help with her expenses a bit — like pay some rent or something. "I guess that boat has left the harbor," she thought resentfully. But ever since his mom and her new husband had moved off to California, she felt responsible for her grandson. Where, oh where, was she going to find some additional income?

Chapter Six

Today the pastors' wives support group was meeting for lunch as they did every Wednesday at 11:30. Elise liked getting away for lunch and she usually enjoyed talking with the other women who all had husbands in ministry at one of the churches in the area. She really couldn't afford to go out to lunch every week, but Nancy, an elderly lady at church, had heard she was missing the luncheons. When she realized it was because of money she started slipping a ten dollar bill in Elise's purse on Sundays.

So, she went. She didn't want to disappoint Nancy. Each week the ladies met at a different local restaurant. Being new to town, she just went along with their suggestions; as far as she was concerned any meal she didn't have to fix was delicious! This week they were meeting at the Garden Cafe which was a nice central location. The Griffiths had been there for breakfast before and Elise was looking forward to trying their lunch special.

As soon as she walked in she noticed that Sarah Jane was much more animated and friendly than she had been when the family had come for Saturday donuts last month. While she waited for the group to straggle in, she heard Sarah Jane fielding some teasing comments from other customers about her "new man."

"Well, there's nothing like a new love interest to lend a spring to your step," Elise thought.

As the group settled in to talk, Elise asked if anyone knew who Sarah Jane was seeing. Kari, the wife of Will Stewart who pastored the Grove City Baptist Church, dismissed her fella as "probably another low life type she picked up in a bar." But another woman said she had seen Sarah Jane and a nice looking, clean cut guy at the pizza parlor last week. Laura, one of the more outspoken women, stopped Sarah Jane as she headed back to the hostess stand to ask.

"We heard through the grapevine that you're seeing someone new, Sarah Jane," she simpered. "What can you tell us about your new man?"

Sarah Jane didn't have much patience with Laura, but she couldn't resist a chance to brag. "Ray is new to town, Laura, so *you* probably haven't met him yet. He's staying at Bella's B&B right now, but I think he's maybe gonna buy a house soon. He's quite wealthy, you know."

"Wait!" Kari interrupted. "Ray — as in Ray Jacobs? Why, he and my Will have gotten quite friendly! I think they're playing golf right now."

Sarah Jane grinned. "Yep, that's Ray! Oops, gotta go - customers!" She sailed back toward the hostess stand with a little wave.

Kari wasn't done. "Ray Jacobs is a thoroughly *nice* man. How he got interested in that piece of *white trash*..." Her hiss was loud enough to be heard at the nearby tables.

Kari's friend Joan placed her hand on Kari's arm in a calming gesture. "So what looks good on the menu today?" she said brightly, then whispered, "We'll figure it out later, Kari."

Elise nearly choked on her ice water. She shot an incredulous look at Gina Kirkland, the senior pastor's wife at Bethel Bible Church. Gina looked bewildered and shrugged helplessly. "What brought that on?" Elise wondered silently.

Sarah Jane maintained her composure, but barely. Inside she was seething. As if that scheming, manipulating, hussie didn't know the whole restaurant could hear her! she thought. Well, Ray *was* a thoroughly nice man, but he was *still* a man! And Sarah Jane had considerable experience in knowing what a man liked.

Ruby had heard the entire exchange, and she could see the play of emotions on Sarah Jane's face. "Oh-oh," she thought, "Now it's war!" She figured Kari had her eye on Ray as a suitor for her spoiled and demanding daughter, Kristen. Probably not much competition there, she thought, although one couldn't be sure of Ray's motives and interests.

As Kari and Joan left the cafe, they stopped in the parking lot to talk. "It doesn't really matter one way or another," Joan said. "Even if Sarah Jane has turned Ray's head right now it won't be long before he realizes that she has nothing much to offer him. From what you've told me, he's intelligent and personable. A dumb blonde won't keep his interest long."

"I suppose you're right, Joan. But I had so hoped that Ray would take an interest in Kristen. She's not getting any younger, you know."

Joan didn't really know Sarah Jane, Kari thought as she drove home. Although her bubbly personality gave the impression of an empty head, Kari remembered that when both Kristen and Sarah Jane were in high school, Sarah Jane often scored higher on tests than Kristen. Unlike Kristen, Sarah Jane had never cared about academics, preferring to spend her time with the dance team and cheerleading squad. Yet school just seemed to come easily for her. And didn't she practically run the Garden Cafe? The owners trusted her to do all the hiring and scheduling.

Will was enjoying golf much more since Ray became a regular member of their foursome. Will's golfing game was abysmal, but the men that completed today's foursome were always interesting. Will and Ray were joined today by Dr. 'Doc' Radcliffe, a surgeon at the hospital in nearby Jackson, and Rob Porter, a lawyer with a long family history in Pecan Grove. Both men lived in the ritzy historic district and both attended Will's Baptist Church. Ray was in a great mood and was, as usual, keeping the golf game interesting. "Will," he exclaimed, "every time we play this dang course either you or I hit a ball into that sinkhole! I tell you, I'm not letting that hole claim another ball. I'm going to play it no matter where it lies!"

When the others saw where his ball had landed, which was just on the edge of the muddy center of the sinkhole, they encouraged him to just take the penalty because there was no way anyone could hit it out of there. "Ray, the rain last night made that dry sinkhole into a pond!" Rob said. "There's no ground for you to get a decent hit."

"No, I can do it! See?" Ray straddled the ball with one foot nearly in the pool and one foot balanced on the steep side of the hole. As he lined up his shot the others watched in a combination of amazement and horror. He took a great swing at the ball and hit it right out of the hole. However the club head was driven into the side of the sinkhole and Ray was thrown off balance, falling backward into the muck! The watching trio couldn't help themselves and dissolved into gales of laughter. No one could even summon the energy to see if Ray was all right. They had almost recovered when Ray sat up in his muddy glory and asked, "Wasn't I right? I DID hit it out of here, didn't I?"

Later, after Ray had changed his clothes, the men sat in the clubhouse over refreshments. Ray was at his most affable as he subtly questioned the men about their interests and difficulties.

He casually mentioned that he was interested in perhaps buying a house in the historic district - if his "prospects panned out." Of course that piqued the interest of all three of his companions, but he coyly refused to say more "at this time."

Laura went home from the ladies luncheon and immediately called her daughter, Lisa. She hoped it was naptime at Lisa's Loving Land, the daycare her daughter operated out of her home, but whatever, this was too important to wait. Daryl, Lisa's husband, had been fired from his job at the hospital a year ago. Laura thought it was a foolish choice when he took classes to get his realtor's license. Everyone knew there weren't that many people moving into Pecan Grove! But Lisa didn't want to give up her business, so Daryl decided this would keep him in town. "Just not in money," Laura often fumed.

"Lisa! So glad I caught you! How are you today, dear?"

"I'm as busy as always, Mom. But I know you didn't call to find out whose diaper I'm changing. What's up?"

"Well, you know that today was the day the pastors' wives met for lunch, right? And we happened to hear that there is a young man in town who just might be looking to buy a house. I think it's new knowledge and Daryl should go see him right away! His name is Ray, and Sarah Jane said he's staying at Bella's — he should be easy to track down."

Lisa nearly groaned out loud. Her mother meant well, but she was always trying to drum up business for Daryl. Lisa knew it stemmed from Laura's embarrassment over Daryl's being fired from his job as a surgical tech at Jackson Memorial. Her standing among her peers depended on Daryl to be a success, for Lisa's business to thrive and for their children to be star athletes and on the honor roll. "OK, Mom, let me write this down...."

Lisa hung up the phone 15 minutes later with a sigh. She had just heard all the gossip Laura had collected at her luncheon. Most of the news centered around what the other women's children were doing, how smart their children or grandchildren were, what new possessions they all had acquired... Lisa thought the pastors' wives support group should be renamed. "Gossip Girls" came to mind.

There was some truth, though, to Laura's assertions that Daryl could have made better choices for his career. The surgical tech job didn't work out because Daryl got clumsy when he was stressed. That resulted in valuable sterile instruments being dropped on the non-sterile floor, rendering them unusable until resterilizing, and sometimes broken entirely.

But real estate was stressful too. Daryl's slight stutter became quite pronounced when he was faced with a high profile client. And therefore, the amount of money his real estate venture brought in was negligible — well, at least he *did* sell *one* house!

And then there was the situation with the daycare center. Lisa was licensed for 14 children. At considerable expense they had converted the first floor of their old Victorian into a well stocked and cheerful day care. There was a playroom with multitudes of toys, two nap rooms, and a separate bathroom/diaper room. The yard had been fenced and outfitted with toys for all ages as well as a sandbox. The kitchen area doubled as their family kitchen too, but the rest of their living quarters were on the second floor. There they had a living room, three bedrooms and a roomy bathroom. The only thing lacking was the fourteen kids. There were Lisa and Daryl's three, who were all under 5, and three others. And only four in Lisa's Latchkey Kids program. They *needed* Daryl to step up and make this sale!

Laura wasn't the only one who got on her phone as soon as lunch was over. Kari immediately tried calling Will, but he must have still been on the golf course. So she left him a quick message, "Invite Ray to come for supper tomorrow." She figured that she needed to step up her matchmaking schedule: it was apparent that she didn't have as much time as she thought. Kristen was already 27 years old and there weren't many eligible bachelors around. Whyever hadn't she snagged a guy while she was in college like normal girls did? Her daughter thought all the fellas were interested in her, but Kari didn't notice any guys hanging around, and there certainly was no ring on her finger. She needed a boost from her mother.

Sarah Jane managed to be charming and friendly to the customers at the Garden Cafe for the rest of the day. She "got back" at Kari Stewart and her cronies as she hinted about her love interest and mentioned that he was wealthy; she casually let it drop that Ray made his money in stocks and she may even have let it slip once or twice that he was coming up on a big deal that would set him up for life. But she wasn't really telling Ray's secret, she rationalized. She was just letting others know that she was Ray's confidante and special friend. Sarah Jane understood that in Pecan Grove what people thought was happening was often more important than what actually happened.

When Jase came home from calling on some teens after school, Elise was waiting with a cup of hot coffee and chocolate cookies the girls had baked that afternoon. All the children were occupied, and she wanted a few minutes to talk before the inevitable rush around supper. She began by asking her husband about the calls he had made, knowing there were a couple of troubled teens he was trying to reach.

"Ah, that Kennedy boy wasn't interested in talking. I finally caught up with him at the pool hall. You know how I hate the way the place is packed with all those smokers and some of them are smoking something illegal, I'm sure. But that's where you find the kids. There was a new kid there though, name of Zeke. Out of high school for a few years, I'd guess, but he seemed to be at loose ends. I talked with him awhile. Seems he dropped out of tech school and is now sponging off his grandmother. He has no money and no ambition, which is when a kid can fall into the wrong company! Claims to have a church home, of sorts. Although it seems it's more his grandma's church than his."

Elise told Jase about her luncheon date with the other pastors' wives. "Kari was positively nasty about Sarah Jane seeing that new man in town! Have you run into him at all, Jase? His name is Ray... something or another...and he's living at Bella's right now."

"Yeah, I think I met him when I went out to breakfast with Kent," (Jase was referring to the "senior" pastor at Bethel Bible Church, although Kent Kirkland was actually a few years younger than Jase.) "He seemed nice enough. Kind of a fakey charm though. Like he's trying too hard or something. Golfs with Pastor Stewart from Grove City Baptist and his buddies, I think. But I heard tell he's been to the Methodist Church too. That's about all I know about him. Why?"

"I don't know. Kari just seemed so ready to defend this Ray guy, and she looked like she wanted to scratch Sarah Jane's eyes out. I just wondered what about him fueled such passion on her part."

Just then Miles came in howling with blood dripping down his leg and a huge rip in the knee of his jeans. "I got hurted when I skateboarded down the hill!" he wailed. Elise picked him up and carried him off to the bathroom for bandaids and a touch of lavender oil. She sighed over the loss of yet *another* pair of jeans.

Chapter Seven

W hen Wayne "the Weasel" Simonson allowed his thoughts to stray from his usual regimen, he wondered again how and what George was doing. He was closer to George than anyone in his family, in fact, with both his parents dead, he hadn't kept in touch with his sister at all. When George came to live with them when Weasel was nine, they had connected at an elemental level and boy did they have fun! Most often it was trouble — but George could make even the most mundane tasks into a game. Like the time they were charged with picking potato beetles off the field of potatoes his family raised. George decided that it was too boring to just pick them so he suggested they make it a contest; they would flick the beetles at the bucket and see who could make the most baskets. They ended up in trouble for that, because they got to laughing so hard they spilled the entire bucket of beetles right back in the potato field.

George always shouldered the blame for all their shenanigans, but after George got sent to Juvenile detention for a stint, Wayne's folks seemed to give up on George. The Simonson family moved to Oklahoma, making no attempt to keep George as part of the family. He got bounced around to a couple more foster homes and then back to detention. When he got out just before his 18th birthday, he was sent to a halfway house until he came of age.

Everyone expected it was just a matter of time before George got put away for good. So it was a surprise when, just after Weasel graduated from high school, he got a call from George. "Hey bro! I think I'm going to enlist in the Army. Want to join up with me? It'll be like old times when we shared a room!"

Wayne was living with his father after his mother's death, and he had to think about that idea for all of about five seconds. "Sounds good to me! Where do we meet?"

The army picked up on Wayne's talent for computers and codes quickly. He was taught to decode encrypted messages, find lost data on computers and given a lot of responsibility. George didn't fare so well. He hated taking orders; he had always hated taking orders. Therefore he was often disciplined for insubordination and worse. Eventually, the Army decided that they needed to part ways, though George didn't seem to mind the dishonorable discharge because he was so glad to be free.

Wayne stuck it out. His work with computers was interesting and he had really expanded his knowledge. But it wasn't as much fun without George and then came the deployments to Afghanistan. He re-upped once, but began to long for something more exciting?... and then George called again. This time, he had a scheme that involved going to Bible school in Minnesota. Imagining George Jacob Ray in Bible school had Wayne doubled over with laughter! But that last tour in Afghanistan had been brutal so, just as he had when he was a kid, he yielded to the irresistible force that was George, took an honorable discharge, and moved to Minnesota.

Kristen Stewart was basically happy with her life, and with herself. She had a job (although not too strenuous a job) as the children's librarian. Since the library was only open three full days and Saturday mornings, she had plenty of time for her active social life. She had a group of friends who *adored* her, always fawning over her clothing choices and laughing as she made fun of other people. Kristen considered herself to be quite witty, and she was *definitely* the only one of her crowd who had a *professional* job. Kristen *knew* that she could have *any* man in town, most likely any man in the *county,* but she was holding out for a *rich* man. Even though her job wasn't hard, she would prefer not to work at all. She felt that someone with her heritage as the last of the great *Lile* family shouldn't have to go to work like some *commoner!*

Unfortunately for Kristen, there were very few people who agreed with her assessment. Most people thought Kristen was lazy, self-centered, and catty. What Kristen considered witty comments, others found to be snide, cutting and mean-spirited. The girls Kristen considered her loyal friends and fans were younger girls who had never fit in with others their age. They liked feeling a part of a clique, especially one headed by someone as well-known as Kristen. And all those admiring men? A mere figment of her imagination; they were merely polite because she was the pastor's daughter.

So when Kari told her daughter that Ray Jacobs was coming to dinner and she was expected to be home, on time and dressed appropriately, Kristen immediately called Beth, one of her group of younger girls. "Sooo," she drawled, as only Kristen could, "what *shall* I wear that will *please* Mother-dearest and *still* knock his *socks* off? *Mother* said he's *rumored* to be *rich.* Maybe he's *worth* my *time.*"

Beth had never met Ray and she never really had any thoughts of her own so she suggested perhaps Kristen should wear the new outfit she had purchased the last time they went to Mobile. "Oh, I think that's too *plebeian,*" Kristen sneered. "*I* think the *sheer* blue blouse with the deep v-neckline, don't you *agree?*"

"Oh yes," Beth breathed, although she privately thought Mrs. Stewart would hardly find that outfit *appropriate.* And Pastor

Stewart was sure to be appalled that his daughter even owned anything that suggestive — if he noticed Kristen at all. Beth was often privately glad that she could count on *her* parents to tell her the truth about her actions, even though Beth made every show of disgust when they corrected her. Come to think about it, one of the things they harped on most often was Kristen's appearance and her influence on Beth. Kristen's parents, on the other hand, seemed too busy working in the church and volunteering in town to pay much attention to her. Beth thought she had heard that Kristen had been mostly raised by her grandma!

When Kristen made her *entrance* at dinner the next night, her mother's gasp of dismay was covered by Ray's bark of laughter which he barely disguised as a cough. He wasn't sure if Kristen's outfit was driven by an ego larger than life or by gross immaturity, but either way, it was a sight to behold. The diaphanous blue blouse and skintight pants only served to emphasize the boyish flatness of her figure; not to mention that the color washed out her pale complexion even further. The elaborate swept-up way she had styled her hair drew attention to her long, overly made up face. And the way she posed on the stairs like a runway model showed that she hadn't a clue as to how foolish she looked. Ray thought it was too bad she took after her father, not her mother. The same features that gave Will Stewart a rangy handsomeness made his daughter resemble an anorexic stick horse.

As dinner began Kari Stewart started her not-so-subtle third degree questioning. Ray had gotten to know Kari in a superficial way at a church fellowship dinner, but he had no clue her charming exterior covered a mother with a lawyer-like taste for cross examination. "Did you graduate from college, Ray? Where did you go? How did you pay for college?"

Ray described his desire for more Bible knowledge, how a church acquaintance with Minnesota connections had suggested

Ray go to a small Bible College in Minnesota, how he quickly found out that his modest savings and a gift from his latest foster parents wouldn't cover living expenses and tuition, so he'd had to find work and continue his education as he was able.

"So Ray," she continued, "someone was telling me that you're quite wealthy. Now how did that happen if you were working your way through school?"

"Well," Ray confessed, "it didn't happen too fast. I was working as a companion to an elderly man and he had made his living off the stock market. He loved to chatter about his gains and losses and the thrill of chasing the next breaking trend. At first I just dismissed it as the ramblings of an old man. But I gradually grew interested although I knew there was no way I had enough money to get started in trading stocks. And I had no education in the matter either. But on the radio I heard ads about the Online Trading College's free course. I took that course then signed up for another. I also took every class the college offered on business along with my Bible studies. But I still had no money to get started for myself. I was praying that God would bless me but I wasn't sure what kind of miracle it would take. I scraped together just enough to get started with a small purchase...and I guess the rest is history."

Kari, Kristen and Will were hanging on every word. "That's very interesting, isn't it Kari? " Will enthused. "Maybe I should look into doing some investing. What do you think?"

Ray laughed and hedged a bit. "Let me research it and we'll get together to talk about it?" he proposed.

The rest of the dinner was unremarkable except that Ray was hard-pressed to remain charming and engaging while deflecting the marriage innuendo directed at him from Kari and the physical contact directed at him from Kristen. Ray wondered if Kristen was really interested in him or if she just needed the attention of everyone around her. He suspected the latter.

As Kari went to get dessert Ray said to Will, "So, I don't mean to bring up a touchy subject or anything, Pastor, but why are there no African-Americans attending your church? I thought there were a lot of Black people of the Baptist persuasion."

Will hung his head. "I'm a little ashamed about this part of Southern Baptist history, Ray. And I'll admit that I really don't know how to go about changing anything. You see, when the country was gearing up toward the Civil War, the Southern Baptists decided to split from the General Baptist Convention. And the reason was slavery.

"Many of the wealthy plantation owners were Baptists, and they wanted to keep their pro slavery views *and* their religion. The Southern Baptists convinced themselves that slavery was supported by the Bible and they had a holy calling to preserve that way of life."

"Interesting! I guess it's no wonder the Black people founded their own Baptist churches then."

"Yes, and I'm afraid that after the war as the Methodists and Presbyterians became more liberal they began to allow black citizens to join their churches. Many of the most aggressive supporters of segregation joined the Southern Baptist churches where they could find more traditional thinking."

"And most of us Southern Baptists still like it that way, right Dad?" Kristen interjected. "I mean, it's great that African Americans can get an education and all, but some things should be separate, right?"

"Yes, I'm aware that there are those in our church who still consider African Americans to be a substandard race. It's sad they can't see the bigger picture."

Ray was somewhat appalled that there were still people in America as bigoted as some he had run into here in Alabama. He had never considered race all that important. If someone was willing to be his friend, why worry about skin color?

Chapter Eight

One of the things that brought the men of Pecan Grove together was the weekly gathering of a group that called themselves the "Book 'n' Brews" which met at the Grove Microbrewery and Restaurant. Although the group was informally run by Reverend Findley from the Methodist Church, there were regulars from almost every church in town. Their motto was that "beer is God's way of telling us he wants us to be happy," a saying loosely attributed to Benjamin Franklin. This kind of group was right up Ray's alley as anything remotely religious was a fair topic of conversation. Reverend Findley had been suggesting topics for each discussion alphabetically. "So, most of you know that for the last several months we've talked about "A" words in the Bible. This month, we're still talking about "B" words. We've talked about Belief and Brotherhood - tonight let's talk about Blessing." After the discussion swirled around for a while, Ray offered the opinion that God is just waiting to bless us. As proof he referred to the Bible passage in James: "You don't have what you want because you don't ask God for it!"

This started a whole new line of conversation with some of the men insisting that God doesn't always bless with material blessings. Ray was quite persuasive mentioning several passages from the Bible, as well as instances and anecdotes, that proved his assertion that God is just waiting for people to ask so he can bless them with riches and honor.

After the discussion died down and the gathering was starting to disperse, Daryl Marshall approached Ray. Ray vaguely knew him from previous Book and Brews sessions and had heard he was trying his hand at selling realty. From Daryl's slightly unsteady gait, it appeared he had done more imbibing than Bible discussing, but who was Ray to judge? "M-m-mister J-jacobs?" Daryl began. "I'm Daryl Marshall, and I h-h-heard that m-m-maybe you would be looking for a h-h-house in town?"

Ray almost felt sorry for Daryl. Almost, but not sorry enough. He thought Daryl might be just the kind of guy he was looking for. "Why, yes!" he replied. "Are you selling one?"

Ray and Daryl agreed to meet at Daryl's office the next morning. He hoped that Daryl's head wouldn't ache too much from the hangover he was sure to have. After all, he wanted Daryl clear-headed enough to sell him a house AND be his first customer for the investment business he planned to start.

Elise and the kids finished up school quickly on Friday. They were planning to head out to Chuck and Nancy Bender's house for lunch and planting in Nancy's extensive vegetable garden. Chuck and Nancy seemed to know everybody, having lived in Pecan Grove forever, and Nancy was often able to get free seedlings and seeds for their garden. Trouble was Nancy was getting older and really needed some help planting, watering and weeding. So when she heard that Elise was used to a big garden, but had no room to plant one, it was a "match made in heaven," she said. Elise looked forward to visiting and working together with the older woman. After moving so far from home and family, it was nice to have a mentor. Elise talked to her mom nearly every day, but it wasn't the same as having her right across town. The kids looked forward to running through the woods and field, jumping on the trampoline and helping in the garden (in that order). Actually, the older ones did drive the 4-wheeler and pull flats of seedlings from the garage to the garden so they thought they were helping! But soon the time would come for weeding, and Elise had all but the little boys trained to pull weeds.

As they worked Elise decided to ask Nancy what she thought of Kari's outburst at the Garden Cafe the week before. It had really been weighing on her mind, and because she had little history of the town folks, she hoped Nancy would be able to enlighten her. She cautiously brought up the subject as they were working side-by-side to get the 6 flats of cabbage seedlings planted, although privately Elise wondered what they would ever do if all that cabbage produced!

"I wonder what you can tell me about Sarah Jane Windham," she ventured. "Has she lived in Pecan Grove for a long time?"

"Oh, let's see....the Windhams have been around since before the town was designated the county seat and that would have been when the town was still called Grantsburg! There are tales of old Elijah Windham who must have been a true eccentric. He was said to wander around town offering to do a little spot of work for whoever needed help, but he was also very wealthy. I think his daddy was a sea captain or something and he didn't need the income. He spoke out against slavery to anyone who would listen, which made him no friend of the plantation owners, you can bet! His son Elijah Junior, however, was a different matter. He acted like the world owed him a crown if not the kingdom. He refused to serve for the Confederate army because he was against slavery, but wouldn't serve for the North either. Instead, he ran off to Canada. When he returned after the war, he found the family decimated;

his daddy dead of the yellow fever epidemic, the family fortune confiscated by the Rebel Army, and the remaining residents bitter that he had run away. He had nothing and ended up becoming the town drunk, begging for handouts, and living off his wife who was a barmaid. His descendants have been around ever since. Some of them have been hardworking and others lazier than a possum. Cora and Sarah Jane Windham are the last of the Pecan Grove Windhams; Cora likes to think that the family's lengthy history in the town makes her important, but others remember that Elijah Jr. was too cowardly to stand with either the South or the North. Seems like we still can't escape the Civil War."

"Wow, that's quite the story!" Elise breathed. "I guess there are a lot of tales in a town as old as Pecan Grove. I wonder if I'll ever get them straight!"

"You're a bright girl. You'll figure it all out with time."

"While we're on the subject, what about the Stewart family? Do they have history here too?"

"Yes and no," Nancy mused. "Will Stewart is from eastern Oklahoma. Kari Stewart grew up here in town, though. She went to school in Dallas and met Will there — her family owned the textile mill, you know."

"No, I *didn't* know that!" Elise was surprised. "What was her maiden name?"

"That would have been Lile." Nancy replied. "It's too bad Kari's dad was a gambler. He had to sell the mill to pay gambling debts and shortly after that he died of a heart attack. Kari was quite bitter at the change in her family status; she went to college as the daughter of one of the wealthiest families in the county and came home to a grieving mother and greatly reduced circumstances. She and Will were already engaged and Will had been offered an assistant pastor position here in town. Otherwise, I think she would have gladly gone elsewhere. When she and Will finally had a child,

Kristen, it seemed Kari didn't really know how to care for her. Her mother, Geraldine, was only too glad to help and raised Kristen nearly single-handedly, aside from Will and Kari indulging her with too many toys, clothes and compliments! It was hard for the family when Geraldine began having memory issues and moved to Florida to live with Kari's older sister. I don't think Jackie had ever married, although she's been away so long I'm not sure."

"So, the other day Kari really lashed into Sarah Jane — called her white trash — loud enough to be sure Sarah Jane, along with half the restaurant, heard. Do you think that had roots in the town's history?"

"I think it's more recent than that," Nancy chuckled. "The girls, Sarah Jane and Kari's daughter Kristen, have never gotten along. Kristen always acts so high and mighty and Sarah Jane is so bubbly and flirty, but they never bothered much with each other. Neither Geraldine nor Kari ever got over losing the historic Lile house, you know, so they were thrilled when young Drew Pearson started showing an interest in Kristen." At Elise's puzzled expression, Nancy backtracked a bit. "You see, the Pearson's had purchased the Lile home from Geraldine. You could almost hear the wedding bells ringing in their brains! Kristen would marry Drew and they would get back their precious house.

"Until… one night, oh I suppose it must have been the summer before their senior year, some kids threw a wild party. There was drinking involved, and for whatever reason, Drew and Kristen were there, and so was Sarah Jane. Rumor had it that sometime during the evening Drew disappeared on Kristen and she was frantically looking for him. He was finally found — with Sarah Jane, of course — supposedly in a rather compromising position. At any rate, Drew was shipped off to West Point, the romance between him and Kristen ended, and Sarah Jane took the blame. And is still taking it, I guess."

Chapter Nine

Pecan Grove was somewhat of an anomaly in Alabama due to its large collection of antebellum homes. Most of the communities in the south had suffered heavy damage when the Union army swept through during the Civil War. However, when General Wilson was making his march through Alabama and Georgia, he met a small contingent of Confederate soldiers just outside of town. The Union army quickly overpowered them and took control of the town, which was at that time called Grantsburg. The town barely escaped destruction — and that was only because of a hoax.

Locals loved to tell the story of their hero, Dr. James Heffelfinger. As the story goes, the Union army had several wounded soldiers so, as the troops swarmed into town, they demanded to see the doctor. He treated the wounded and casually let the soldiers know that the town was in the midst of a smallpox epidemic. Although this was untrue, the army didn't take a chance on finding out for themselves, and left quickly.

After the war the town folk wanted to get rid of the Grantsburg name so no one would think they were honoring a Union general. A petition was circulated encouraging the town council to rename the town Jameson after the good doctor. It seemed they at least recognized that Heffelfingersville wasn't going to fly! However, some of the town fathers demurred, citing nearby Jackson and saying it would be confusing. The good doctor himself suggested that if they were determined to change the name they should rename the town for the natural stand of pecan trees on a nearby hill.

Many of the historic homes were still standing and, by the 1950's, they were beginning to draw tourists into the town. It wasn't long before the citizens of Pecan Grove realized their gold mine. They placed many of the homes on the historic registry, began to actively promote their heritage and initiated celebrations in honor of the history represented there.

The grand old buildings on Main Street were carved up into shops that served the tourist trade. The Grand Hotel was home to an elegant restaurant and some of the rooms had been refurbished as a luxury hotel while another wing hosted office suites for lawyers and other professionals. The old Courthouse, a prime example of Queen Anne architecture, was a popular destination with two stories of shops including a fudge shop, a quilting shop, a pecan roastery and many more. Most of the historic residential properties had been passed down from one generation to another. Oftentimes they were still known by the names of the families that built them or the family who had lived there the longest.

When Ray and Daryl met to discuss real estate in Pecan Grove, it became clear that Daryl wasn't expecting much from Ray. "So, are you l-l-looking for a townhome? Maybe a small c-condo? S-something where you won't have yard work, I'd guess?"

"No, Daryl, I want a place that can be, or already is, a showplace. I would *really* like a place in the historic district with a garden and room to entertain. I want to show what God will give us if we *ask*!"

Surprised and pleased, Daryl thought through the residential properties in town. Were any of the bigger showy homes for sale? No — but then he thought of the old Lile place. It had been sold to the Pearsons for something less than its true worth when Henry Lile died and his widow was facing more debt than even the sale of the mill could cover. It had been one of the grandest properties in town years ago, but when the Pearsons' son died in a military helicopter accident, they began to withdraw from town functions to spend more and more time at their lake property. The house had been neglected for several years. Now Daryl wondered if they might be ready to give it up. What a coup that would be. Sell the Lile House!

"Let me call about a certain place I have in mind. It's not actually listed yet, but I think the owners might consider selling, for the right price. It's a large Italianate style home on the edge of the historic district near the river. It has quite an extensive garden — but it might need a bit of refurbishing. Do you think you would be interested?" Daryl was so focused that for once he didn't even stutter!

Chapter Ten

Weasel had been an introverted child, so shy he would never even raise his hand in class. His mom tried to get him out of his shell by enrolling him in various activities, all of which caused him extreme anxiety. He was happiest with his books and legos, and whenever he was allowed, the computer.

Looking back, he figured that taking in a foster child his own age was his parents' last ditch effort to draw out their son. And it had worked. George was quiet and polite at first which drew Wayne to him. Then, as George got comfortable, his charm and adventurous spirit showed up. George could talk Wayne into all kinds of adventures by sheer persistence and a gift for making every idea seem like the best one yet.

As an adult and especially after Afghanistan, Wayne had gone back somewhat to his introverted ways. He had found that, being a big guy, people expected him to be tough. So he had an impressive collection of tattoos which gave out some serious 'bad guy' vibes. He had gotten his first tattoo before his fifteenth birthday when he realized George wasn't coming home. That was also his first time using a fake ID that he had made. It wasn't very sophisticated but the back alley tattoo artist didn't look very closely.

In the ramshackle farmhouse on the outskirts of Pecan Grove, MaryEllen Huggens gradually became aware of the familiar sounds that meant morning. She could hear Auntie Mae banging the cast iron skillet on the burners getting ready to fry up some pork and grits. She could hear the whine of the shower head and the splash of water on the tin shower walls that meant Uncle Bob was getting cleaned up after chores already. She still smiled a little to herself when she thought of how proud Uncle Bob was of "that there indoor plumbing" that he'd had installed when Grandpa Huggens left him $1,000 in his will.

Something told her she'd been out too late the night before — maybe it was the way her thinking felt disjointed or perhaps because she hadn't popped out of bed instantly ready for whatever would come. She smiled to herself as she thought of what had kept her and LeRoy out past her normal bedtime. This relationship had real promise... for a change.

MaryEllen knew that her dawdling would not go unnoticed so she reluctantly left her daydreaming and got herself up and dressed. She could only afford one class at the community college this semester and it didn't start until 10:00 am, but she knew Auntie Mae would appreciate her help cleaning up after breakfast so she could get to the garment factory on time. Then maybe MaryEllen would study for a while if she could keep her mind on it. Her thoughts kept drifting back to last night... if things worked out maybe she wouldn't need her nursing degree after all! Leroy was a great carpenter and he was *fantastic* at remodeling houses. Last night they had dreamed about her becoming his designer and helper. They would be just like one of those couples on TV; maybe even have their own show like that one called *Flip or Flop*.

Just as MaryEllen entered the kitchen, Uncle Bob's dogs set up a racket in the backyard. The makeshift pens where they were housed featured walls made of corrugated tin roofing and the barking and baying and banging was gosh-awful loud for so early in the morning. Good thing they lived in the sticks, although MaryEllen thought that even the town folk would be able to hear the dogs this morning. She vaguely wondered what had set them off — but sometimes it just happened. If only Bob raised Cocker Spaniels instead of Bloodhounds!

MaryEllen's somewhat disjointed thoughts jumped to the hounds and Uncle Bob. In some ways she thought Uncle Bob resembled his hounds. Although he was long, lean and loose-limbed, that wasn't the only way he was like a bloodhound. When he got a scent of something there was no stopping his questions. He would sniff and ask and poke around until he found out what a body was up to. She had to be careful around Uncle Bob because there was no sense spilling the beans and getting subjected to his third degree until she and LeRoy were ready. Maybe she could distract Uncle Bob by teasing him to sign up for the pet/owner look-alike contest at the Heritage Days Festival!

Elise took her kids to the library every Thursday afternoon. The home school curriculum they used was based on unit studies so they always needed books on whatever subject they were due to study next. She found the librarian, Kristen Stewart, to be knowledgeable and helpful, if a little condescending.

"It's so *nice* that you *bring* your *children* to the library *regularly*! I *imagine* they don't have *much* of a *social* life, being *homeschooled* and all!" Kristen's comment grated on Elise's nerves. Why did people assume that homeschooled children would automatically be socially isolated?

"We need the library for our curriculum, Miss Stewart. But the children get plenty of social opportunities with the homeschool co-op and church activities. Now, what do you have about the Civil War for multiple age groups? That's our next unit."

"Oh, the *Civil* War! Such a *tragic* time! You *know*, being from the *North*, you *might* want to *study* the War from the *Southern* viewpoint. It would *give* you a *new* perspective! Did you *know*, most *Yankees* actually *believe* that *propaganda* about the war being *fought* over *slavery*?"

"And it wasn't?" Elise managed to keep the impatience out of her voice.

"Oh, no, *slavery* was a *good* system for the *black* people. The South *fought* to preserve the *Southern* way of life from *Northern* encroachment!"

Elise wondered how anyone could have really believed that. She followed Kristen to the section where the history books were shelved and dutifully selected several of the titles Kristen suggested, but she made sure that the preponderance of books she chose were from the more traditional point of view!

Still, she thought it might be interesting to find out what this "Southern viewpoint" was all about.

As was her custom, Elise spent the weekend skimming through the stack of books from the library to choose the ones to use in planning the kids' lessons for the following week. She found the books that Kristen had recommended to be pure Southern propaganda and wondered who some of the authors were - the Ku Klux Klan? While Elise was researching for her unit on the Civil War, she came across a web article about the United Daughters of the Confederacy. It detailed the history of a group of Southern socialites who popularized an effort that came to be known as the Lost Cause. This campaign aimed to show that the Confederate soldiers and leaders were heroes.

The UDC was responsible for erecting memorials all over the South often in public places like courthouses and Capitol buildings.

The article said that they targeted children by endorsing school books that shed a positive light on the Confederate effort. Elise checked: yep, the books Kristen had recommended all had a notation "approved by the UDC." From what Nancy had told her, Elise surmised that Kristen's Grandma Geraldine must have been a supporter of the UDC. And she had successfully passed their view of the Civil War to her granddaughter.

—∿—

The way Elise looked askance when Kristen talked about the Lost Cause wasn't missed by the young librarian. She had seen that look before. She knew her grandmother's opinions weren't as popular as they used to be, but she felt she owed it to Grandma Lile to hold on to the way of life that was so important to her. She sometimes wondered if she herself actually believed that anyone was happy being a slave — but Grandma said it, so it *must* be true. If she started questioning Grandma Lile, she wouldn't know who she was anymore!

—∿—

When Bob Huggens arrived at the farm store one morning in mid-April he expected to pick up a few bags of dog food, some fertilizer for the pecan trees, and the roll of fencing that he needed to keep the coyotes away from the puppy pen. He figured maybe some of the old timers who liked to sit on the front porch and gossip would spare some time to keep him up on what was happening around town. He liked his privacy well enough, but he considered it his "ceevic dooty" to know what was going on with his town and county.

"Wa'all Bob," drawled old Amos Walker. "Haven't seen y'all in town for a spell. Yep, yep. Reckon y'all's keeping busy with them trees you planted, eh? How're them trees agrowin' anyhow? How's Mae? How's that perty little niece o' yourn?" Amos was a lifelong bachelor and one of the biggest gossips among the men who hung out at the feed store. Everyone knew he had "secretly" been in love with Cora Windham most of his life.

"Hey, Amos, fellas! I been feelin' mighty pleased 'bout my trees this year - Good Lord willing I might have a true crop come fall! But I been missing a good old gab session. Seems since MaryEllen's been schoolin' over to the commun'ty college it's easier to have her pick up stuff around town and I got no good reason to come anymore."

"Haven't I seen her hanging with that LeRoy Roberts?" chimed in Don Willis.

"Yep, she's been seein' him for a few months — like him better'n some of her other flames." Bob thought of Fred Jamison — that was a freak show he was glad was over! "What's new in town these days?"

"Biggest thing keeping tongues wagging is that there Daryl Marshall seems to be growing a backbone!" cackled Amos. "Yep. Yep. He done asked the folks who've been neglecting the Lile place — what's the name anyhow? if he could list the house for them!"

This was an oft-discussed topic Bob could tell. None of the other fellas had much to add at first, besides guffaws and jokes about spineless Daryl. "So what's he gonna do if Pearsons agree to sell?"

"Oh they agreed all righty," Gerald Bronson said. "Think Daryl's got his eye on that Ray fella for buying it!"

"Ray who?" Bob was beginning to feel lost. "Ain't heerd of no Ray."

"Bob, ya gotta get your behind into town more often! Ever'body knows Ray Jacobs!" This brought on more guffaws and knee slapping. There were times when Bob would have enjoyed the slow exchange of information, but today he felt he was on the outside of the town he grew up in. He wasn't a man to rush into things as a rule and he knew it wouldn't do any good to rush these fellas. Still, he didn't much like the impatient feeling he was getting.

Finally, after settin' a spell and listening to other gossip swirl around him, Bob was able to ask a little more about Ray. "So this fella who might buy the Lile place? Big city guy? What's he do for work? "

"Naw, he mostly sits around on his 'puter, I reckon," Gerald said. "Says he made some money tradin' on that there Wall Street."

"Yeah, heerd him rambling' about how God gave him the 'desires of his heart' right here in Pecan Grove!" Elroy Tyson was clearly unimpressed, as he spat a stream of tobacco juice toward the spittoon in the corner. "Never done heerd such nonsense."

"Waal," drawled Amos, "he cain't be all bad. Sarah Jane sure thinks the world of him!"

Bob wouldn't give a plugged nickel for Sarah Jane's taste in men. Most of them were worse than MaryEllen's old boyfriends. But, remembering Amos's crush on Cora Windham, he supposed Amos was a bit prejudiced toward Cora's daughter!

Chapter Eleven

Weasel felt uneasy, the way he felt in the army when there were enemy soldiers nearby. "Of course there is no enemy here," he reasoned silently. "I'm at the corner bar where I go every Friday night," but his skin was crawling with the sensation of being watched. He tried to be casual as he glanced around at the usual clientele. That guy - the flabby fellow with the meth mouth - was he the one watching? Naw, he'd seen that guy a few other times without getting bad vibes. His PTSD must be kicking in!

Ray had settled on attending the Sunday morning Methodist service at 8:30 am with Sarah Jane. Reverend Findley was kind of boring but the people were friendly. Then he would walk across the square in time to make the 10:00 am service at the Baptist Church. He liked Will Stewart *and* his preaching. His challenge at the Baptist Church was keeping a distance between himself and Kristen — and her mother! He would occasionally make a visit to another church service as well, but he found some to be too lofty and ritualistic, while others catered mainly to the black community. Anyway, he had his hands full concentrating on two churches.

He was surprised one evening when the Reverend Findley approached him after the Book 'n' Brew session. "Ray, I notice that you know your Bible pretty well. I'm in charge of lining up speakers for the annual men's retreat coming up in May. The retreat draws men from churches across the entire county and one of my speakers just cancelled on me. How would you like to lead a couple sessions on how God wants to bless us?"

"That sounds interesting, Reverend! What weekend is it? " he answered. "I'd really like to speak on that topic because it's something I'm pretty passionate about!" Ray was more than pleased. He had thought it might take nearly a year to gain the confidence of the church pastors. Here it was not even May...

Ray had developed much of his theology, if one could use such a lofty word to describe his views, by listening to televangelists. He had grown up with the television tuned to the likes of Billy Graham and Oral Roberts at every opportunity. He had been further immersed in religion while spending a couple months in the Minnesota prison. It seemed like the wardens there believed that "religion is the opiate of the people," and they tried to keep the inmates subdued by playing 24-hour programming of Joel Osteen and other televangelists through the speaker system. He had seen opportunity in the messages that he had practically memorized.

Ray had the idea that he could start his own investment business here in Pecan Grove. He wondered if speaking at the retreat would get people interested in coming to him for investment advice. He had a fledgling idea that somehow wealth and Christianity could intersect and launch his business.

The one thing missing right now, he mused, was Weasel. He had grown impatient with Weasel acting like a parent and wondering what he was planning and where he was going. It had grown much worse after he spent those months in prison. But, at the same time, he needed a confidante, and Weasel fit the bill. He would never betray Ray, even when he didn't approve of his actions.

———⁓⁓⁓———

Meanwhile, preparations for the Pecan Grove's Heritage Days festival also were moving along. Along with the Home and Garden tour held in the fall, the emphasis on Civil War history brought Pecan Grove a needed flood of tourist money each year. Although the festival wasn't held until the third week in June, committees had to decide the innumerable details beforehand; which vendors got booths in which locations, what activities were money makers and which could be dropped. Because she always volunteered, Kari Stewart was rushing off to attend one planning meeting or another. However, this year she had been asked to be in charge of a different committee — children's games. She wasn't as comfortable working with this as she had been with the food vendors. It had been a long time since Kristen was a child, that is, if she had ever acted like one at all. Kari had never been very comfortable with children; that's why she let her mother take care of Kristen.

Unfortunately for Kari she wasn't getting as much help from her committee as she had been led to expect. Turns out that when old Charlotte Decker ran the children's carnival, she pretty much did everything herself, so her volunteers were prepared to do little more than read their names on the festival literature. Kari was entrusted with giving the Kids Karnival a more modern appeal. Worse yet, she was saddled with that loathsome, meddlesome Cora Windham. "She should change her name to Cora Windbag." she thought uncharitably. "All she does is talk about the glories of Windhams past and present. And precious few of them, including Cora, ever actually did a thing for Pecan Grove!"

She wished she could interest Kristen in volunteering. She could use some fresh ideas for the activities — and Kristen had gone to college for Children's Library Studies. She should have some ideas! But all she would do is wave her mother off saying, "Oh mom, that's too *quaint*. I'm sure no one *here* would want my *progressive* ideas!!" Progress, shmogress. Kristen had the most old fashioned ideas of any person under ninety that Kari knew, except maybe in the way she dressed. She just needed to get in gear and DO something! Kari thought, not for the first time, that perhaps her mother hadn't been the best influence on young Kristen.

Sarah Jane and Ray had begun going out together at least once a week. They might catch a movie, go out to eat in Mobile or Jackson, or have popcorn and play a game at the boarding house. They had very little truly private time since Ray was still living under the gimlet eye of Bella and Sarah Jane under the same roof as her mother (and a tiny roof it was at that!). Sarah Jane really liked Ray. He was funny, smart, and didn't look down on her for not having much money or for her past escapades.

"What happened that your mama never married your dad, Sarah Jane? I would have thought that went against the values I see here in Pecan Grove," Ray ventured to ask one night.

"I'm never sure if the way my mama tells the story is true for real or only true in my mother's mind," Sarah Jane answered. "But what I can piece together is that Mama was a real beauty back then. She attracted attention from a lot of men and some of them were older and wiser in the ways of the world than she was. She had dreams of being a famous chef like Julia Childs, so to help put herself through school she was waitressing at a fancy nightclub outside of town — it's been closed now for years. One man in particular paid a lot of attention to her. He said he was a traveling salesman and only in Pecan Grove every other week. She dated him for a couple years before she found out he was married. He had a whole family just over in Jackson! It was all fake. Even after she found out he was married he said he loved only her, that he was going to divorce his wife and marry her…. guess that's the oldest story in the book, right? Anyway, she got pregnant and he was gone. Moved away from Jackson and never contacted Mama again."

"I guess I'm the lucky one that she didn't decide to have an abortion, right?" Ray said as he kissed Sarah Jane.

Chapter Twelve

*H*e hadn't learned anything in the months since George disappeared. It seemed he had vanished into thin air. Even the Weasel hadn't let a single word slip about the guy! He needed a different plan. Maybe he could smoke him out...

As Weasel turned the calendar to May, he wondered again what George was up to. Weasel had half expected to get either a distress signal or a bragging call from him within a couple months, but George had been gone since January. He hoped that his brother was building a new life for himself, that he was finding some purpose to cure his restlessness, but when he really looked at George's character and past inclinations, he knew that was doubtful. Oh, George could work hard when it suited his fancy. But most of George's hard work in the past had been in pursuit of easy money!

He wondered at the attachment he still felt for George. They were different in so many ways. As a kid, he had been attracted to the easy way George drew a following. There was a certain adrenaline rush to plotting and carrying out some harmless prank or another. He felt that in some way he was responsible for not keeping George as a part of their family — perhaps that is why he had so quickly joined George both in the Army and here in Minnesota. But from the stories George told about the time they were apart, it was apparent that George had engaged in some wild and questionable behavior, while Weasel had more or less settled in to doing what was expected of him. The way George told stories... at first Weasel was inclined to treat the vast majority of what he said as a joke, but he gradually realized that there was an element of truth to the tales. Oh, they were sanitized so George was never at fault and embellished to make the tale more interesting, but, pieced together with the infrequent emails and phone calls from George over the years, he realized that the events probably all actually happened. If so, George had tried his luck in Hollywood, landing bit parts in a couple of low budget films, had done a stint as a poker player in Vegas, and there was a possibility he had even been a race car driver. It made his schemes in Minnesota seem positively tame by comparison. Weasel had caught hints that George had some money saved up from these ventures, but that didn't seem to dim his appetite for a real humdinger of a money making idea. He pondered what kind of big idea George had concocted now. Sadly, he recognized that some of that easy money inclination had worn off on him as well. After all, the times he felt most challenged to work hard were when he was building a false identity for someone willing to pay the big bucks!

And there was another thing that had changed with George. His interest in religion had become intense. As a kid, he had sat through church with Wayne, half paying attention, and half looking for mischief. Afterward, he always knew the sermon nearly word for word, and would mock the pastor privately. But now it seemed that he was analyzing what made people believe. Weasel had given up all pretense of believing when his prayers for George to return to the family went unanswered. With George, it wasn't as if he had ever really believed, and his interest now seemed almost sinister.

———

Kristen Stewart didn't recognize her feeling of restlessness as boredom. She hated to admit her life was not turning out the way she had envisioned it. To admit that would be to recognize that she was less than perfect; another thing she usually refused to think about. After her romance with Drew Pearson fizzled out — she still blamed Sarah Jane for that — she had figured she would go to college, find a handsome, well-to-do man and get married. They would return to Pecan Grove and eventually her husband would buy the Lile house and return the Stewart family to its rightful place in society. She had loved imagining the gratitude her mother would feel at once again having access to the beautiful home and grounds where she was raised.

Kristen couldn't understand what had gone wrong. She had followed all the advice from *Cosmopolitan* about finding a man. She copied the fashions of her favorite movie stars. Mom and Grandma had said she would be better off with a wealthy man because then she could be sure he wasn't just after her inheritance. Maybe the problem was just that Pecan Grove didn't have enough *men* that fit that criteria. But that Ray Jacobs seemed to be right up her alley...

If only Grandfather Lile hadn't messed everything up! At least he'd had the foresight to put aside money in an unbreakable trust for any grandchildren he might have, and there were no other grandchildren. A small portion of the interest it earned had paid for her college education, but next month, when she turned 28, she'd get it all and by now it was nearly a million dollars! Then SHE could buy back the Lile house!

Kristen thought about the stories she had heard about Grandpa Lile. All her life he had been portrayed as fun and generous although not much of a businessman. She had never met him, but she didn't think he was as dumb about money as everyone said. After all, he'd provided for his eventual grandchildren while his children were still in high school. Maybe he knew the mill was failing, or that it would be discovered that he had been using the profits for gambling. Whatever. Aunt Jackie had never married so she had no children. Uncle Jon was killed in a car accident on his honeymoon. Mom and Dad didn't have any children for years until she was born when her mom was 35. She might have enjoyed having cousins, but as it was, she was going to be very rich!

Meanwhile, games on her iPad, reading women's magazines and languishing about the parsonage just wasn't very *fulfilling*. She was sure having her own home would be *so* much more *exciting*. She had almost considered helping her mother with the Heritage Days activities, but that would involve interacting with children in a hands-on way and she felt more comfortable with a library desk between the little monsters and herself. Besides, if she helped in the park she might get *sweaty*.

Kristen didn't like thinking too hard about her life. Deep down, she knew there were things she had done to hurt other people. Sometimes when her dad was preaching, she had all she could do to keep herself distracted so she wouldn't have to actually deal with her wrongs. So, Kristen grabbed her favorite *Cosmopolitan* magazine — the one with the list on how to snag your love interest — and started reading.

The men's retreat was always held the third weekend in May. The spring farm work was done by then and those who had farming responsibilities were ready for a weekend of fishing and preaching. Though it was held at the Methodist campgrounds, it drew men from the entire county in all walks of life and religious persuasions. It was the highlight of the year for many men and the boys eagerly looked forward to their 15th birthday so they would be old enough to attend.

The area pastors took turns lining up speakers for the retreat so no one could complain that it was always run by one denomination. They made a point of not announcing to the world who was in charge each year.

"You goin' to the retreat this year, Bob?" Mae Huggens asked her husband one morning.

"Don' know who's agunna do the chorin' iffn I do," Bob grumbled.

"Thought mebbe Sam's boy could come in the mornin's and MaryEllen'n me could handle the evenin's" Mae encouraged. "You've hardly been off the farm since plantin' season!"

"Oh, I suppose," Bob grumbled. "'Twould be nice to set a spell, hear some preachin' and mebbe drown some worms."

Mae was pleased. She knew he really wanted to go, but worried about her and MaryEllen being alone on the farm.

At the Griffiths' home a similar conversation was taking place. Elise was encouraging Jase to go to the retreat, "and take that young man you've been trying to reach, Zeke someone... We'll come up with the money somewhere."

"Guess I'm getting it from both sides," Jase muttered. Pastor Kirkland had also been pressuring him about attending the retreat. "I'll go. I'll call Zeke too."

With the increase of tourists who were interested in the antebellum time period coming to Pecan Grove, many attractions had sprung up nearby. Two historical museums opened with competing views of the Civil War and totally different stories about the history of Pecan Grove. There were a couple of older homes which had restored their slave quarters and offered tours for a hefty admission price. Then there were the usual gaudy attractions for families including a mini golf course designed like a battlefield with multitudes of cannons and fake soldiers guarding the putting greens. One of the small farms had even started a petting zoo advertising real live Confederate animals. Visitors were left to wonder if the animals were alive for over 150 years or if they were somehow proven to be Southern sympathizers!

Sarah Jane figured it fell to her to educate Ray on the "true" history of Pecan Grove; although, like many Grovers, she subscribed to a mix of truth and convenient fiction. Tonight she had taken Ray to the mini-golf course since it was *supposed* to be a semi-authentic replication of the skirmish that had left the Union in control of Grantsburg. Ray was keeping all the surrounding golfers laughing with his ongoing commentary on the decorations, the battle and mini-golfing in general.

Sarah Jane had captured numerous pictures on her phone of Ray: posing next to a statue with his putter held like a musket, peering into the end of a cannon with a quizzical look, gathering a group of children as he spun a yarn about what *really* happened when the Union general went golfing with the Confederate soldiers. Her favorite memory was one not on film. Ray had spotted a fifer among the statues and began to whistle "Dixie" whenever a child came close. He seemed to be able to make the whistling sound like it was coming from the statue. The children were enthralled. Many parents were trying to see how the mechanism worked. And then abruptly the whistling stopped and the drummer boy began to beat his drum. Even Sarah Jane had to look twice, although she knew it was just Ray. How *did* he do that?

As far as Ray was concerned, dating Sarah Jane opened up a totally different way of thinking for him - that he could spend time with someone of the opposite sex and not have, well, sex! Any other time he had dated the relationship had quickly become physical and, just as quickly, fizzled. But because of the public nature of his outings with Sarah Jane they had been forced to become friends. He thought he could get used to this.

That night as they enjoyed a root beer float at the drive-in after golfing, Ray asked Sarah Jane if she had ever thought of living anywhere other than in Pecan Grove. "I've always had a hankering to see different places." he stated. "What about you, sweetie? Are you happy with just staying where you've always been? Or do you have a little wanderlust buried deep inside?"

"There has never been an opportunity for me to think about moving away," Sarah Jane replied slowly. "It's always been just Mama and me and I've always felt it was up to me to take care of Mama. When I don't keep her eating well, lay out her pills, make sure she's taken her insulin and all that, well, she either "accidentally" forgets, or purposely fixes a load of sugary foods that send her blood sugar on a ride. I've come home from a night out to find her loopy and nearly passed out from an insulin reaction more times than I care to think about!"

"But you didn't answer the question. If you were free, would you stay? Or where would you like to go?"

"Oh, I think the dust of Pecan Grove would be left far behind my fleeing footsteps if I could ever move away! Ever since Kristen Stewart started spreading rumors about me in high school, all I've ever had from most people here have been taunts and teasing. It was all a lie, but by the time I realized what was going on, most people believed it."

"What's all this about?" Ray was shocked at Sarah Jane's bitter outburst. She usually seemed so unflappable.

"Oh, it stems from a stupid party I went to in high school. You know, the kind where some older kid brings a keg of beer and everyone tries to show how cool they are by drinking too much. Anyway, Drew Pearson and Kristen came for some reason, even though they weren't a regular part of that group. After a while, Drew and I got to talking. He wanted some private advice - he was heading off to military school and wondered how to break up with Kristen gently. He thought she was way more serious than he was ready for. She found us talking a ways away from the group and started spreading rumors that we were intimately involved. By the time I heard the story, she had managed to turn some of my closest friends against me. And that was just my first experience with Kristen's acid tongue. How do you stand being around her, anyway?"

Ray's explanation that he needed the contacts the Stewart family provided so that he could start an investment business seemed to fall flat with Sarah Jane.

That night Sarah Jane couldn't stop wondering why she felt she needed to stay in Pecan Grove. Yes, there was her mother, as she had told Ray. But there was something else, which she finally recognized as pride. She was determined not to leave town and have anyone think she was running away! She would leave as success and with her head held high. And she was willing to work her tail off to get to that place.

Chapter Thirteen

After yet another committee meeting in which they had decided to have a bounce house (Kari would rent one - she had seen one designed to look like a haunted Victorian home), face painting (Ruby volunteered herself and commandeered Elise to help), and pony rides (Mae Huggens was sure her neighbor Sam would bring his Shetland ponies), Kari sank down on a chair in the lobby to check her lists. She was dismayed to see Cora Windham plowing toward her. She had noticed that Cora was fairly bursting during the meeting (not that she was bursting with eagerness to actually work) so Kari figured she had some inane particle of self-importance to share.

"I'm sure you're excited about the sale of your childhood home, aren't you Kari!" she exclaimed loudly. "I'm sure hoping Sarah Jane will get to live there!"

"What in heaven are you talking about? I hadn't heard the Pearsons were planning to sell."

"Oh, it was pretty hush-hush, I guess. That Daryl! Who would have guessed?"

Kari really didn't like being put in the position of adding to Cora's self importance by asking for more information, but her curiosity was wild. "Oh, that," was all she said dismissively. "I suppose Sarah Jane is applying as housekeeper?"

"Not at all," Cora huffed. "With Sarah Jane and Ray practically engaged, you know."

Kari wasn't following, but she refused to ask. "Whatever. I need to get back to business. This carnival isn't going to organize itself!" And she stalked off. She figured she could call Joan for an update. Joan was plugged in to the gossip mill more closely than Kari.

"Daryl, I'm *so* proud of the way you took charge and sold the Lile house!" Lisa bubbled to her husband. "When do you think the commission check will come? We really need a van for the daycare, and if we could use part of the commission for a washer and dryer, maybe daycare money could be used toward a van and…"

Daryl interrupted his wife. "I've been meaning to talk to you about that. You see, Ray made a fortune by investing in that new cyber security system…"

"Yes, I know, I know! You've been talking about that for two weeks."

"That's just it Lisa. You never want to listen to me tell you about it. It's just that, w-w-well, you see, R-Ray offered me a chance to get in on the ground f-floor of investing in this great security system. So I p-p-put the commission toward b-buying some stock in the company that developed it."

Lisa was stunned. "You did what?" she whispered. "You invested our money in some company? Do you have any idea how risky that is?" She knew Daryl wasn't overly responsible with money, but this was beyond belief.

"You *knew* I was counting on that money. You *knew* our washer and dryer are falling apart! You *knew* the boys needed bunk beds!" Lisa's voice was rising to a screech. "I thought that selling the Lile house would make you more responsible, not less." Lisa could not stop the stream of insults that poured out of her mouth. "I guess that shows us where we stand in your opinion, Daryl. That money was for family. How *could* you!" She burst into tears and ran out of the room.

Daryl felt helpless. He tried so hard to please his wife and take his proper responsibility in his home. Now it seemed that he had failed again. He had been so sure this was right because Ray *did* make a fortune! All he wanted was a good rate of return to prove that he wasn't the hopeless failure that his mother-in-law believed him to be. And now it seemed Lisa was coming to believe it too.

Daryl thought back over the last few weeks to figure out where he might have gone wrong. He had called the Pearsons with great trepidation, but they had been more than gracious and agreed that yes, they were ready to sell their home. Then he and Ray had met together to go through the Lile house. Ray declared the house was perfect for his needs and was enthusiastic about getting into the house quickly so it would be ready for fall entertaining. He had seemed knowledgeable about the antiques in the house and requested that the Pearsons consider selling him the furnishings along with the house. Daryl was excited because that would up his eventual commission. Ray had also noted that the kitchen needed an upgrade and there was only an old steam boiler system for heat so he'd asked Daryl to look into how much that work would cost. So far so good, thought Daryl.

It was when they were sitting down together to write up a purchase offer that Ray started enthusing about the great investment opportunity God had led him to — the one that was making him so much money that he could afford to buy this house; the one that was allowing him to volunteer his time instead of working; the one that was making people billions and that corporations around the country were scrambling to invest in. He made it sound so easy and attractive that Daryl had wanted a piece of that action. The only money he had to invest was what he would make off the sale of the house. He had hoped that Ray was right; now he *prayed* that Ray was right and he would make enough money to vindicate his decision.

Kari came home from her committee meeting and raced through the house, barely acknowledging her daughter. She closed and locked her bedroom door, sank down on the chaise lounge and called her friend Joan. She was long overdue for an update on the local news.

"Hey Joan! I've missed you!" Kari began lightly. "I've been so busy with Heritage Days I haven't made the last couple pastors' wives lunches. What's new?"

"Oh Kari, you *won't* believe it all! I've been *dying* to chat, but your phone *always* goes directly to voicemail. It doesn't *work* if you don't turn it *on*!" Joan knew her friend was something of a Luddite. Kari owned but rarely used a cell phone and computer and Joan loved to tease her about it. "But I digress. I *suppose* you want to know about how old Vera McNeely was found *dead*? Or did you want to hear about June Sawyer's *engagement* party?"

Kari *did* want that news, but it wasn't what was driving her burning curiosity. However, that was the way the gossip game was played so she schooled herself to keep her tone light. Even if Joan was her best friend it wouldn't do to let her know how unsettled she was. After all, Joan *was* the best gossip. "Oh? Is there news about Vera? I thought she died of natural causes."

Joan's reading tended to be mystery fiction and she thought all dead people had been murdered and the murder should be solved in a tidy way preferably in less than 300 pages, so she was open to any interpretation of someone's death, no matter how old they were. "That's just it! They *thought* it was natural causes because she was 87, but you know how they have to do an *autopsy* if the death was unattended—and they found *lethal* levels of morphine in her system!"

After what seemed to Kari to be an eternity of speculation on Joan's part: what the police were doing, whether they found any motives, who she suspected, whether it might have been accidental and on and on — Kari thought her head would burst. The headache that started with Cora's odd pronouncements was throbbing in full force now.

Finally Joan had exhausted her supply of information about Vera and June. "Let's see, what else...oh I heard the Pearson's *finally* sold your old home! I sure hope the *new* owner will keep up the gardens better. I guess Daryl Marshall finally got the *gumption* to live up to his title as *realtor*," Joan laughed. "I *wonder* if Laura will be crowing about her *brilliant* son-in-law at our *next* luncheon!" While Joan was getting to the point Kari wondered inanely if Kristen got her exclamations and italics from listening to Joan.

"Oh really," Kari responded, forcing a disinterested tone into her voice (finally they were getting to the important stuff.) "I wonder if the new owners are moving to town soon. I suppose we'll have to invite them to some of the fall festivities. I don't know who around here has enough money to buy that house except those who already live in the historic district."

"Well, Daryl is being really *secretive* about his client, but *someone* said he's been meeting with Ray Jacobs a *lot* lately! If Ray has *decided* to *settle* in here - well, from all *you've* said about him I reckon *he* has enough *money* to buy it."

Suddenly all of Cora's innuendoes clicked into place for Kari. She was stunned and chagrined that she hadn't seen this coming — could Ray really be buying *her* house? Barely able to keep her voice from shaking she extricated herself from the conversation as quickly as she could, which wasn't at all quick enough, in her mind. "Looks like I can't afford to miss any more sessions of the ladies luncheons!" She tried to laugh lightly. "I've been out all day — I'd better see about some supper here, Joan. Keep me informed, okay? I'll go turn on that cell phone... if I can find it."

Chapter Fourteen

Weasel was increasingly uneasy. His Friday evening jaunts to the corner tavern were becoming a nightmare with the constant feeling that someone was watching him. He had even skipped a couple weeks, but then he worried more about what was happening behind his back. He had a niggling feeling that he should know the fat jerk whispering in the darkest corner. He had overheard that the guy claimed to be "with the FBI." Most of the guys thought he was just a self-important blowhard, so why would he trigger Weasel's 'spidey' sense? If only he could remember where he'd encountered him before.

Will and Ray had taken to golfing in the early mornings as the weather became warmer. Will looked forward to their outings and Ray's light-hearted banter. Ray knew every golfing joke ever printed... and some that were never printed too. It was all a welcome relief from Kristen's dramatics and Kari's seriousness.

After their round of golf they were chatting in the clubhouse over coffee and sandwiches when Ray brought up the subject of his investment and how this cyber security device was outperforming all stocks on the market. "I tell you Will," he said, "as my friend I sure wish you could get in on this. I just know God is waiting to bless you too! I've increased my portfolio by 45% in the last three months alone. You don't know how glad I am that I cottoned-on to this possibility."

"You know, Ray, I've been thinking about that. I've got some money set aside for Kristen's wedding, if she ever gets married, that is. I don't think it will be enough, seeing as she has some pretty high-falutin' ideas. Perhaps I should invest half of what I've saved and see where that goes?"

"I'm sure God won't disappoint you Will!" Ray enthused. "You'll begin to see results very quickly with this stock."

Ray's sessions at the retreat were well-attended. It seemed most everyone was interested in having God's blessing and if they weren't, they came just to see what he was going to say. He was new enough to town to still be a draw due to curiosity alone.

He started his session on Friday night with his favorite Bible verse. "'You don't have, because you don't ask!" God is waiting to bless us, but our problem is that we forget to ask Him. We ask God for health, and if that doesn't work we ask God for healing. What else do you ask God for? You say prayers on behalf of your friends, but do you ask for money for them? Yet we often refer to an unexpected monetary gain as a *blessing!* So why don't we ASK God for money?" Ray spoke with conviction.

"Let me tell you my story. I was raised in foster homes and it always seemed to me that others who had money were happier than those who were struggling. I noticed that the people in church who were unhappy could have been happier with money. 'Oh, if only I could afford to have a hip replacement, then I could play with the grandkids.' 'Oh, if I had the money I could go away on vacation with the family.' 'If I had more money I could help the church.' 'If I could put my child in a private school, they would have a better future.' 'If I could go back to college…' 'If I could afford a bigger house…a boat…a nicer wardrobe…' You name it. It all could be made better with MONEY. Most of these things would do good for people. But no one ever asks God for MONEY.

"Finally, when I was in college, I realized that God has commanded us to *ask*, not just wait for it to happen. "Ask, and it shall be given unto you." So I started asking God for money. And then, just when it seemed I was wrong and God wasn't going to answer, a grandmother I didn't even know died and her lawyer tracked me down. She had left me everything she had. Not much, really, but it renewed my faith that God WANTED to bless me!" Ray paused and noticed he was running out of time. "Did my grandmother's inheritance make me wealthy? No, $100,000 isn't enough to be considered wealthy. So now what? Wait for another gramma to die?" This drew a laugh from the men. "Blow the money on a fancy car and some expensive clothes? That's when the second revelation came to me. But I'll have to tell you about that in the next session."

Ray's dynamic presentation was the talk of the retreat. All that evening there was spirited discussion going on around him, but Ray made a point of ignoring it and drawing Will into telling him about the session on "Loving Your Children Back to God." He didn't want to answer questions yet.

Ray's second session was scheduled for Saturday morning. There were even more attendees this time. Word was out that Ray was going to give them the secret of enormous wealth.

Ray began right where he left off. "So here I was sitting on $100,000. How can I use that money best? Do I save it for a rainy day? Why did God trust me with that money? By this time I was taking some classes from the online Trading College as well as finishing up my Bible degree. One of the assignments for Bible school had me writing on the parables of Jesus. That's when it hit me!" Ray paused for emphasis.

"I was studying the passage where the rich man gives his servants charge of his money. And one servant invested his ten talents and returned it double. Another invested his five talents and returned it double. And the third man was too afraid to do anything with the small amount of money he was entrusted with and *he* got *scolded* by his master. This made me realize that when God entrusts us with some money, he waits to see what we will do with it. He wants us to look for opportunities to increase that wealth. He wants us to TRUST Him for the results as we step out in faith. So I researched and I trusted, and I invested my grandma's money. God kept increasing the money and giving me better opportunities and waiting to see if I would continue to trust Him. And the returns kept getting bigger — and bigger! God is waiting for YOU! Do YOU have some resources you're just hanging on to? Are you ready to TRUST GOD with what He's given you? Are you ready to ask GOD to bless YOU with money?"

By the time Ray was finished, he was dripping with sweat and exhausted from his impassioned speech. But he felt good. He felt he had really connected — and the buzz in the room told him he was right..

Chapter Fifteen

ari composed herself with a hot shower after her talk with Joan. If only Will didn't have that men's retreat tonight. She wondered if he had known about this all along and was trying to shield her. She hated that. She went to the kitchen to find some supper for herself and Kristen, but she felt too unsettled to cook. When Kristen came downstairs, Kari said, "Get ready to go out. I'm not in the mood to cook tonight."

An hour later they found themselves at the seafood restaurant that had recently opened up on Main Street. After ordering shrimp and hush puppies for both, Kristen said "I *heard* you on the *phone* this afternoon, Mom. Was that *Joan*? What kind of *gossip* was she peddling *today*?"

"She was dying to talk about Vera McNeely's death. You know, Joan, she loves a good mystery. And if she can't find a legitimate mystery, she'll create one. She was trying to get me to believe that there was foul play in Vera's death. Something about there being 'lethal levels of morphine' in her system or something like that."

"Wouldn't that be *murder* then?" Kristen gasped.

"Oh, you know that Vera was struggling with Alzheimer's. And then with that fall she took last month her back was causing her a lot of pain. She was getting so forgetful and her family just let her keep on living alone. I'm sure they will discover that Vera just forgot she had taken her pain pills and took too many.

"So, Kristen, what have you been up to this week? Have you seen any more of Ray?"

"Not much, but I *did* run into him at the *Garden Cafe* one morning. I *asked* him if he *wouldn't* like to get out of that *depressing* Bed and Board place for a *movie* or something. He *said* he was *busy* preparing for the men's retreat."

"Is that all he was busy with? Joan said he was meeting with Daryl Marshall about buying a house."

"Really? He doesn't have a *wife* or anything, why would *he* want a *house*?"

"That's what I was hoping you could tell me. And it's not just any house. The rumor mill is saying he's buying **our** house! I mean, the Lile house." Kari found her voice shaking at the thought of another unworthy owner for the house she loved. But her reaction was mild compared to her daughter's.

"What?" Kristen whispered, her face having gone all shades of white. "But next *month* I'll be 28. Next *month* I'll get my *inheritance!* Next *month* I was going to try to *buy* the Lile house!" Her voice had risen several decibels and several octaves as she spoke.

Kari was shocked. She had never anticipated Kristen wanting to buy the house. Of course, it made sense. All her life Kristen had heard stories about the parties and fine living Kari had enjoyed growing up. It was just the kind of life that would appeal to her "Cinderella" daughter. She thought she'd had a headache this afternoon, but it was nothing compared to the whopper she was developing now.

It was difficult to eat the meal when it arrived although it was superbly prepared. Kari knew she needed to eat or she would be thoroughly sick. Kristen, as usual, was barely picking at her food while she schemed. "Maybe *Ray* won't have enough *money*. Maybe

I could *outbid* him? Maybe I can *just* get him to *marry me,* and *then* I won't *have* to *worry* about it. That's it, Mom! *You* can *help* me. He *won't* know *what* hit him!"

Kari thought that was the best idea yet.

———

After Ray's impassioned talk at the retreat, Jase found himself walking to lunch with Bob Huggens. Bob was muttering almost to himself but loud enough for Jase to think he wanted him to hear. "Seems like there's other Scriptures he oughta be thinkin' on. Like 'the love of money bein' the root of all evil' and such. Seems like someone oughta be looking closer into what that Ray fella is teachin.'"

Jase agreed. Nothing he had seen or heard had changed his initial impression of Ray. His speech had all the elements of the prosperity gospel preachers Jase had never agreed with... A little too slick for his own good. Even more worrisome was the way Zeke and many of the other younger guys were eating up Ray's talk. "I think all we can do is keep our eyes on the whole truth and tell people when we have the chance. You can't just take a verse here and there and string them together to suit your own ideas. Especially if what you're saying is contradicted elsewhere in the Bible."

Later in the afternoon, Jase saw Ray headed to the lake with a group of men carrying fishing gear. He grabbed a pole from the rack by the door and quickly made his way toward them. "Mind if I join you? Or should I say y'all?" he asked. "Still not used to talking Southern!"

He was hoping for a chance to talk to Ray and maybe to give him some additional Bible verses to consider. However, Ray stayed busy laughing and joking with a couple guys and deflecting questions about the stock market. Jase could almost feel the younger man avoiding him.

Something about Jase Griffiths made Ray's brain go on hyper alert. The man reminded him of a foster dad he'd had when he was very small. As little George was telling an elaborate tale about how such and such infraction wasn't his fault, Dad would just look at him with a mixture of sadness and compassion and say, "I wish I could believe that…" Ray was afraid that somehow Jase could see through his current ruse in the same way.

———

Kari and Kristen put their plan to combine forces into action at church Sunday morning. They were watching for Ray to come in as he usually did, just a little late. Kari immediately invited Ray for dinner after the service that morning. "Kristen was cooking up a storm yesterday. We have WAY too much food for the three of us." Just a little white lie there. Kristen had stood around criticizing her mother while, despite her headache, *Kari* cooked up a storm. The piano was already playing, and Ray had no time to come up with a plausible excuse, so he was stuck.

Will was looking forward to the opportunity to talk to Ray about his sessions at the Men's Retreat. Kristen, however, had different ideas. They had barely said two words to one another when Kristen interrupted with some inane talk about Heritage Days. "Thursday is geared toward the *kids* with pony rides and *face* painting, but on *Friday* there's a parade and Saturday there's going to be a Barbershop Quartet *contest*. There's *lots* of food because *restaurants* from all over western *Alabama* set up *tents* and you can get little *sampler* plates. There are *carnival* rides — and on *Friday* night there will be a *great* fireworks display too! We can go *together,* and *I* can *show* you the sights!"

Heritage Days wasn't for nearly a month. Kari thought that Kristen could have come up with an activity that would get her out with Ray sooner. She nearly said so out loud. But perhaps it was best. Because it was far in advance, most likely Ray hadn't made other plans. He would be hard-pressed to get out of this invitation.

Truth was, Ray had heard about Heritage Days and was hoping to go with Sarah Jane, although he hadn't asked her yet, so he didn't have that excuse. "Okay, I guess we could do that, Kristen." He didn't know how he was going to take hours of listening to Kristen emphasizing every other word when she talked, but there *was* that tidbit of gossip he had overheard, that Kristen was due to come into an inheritance before too long... and well, lots could happen before the Heritage Festival.

Across town at Bethel Bible Church people were still talking about the retreat, as they were in most of the churches in the area. Jase felt he could hardly turn around without hearing a conversation about trusting God to make you wealthy or having someone pin him down about his thoughts on God's monetary blessings. Pastor Kirkland even mentioned Ray's talks from the podium when he gave announcements.

"I'm SO glad I attended the men's retreat this weekend. Guys, if you missed it this year, you really missed out. Ray Jacobs gave some excellent sessions on God's blessing. I am so pumped about what God is gonna do for me personally and for our congregation too!"

Jase groaned. He wished people would be more discerning about Ray's claims. It seemed this was one runaway train no one wanted to stop. He wondered what money Kent was going to come up with to invest when he and Gina were always complaining that they needed more money.

Chapter Sixteen

Elise and Ruby had been recruited to assist in the face painting booth at Heritage Days. "I've never done face painting before, Ruby," Elise confessed. "I know I said I'd help wherever needed, but I'm not sure I'll be any good at painting wiggly little faces."

"Nonsense, girl! A little practice today and you'll be ready by the time the festival gets here. I've seen the signs you lettered for the town rummage sale — you've got a steady hand and that's all it takes. I've got a poster of designs the kids can choose from and I'll bet you'll come up with some cute ideas of your own. It'll come easy for you. Now, let's get those kids of yours to sit for some practice here."

As they worked, Ruby kept up a constant stream of patter about the festival, about the town, about the Garden Cafe, and of course, about the people of Pecan Grove. Elise didn't recognize all the names so her mind was wandering a bit, but she perked up her ears when she heard Kari Stewart's name.

"...think Kari is mostly flummoxed about how to handle Kristen." Ruby was saying. "She was older when Kristen finally came along and she doted on her something awful. Now that Kristen's grown up I think even Kari can see how spoiled she is but can't easily undo the damage. I personally think she let little Kristen spend too much time with her high and mighty Grandmother Lile. That woman had some strong opinions and filled Kristen's head with ideas about the 'Southern Way of Life,' and how anyone with Lile blood was special. Ah well, some people just seem to have to learn through experience and I would guess Kristen's one of 'em! I heard there was a trust fund started by her Grandpa Lile. I wonder whether she'll get control of that anytime soon. Some of those trusts are written funny and maybe she has to marry first or something."

Weasel heard a rumor at the bar Friday night. He didn't know how much credit he should give it, since things got exaggerated when people were tipsy, but it worried him. They were saying that the Feds were looking for George on some charge of tax evasion, and money laundering or some such thing. He didn't think the FBI would really concern themselves with a small-time scoundrel like George, but still...he had skipped out on his last few appointments with his parole officer.

He had started a rumor. His ego told him that he was the perfect one to know private information — after all, he had let it be known (confidentially, of course), that he was with the FBI. Yeah, so he was only a janitor at the FBI building. No one needed to know that! So he said, "Remember that guy who used to come in here sometimes? Wasn't that George Ray? 'Cause I heard that a George Ray was wanted by the Feds. My colleague said they're going to hunt him down for tax evasion, parole violations and money laundering!" That should get the Weasel running after his brother.

The next couple weeks sped by for Ray. He was inundated with men who had been at the retreat calling to make appointments to talk about high reward stocks, stock options and Ray's favorite - cyber security stocks. Ray interviewed each prospective investor making sure that their motives were right: that they wanted to be blessed by God so they could be a blessing to others. Somehow he always managed to bring the conversation around to the success he had with this great new company, how he found it through a former Wall Street mogul who was now dedicated to helping ordinary Americans become millionaires, and how well Ray himself had done with it over the last months. He made sure his customers knew that he was confident they would make a killing with this stock. After all, every company was going to be installing this security system. Even the government was investing in it! He was even willing to back up their investments with his own money. He pointed out that he was already able to buy the Lile house for cash and he had only discovered this stock a few months ago.

Some of the men invested with Ray on the spot, others planned to talk with their wives, some planned to free up some money so they could invest, and only a few were skeptical. Ray assured the hesitant ones that he wasn't taking it personally and that they would soon see their friends becoming rich and might change their minds. He gave everyone his business card which read simply: Ray Jacobs, broker.

When Ray and Sarah Jane finally had time for a movie night, Sarah Jane said, "By the way, you never told me how your talks went at the Men's Retreat. I had to hear second-hand how impressed everyone was. Does this mean you're about to change your mind and become a preacher?"

"Well, I thought as a kid that I might want to try preaching when I grew up. And that's part of the reason I enrolled in Bible College. But talking with Will, well, there's a lot more to heading up a church than the preaching. And I'm not really into studying as much as he has to either. No, I think I'm happy just helping people make money."

"Good!" Sarah Jane's reaction showed that she was worried about the possibility. "I'm quite convinced that I'm not cut out to ever be a preacher's wife!" Oops - she couldn't believe she had actually referred to herself as Ray's potential wife. He didn't seem to notice. She hoped he hadn't!

Elise and Jase were talking about how the Kirklands had sold their RV and the kids' 4-wheelers so they could invest in cyber security stock. "They only bought that RV a couple months ago!" Elise exclaimed incredulously. "They bought it new, too. They must have had to sell at a loss to get rid of it this quickly."

"Yeah, I think he said he didn't even get blue book price for it. But he didn't want to 'miss the one-of-a-kind opportunity to get in on the ground floor of this hot stock,' as he put it," said Jason. "And I think his kids are going to be unhappy, maybe even bitter, when they find out their high-end 4-wheelers are gone too."

"Is it worth alienating your family for the hope of wealth, Jase? I know Gina was really looking forward to quality family time in that RV."

"There's that verse in the Bible that says, 'those who want to get rich fall into temptation and a trap.' I wonder if this could turn out to be a trap for a whole lot of people."

"Is there anything we can do to protect the church people in case they get in over their heads?" Elise asked.

"Bob Huggens and I talked about that a little bit at the retreat. For all that he's a crusty old farmer, he's got a good head on his shoulders. I think the main thing we have to do is teach people truth, but maybe I should start doing a little research into our Ray Jacobs and his claims. When I have time, that is."

Chapter Seventeen

Ray found Zeke to be the perfect web designer. Savvy about computers with a flair for design, he was able to build a website that was so complex it was difficult for even the most experienced computer users to plumb its depths. Zeke had added various logon options, user-specific reporting capabilities and even connected e-mail marketing. Yet with all his skill, he was naive about people and never questioned Ray about his business, or why he wanted so many layers to the website. Ray had him convinced that financial sites were all set up that way for security.

Zeke had been spending a lot of time with Ray and Ray got him the job of designing a web page for Daryl's real estate business too. Then Daryl wanted him to design one for Lisa. Zeke only wished he had money of his own to invest with Ray. Ray was fantastic. Ray was rich. Ray was everything Zeke wanted to be.

"Grandmaw, why don't you invest some money with Ray Jacobs?" Zeke queried. "I know you've still got a little money sitting in that savings account. What kind of interest is that earning you? Three percent? Less than that, I bet! Ray is telling people they can get 40 or 50% in just a few months! You'd be WAY better off."

Ruby was sorely tempted. Cautionary statements ingrained in her by her father were holding her back, however. Things he used to say regularly: "A bird in the hand is worth two in the bush" and "There's no fool like an old fool." No, Ruby decided. There would have to be more proof before she was going to trust what little money she had left anywhere but where it was right now.

Zeke barely kept his impatience with Ruby's conservative ways in check. But he knew where Ruby kept her 'private information,' like passwords, codes and such. Maybe he could repay Ruby's kindness to him by investing the money himself! He just KNEW Ray would turn that couple thousand into a decent retirement for his grandmaw.

———

Weasel worried over the rumor that the Feds were after George. He figured it had about a 50-50 chance of being true; after all, hadn't he warned George that it wasn't a good idea to skip out on his parole? And although they'd never be able to make a money laundering charge stick, they probably could make a case for tax evasion. That alone would be enough to put George away for quite some time. He knew there was a limit to how much prison his brother could take without going mad or succumbing to the violent elements around him. Didn't that counselor George saw back in junior high warn him that being born to an addicted mother would make him prone to addictive behavior? Besides, even if the rumor was false, it meant someone was out to get George. And wasn't it his duty to check on his best friend and brother? He decided it was high time to track down George's whereabouts.

Weasel didn't expect it would be too hard; after all, he knew the alternate names he had supplied for George. And he knew George was heading south. A simple matter of hacking into some driver's license bureaus and he'd be able to make a little trip to see his brother.

Weasel thought back to the difficult time when George was on trial for embezzling funds from the man he was working for. Others had come out of the woodwork claiming George had stolen from them or their relatives as well. Weasel had called in some favors with the less savory elements of society and gotten most of them to drop their charges against George. There was that one man, though... Al Something or other, who was pretty belligerent. Weasel always thought that he had something to do with the time George almost got run over while crossing the street. George, with his supreme ego, had insisted that no one could be *that* mad at him. But wait! Could that Al and the guy at the bar be one and the same? He felt a chill travel down his spine. If it was the same man, he had gained a lot of weight and shaved his head but it *could* be the same guy.

———

Will kept talking about how much fun it was to golf with Ray, Doc and Bob. "You know I only started golfing because it would give me opportunities to minister to the more well-to-do segment of our congregation, right, Kari? Well, I'm not too good at it and it was never much fun until John moved away and Ray became a regular in our foursome. He is SO much fun! I have never laughed so hard as when we're all golfing together. Why, the other day he had an impossible putt, it was uphill and with a curve to the left. He started singing "I Feel Lucky," broke into a soft-shoe dance, and was twirling his putter like a cane, making up new words to the song as he went. Bob and Doc were laughing so hard I thought they might collapse! Even the women at the next tee were watching with wide eyes and huge grins."

Kari suddenly had an idea. "How about Kristen and I golf with you and Ray this week? Kristen needs some fun in her life."

"Aw, Hon, you know Kristen doesn't enjoy golfing or any other sport. Not that we haven't tried to get her interested." He added the last bit under his breath.

"But Will, you said you didn't enjoy golf much either - until Ray joined you. Maybe he would do the same for Kristen." Kari was at her sweetest and most persuasive.

Will knew he was beat. "I'll see what I can set up."

Will thought about his daughter and wondered where things had gone so wrong. He had been thrilled when Geraldine Lile had decided to move to Florida to live near Kari's sister. He thought it would be good for Kristen to be away from her grandmother's idea of "proper" behaviour for a "Southern gal." Geraldine thought that girls needed to marry, preferably right out of school, have a couple children and then entertain and volunteer the rest of their lives. It had been a great disappointment to her when Jackie never married and Kari didn't have children for so long. He often felt that he was a disappointment to Geraldine too, because he wasn't wealthy enough or handsome enough to fit her prototype. However, the damage seemed to be done in Kristen's life. Grandma Lile had filled her head with all that Southern gal nonsense for 16 years. And now Kari was reverting to the way she had been raised and acting as if there was nothing more important than getting Kristen married — and to the wealthiest man she could find.

Geraldine had drummed the thought into Kari's brain that any man who was interested in her was probably out to get her money. Will thought it was only when his father-in-law lost the mill and the house that Kari decided for sure to marry him. He was only surprised that Kari had married him instead of holding out for someone wealthier. He suspected that Geraldine had told Kristen the same thing: marry a wealthy man so you know he isn't after your money.

When the closing papers had finally been signed on Ray's purchase of "one of the finest examples of Italianate architecture in all of Alabama," also known as the Lile house, he also had good news for Daryl. "So Daryl, now that my business is taken care of, how about we look at the returns on your investment?"

Daryl felt a moment of panic. Is this when Ray would tell him the company had folded, his stock had crashed, and he had lost his commission for good? That's what Lisa was sure was going to happen. But no, one look at Ray's grin told him the news was better than that. "OK, hit me!" he joked.

Ray handed Daryl a check for almost half of the amount he had invested. "And this is without touching your original stake, Daryl. You can look forward to returns like this for a long time to come!"

"Fantastic Ray! Simply f-fantastic! I can surprise Lisa with a new w-washer and dryer this afternoon. And maybe I'll put a d-down payment on that van she's had her eye on as well."

Lisa couldn't believe her eyes when a delivery van pulled up later that day with a brand spanking new front loading washer and dryer. "But, but, who sent you?" she sputtered. She was afraid her mom and dad had taken pity on them even though she had told them to quit trying to finance her life.

"Order signed by Daryl Marshall," intoned the delivery man laconically. "You want 'em or not? Extra charge if we have to return 'em."

"Oh, I'll take them alright!" Lisa was pinching herself to make sure this wasn't her imagination.

Just wait until her Mom heard about this! Finally Laura would have something good to tell her gossipy friends about her 'brilliant' son-in-law.

Chapter Eighteen

On Sunday afternoon Jase was resting on the couch. The little boys were down for naps, Elise had gone up to the bedroom to rest, the girls were busy with homework in their rooms, and Mark and Matthew were quietly playing video games. It was the first time in weeks that he didn't feel pressured by some looming deadline. He set his laptop on his knees and started an "investigation" into Ray Jacobs. He would be the first to admit he wasn't really computer savvy. Yes, he could use one. No, he didn't know how they ticked or where they stored their secrets. But he'd see what he could find through a simple search.

First, he googled Ray Jacobs. Oops. Do you know how many Ray Jacobs there are in this country? In this world? He spent too much time browsing through bios of various men with the same name, but nothing stood out. He thought a bit and decided to try Facebook. Most people were on Facebook, he supposed. He had an account, but rarely, if ever, posted anything. He left that up to Elise.

Ah, here was the right Ray Jacobs. He had 1200 friends! Wow! Who really knew that many people? He browsed through Ray's history. There were statuses about the retreat, about his move to Pecan Grove, about buying the house. There were some funny stories about life at Bella's — I wonder how she likes that? Oh well, Bella probably considered Facebook a tool of the devil and would never know. Nothing that seemed out of the ordinary or out of place. He wondered if Ray had just signed up for Facebook when he came to Pecan Grove, because there didn't seem to be any mention of his life in…where was it? Minnesota? Where would you go from here? Jase was at the end of his investigational abilities. Maybe he'd have more time soon to sort through some more of the Ray Jacobs listings.

He was exultant that his plan to smoke out George seemed to be working. Apparently Weasel couldn't stand the thought that George might be in trouble again. He had managed to be close enough to eavesdrop and overheard Weasel mentioning to the bartender that he was planning a little trip so he'd have to lay off his workers for a bit. He was smart enough to have had the foresight to concoct a story when he spoke to the head of the janitorial department about his plans. "You know my grandfather has been really sick back in Tennessee? Well, his caregiver has been talking of quitting and I may need to go down there kind of suddenly to settle things, either hire a new companion or settle him in a nursing home."

He was granted two weeks leave whenever he needed it. Should be enough, he thought.

Daryl had fulfilled his promise to himself and visited the local car dealer. He put a nice down payment on a slightly used fifteen-passenger Ford van in navy blue. He asked for a decal to be made with the logo for Lisa's Loving Land and asked for it to be delivered. Lisa was in heaven. His marriage, so recently on the rocks, had never been better. "Ray was right, people could be happier with money. Amazing what a difference a little money could make," he thought.

"Hey Daryl," Dr. Swanson hailed him when he came to pick up his twins from Latchkey Kids. "Where'd you get that sweet van? That's really going to help Lisa, isn't it?"

"She deserved it," Daryl replied. "I used the commission I got from selling the Lile house to invest in some stock that I had heard about." Daryl lowered his voice. "I had it on good authority that the market was exploding on this new cyber security device and I was offered a chance to get in on the ground floor. Boy, was Lisa mad! But I was able to buy her a new washer and dryer and put a good amount down on this van after only a few weeks - and that without touching my original investment."

"Whoa! That sounds too good to be true. Can you give me the name of the stock?"

"You know, I think it was something like CySmart? I could look it up for you but I really don't know anything about the stock market. I would be scared silly to invest on my own. But you can talk to Ray — Ray Jacobs — do you know him? I've heard he's helping a few others around town. He specializes in helping people who are asking God to bless them so they can do good to others; he might help you too."

"I've heard Ray's name mentioned. Maybe I'll look him up one of these days." Dr. Swanson wasn't quite sure if he qualified for "asking God to bless him." He figured his plans might qualify as wanting to do good, though. He wanted to build a new clinic to compete with the HMO moving in on Pecan Grove. Maybe he could convince that Jacobs guy that he would also treat charity cases, although that wasn't really on his agenda.

The golf outing was scheduled for a Thursday morning and Kristen complained about having to get up so early. Kristen complained that the day wasn't sunny. Kristen complained that her complexion would suffer if she didn't wear a hat and if the sun didn't shine a hat would look silly. Kristen complained that they couldn't stop for a nice leisurely breakfast. Will had finally had enough.

"Kristen, I will not abide your constant griping this morning! We are supposed to be going *golfing!* For *fun!* If this is so distasteful to you, why did you agree to come?"

"I don't *know* why we *have* to go *golfing! Why* couldn't we go to a *concert* and a nice *dinner?* Or even a *museum* or *something?*"

"I thought you were interested in Ray Jacobs. Golfing makes Ray happy. Are you truly interested in the man, Kristen? Or just in his money?"

Will rarely got involved in the romance department of his daughter's life, but Kari wasn't doing much to direct Kristen right now. Come to think of it, Kristen was too old for either of them to be meddling. Maybe he should suggest that Kristen move out of the house. Get an apartment and find out what life was *really* like! That would likely go over big.

Kristen was frustrated. Yes, she had asked her mother for help snagging Ray, but why, oh why, did her mother have to pick *golfing?* Kristen had never attempted much in the way of sporting activities having discovered in grade school that she had no natural tendency toward athletics. Although her parents encouraged her to try various sports, she always had an excuse why she couldn't. She just never wanted to open herself to the possibility of failure. It was safer to just pretend that *sports* were *beneath* her.

But, here she was, on a *golf* outing, about to display her utter ignorance in front of the man she wanted to impress. Earlier she had been crabby and irritable, but when her dad reprimanded her sharply, she decided it would be better to put on her sweetly innocent persona — that worked pretty well with men, didn't it?

"Oh, Ray! I *bet* you are about the *best* golfer in Pecan Grove, aren't you?" she cooed.

"Not so much," he replied. "I just enjoy the challenge. Don't you?"

"Not so much", she thought. The challenge would be not to look foolish.

On the first tee, Kristen held back until the others were excitedly jabbering about where their balls had landed, then attempted her first swing, which missed the ball. "Good idea to take a couple of practice swings, Kristen," Ray called encouragingly.

Too bad I wasn't practicing, she thought, as she carefully lined up again, this time hitting the ball a decent distance, although it appeared to land in the tall grasses at the edge of the fairway.

There was some discussion as to who would ride in the cart as Kristen assumed she would ride with Ray, but their balls had headed in opposite directions. "But Daaad, I don't *want* to golf with *you!*" She stamped her foot and pouted as she took her place in the cart with Will.

It took Will and Kristen quite a while to catch up with Kari and Ray at the next tee. Kristen couldn't get her ball out of the rough and opted for the penalty. Then it was several more crooked hits before she got to the green. Will tried to console his disconsolate daughter. "I know how you feel, honey," he said. "Sometimes I think the only place God doesn't answer prayer is on the golf course!"

"How's it going, Will, Kristen?" Ray inquired.

"I'm pretty tired of my dad, Ray. All he does is correct me! 'Stand with your head down. Stand closer to the ball. Stand still when you swing.' I'm sure you'd be more fun as a partner."

"Well, I'll just stay with you, then," Ray offered magnanimously. "Your mom and dad would probably enjoy some time together anyway." Ray watched as Kristen hit her ball from one side of the green to the other and back. He couldn't help but compare Kristen's grumbling to Sarah Jane's light hearted laughter as she made fun of herself while mini golfing.

Kristen was determined to show that she could, indeed, golf. So she stepped up to the next tee resolutely. Ray encouraged her by telling her to 'swing hard, in case you hit it!' So she did. Swing hard, that is. And she sort of hit it too. But the way she hit it caused the ball to *somehow* squirt *backwards*! When she looked up, she saw her mom and dad were laughing along with a couple waiting for them to tee off.

"Take a mulligan, Kristen," Ray managed to choke off his laughter.

Sure, she thought. Whatever that is.

The rest of the hole proceeded slowly with Kristen hitting her ball from one side or the fairway to the other and gradually approaching the green. For Kristen, the best part was that Ray had opted to stick with her and was continually encouraging her. Even when her ball barely dribbled forward, he would say, "Great job, Kristen. You won't catch the wind if you keep it low." Only once did she feel a little uneasy -- when he complimented her on drive (that landed in a pond) by saying "Good shot!" and then he muttered what sounded like "if that's where you were aiming." But she must have been mistaken. Ray was too much of a gentleman to be making fun of her.

After a couple more holes with Kristen getting increasingly frustrated as her stroke count mounted astronomically, Ray took pity on her. "Here Kristen, let me help you hold that club right so you get a decent swing." He kept as much distance and professionalism in his actions as possible, but stood behind her and placed his hands over hers to help her with her swing. "There you go! That was your best tee shot yet," he encouraged, even though the ball went only about 50 yards down the fairway.

But Kristen was tired. At the next tee she announced that she was through golfing. "I've hit that ball three times as often as any of you!" She could tell the others were secretly relieved that they'd be able to finish nine holes before dark.

Kristen volunteered to drive the golf cart and watch the golfers. All went smoothly for a while until, close to the clubhouse, Kristen was jolted out of a daydream about living in the Lile house by someone yelling "Watch out!!" and she realized that she had let up on the brake and the cart was creeping toward a foursome of men. Quickly she stomped on the brake but somehow hit the gas pedal instead. To her horror she hit the closest golfer from behind, sending him toppling over the front of the cart and into her lap! Startled, but basically unhurt, the man said, "Well, honey, that's one way to pick up a guy!" Mortified, she muttered apologies and stomped off to the clubhouse, leaving at least two groups of golfers laughing uproariously.

Later, on the way to the car, Kari remarked quietly to Will, "well that was an entertaining outing. But I don't think it was because of your friend Ray."

Chapter Nineteen

As Weasel drove south from Minnesota, he contemplated ways of approaching George when he arrived in town. It had been fairly easy for him to find his brother's whereabouts — he knew he was heading for warmer weather, but he didn't think George would return to Texas. So he hacked into the DMV websites of several southern states, entering the names he knew were on the driver's licenses he had made for George. He got a hit for Ray Jacobs in Alabama, specifically in a small town called Pecan Grove. So he set his GPS and headed out.

But before too many miles had passed, Weasel noticed a gray sedan that seemed to be lurking just a few cars behind him. He slowed down, hoping it would pass him, but it seemed to have disappeared. He exited the freeway to use the rest area on the Iowa border, then browsed for a while in the kitschy gift shop attached. That should give 'Mr. Gray Car' time to get lost, he thought. To be on the safe side, Weasel then took a county highway to the next town. He was shocked when he again thought he caught sight of the same gray sedan!

Accelerating through a yellow light, he sped down a side street, zipped through a couple parking lots and headed east on a gravel farm road. He saw no plume of dust behind him and felt safe again.

But to be certain, he stopped at a used car dealership in the next small town and ditched his red Jeep.

———

At first he found it easy to follow Weasel. He figured it was a smart idea to attach a tracking device to Weasel's car. There was some trouble when, after driving a few hours, Weasel stopped in a small town and traded the car for a different one. He'd had to pretend to be interested in the piece of junk Weasel had left behind so he could retrieve the tracker surreptitiously while chatting up the salesman about the former owner and what he had bought. Then he had to drive like the devil trying to guess where Weasel was headed. Luckily he spotted a car something like what the salesman described as Weasel's new wheels at a diner. Otherwise… Well, best to just say, he was in a very bad mood.

———

Whistling as he walked toward the Garden Cafe, Ray was excited to tell Sarah Jane about his recent phone call. Will had asked him to fill in for the usual tenor in their barbershop quartet because Bill Wilson had been called out of town for a family emergency. They would be singing in the competition held the Saturday night of Heritage Days. Ray could sing and he loved to perform, so he was a perfect choice for the vacancy.

Suddenly Ray stopped in his tracks. He realized that he was excited by something other than the prospect of making more money. When did that happen? And furthermore, he realized he was excited about telling Sarah Jane! He thought about turning around and waiting to share the news in a more casual manner. Maybe sometime when the subject came up naturally. But he realized that the thought of *not* seeing Sarah Jane, of *not* telling her the news right away was acutely disappointing. Was he growing roots? Was he falling in love? This was *SO* not a part of his master plan.

As he continued walking, much more slowly now, he contemplated the ramifications of falling in love. What would he have to change to make a life with Sarah Jane? Would he really be able to settle in one town for any length of time? And love itself. He had always felt that love was like that 60's song: only true in fairy tales. Was there any such thing for a man like him?

<center>~~~</center>

The weekend of the Heritage Days Festival had finally arrived. After a flurry of activity, the town square was transformed to appear as it was in Antebellum days. People poured into town from all over to attend the craft show, to bring their kids for pony rides and to crowd the downtown park where the carnival was in full swing. Many townsfolk were dressed in Civil War costumes ready to take part in the parade and in staffing the booths that lined the edges of the park. Ruby had taken off work early to paint faces Thursday afternoon and she and Elise were swamped the entire time they were open for business. They had all they could do to keep the line of children moving while catching snippets of the conversation swirling around them as they worked.

From what Elise could tell the hot topics were, in order, that: Daryl Marshall had bought his wife a new van last week for her daycare business, speculation surrounding the death of old Vera McNeely, that Cora Windham was telling people Ray and Sarah Jane were engaged, that Amos Walker was bragging that he was going to win the shuffleboard contest, and lines for the booth selling reproduction Civil War dolls were even longer than for face painting. 'So what about the new van?' she thought. And, 'More power to Amos!' Then, 'Cora's bragging is getting insufferable' and 'At least the town is making money on the Festival so far!'

Friday found Kari exhausted from the children's festivities the day before. But Kristen was in a tizzy over her date with Ray that night. Although she had seen Ray at church and around town since the golf outing, she'd been disappointed that he hadn't asked her on any dates yet. "I'm *sure* I'll have a *chance* with him after we *spend* the day *together*," she had confided to Beth. "It was *so romantic* when he put his *arms* around me and *held* my hands, all on the *pretense* of helping me *golf*!

But today Kristen felt everything HAD to be perfect! Where was her sunbonnet? Did she dare paint her nails or was that not authentic? Should she take her mother's advice and be discreet in her affectionate gestures? Or should she believe *Cosmopolitan* (and her friends) which advised her to leave no doubt about her interest? And "Mother, could you *please* press my costume *one* more *time*? It got *wrinkled* again!"

Ray had rented a costume for Heritage Days, complete with handlebar mustache and suspenders, when he went to Mobile to do some shopping. He dreaded the day with Kristen, but he still thought that a good relationship with the Stewart family was important to his success in Pecan Grove. He and Sarah Jane had arranged to meet at the festival just after the shuffleboard contest started. Sarah Jane assured him that her mother would abandon Sarah Jane to watch the men, especially Amos, play shuffleboard.

Ray had felt awkward about telling Sarah Jane that he had been inveigled into taking Kristen. On one hand he figured he could take anyone he wanted—but did he owe Sarah Jane an explanation? He thought he would casually ask Sarah Jane to join him and Kristen. It was the only part of the day that Ray looked forward to.

———

Weasel had not counted on the number of back roads he had felt compelled to take as he honed in on George. He'd still had a spidey sense of being followed, although he never could catch a glimpse of anyone behind him. He had driven at varying speeds, through towns and down dusty back roads, using every maneuver he could to avoid being followed. He wondered if it was paranoia but he couldn't shake the thought that it could be the man named Al who had vowed revenge on George - or could it be the Feds?

When Weasel finally arrived in Pecan Grove, he was hot and tired. He was doubly dismayed to find the town swollen with tourists for some festival going on in the park. "There goes any chance of a hotel room and shower," he thought resentfully. Driving across the field they were using for parking, Weasel felt a glimmer of hope. Wasn't that the car George — well, Ray now — arranged to buy off a friend before he left Minnesota? Surely it couldn't be a coincidence that there was another vintage black Mustang in the place he expected to find his brother!

———

When Ray arrived just before 5:00 to pick up Kristen he found that her dress was an elaborate hooped affair that would barely fit in his Mustang. When the hoop popped out the door for the third time, he finally gave up and kicked it inside the door. That earned him a dirty look from Kristen — and her mother. Not elegant, but effective, he thought with a grin. He soon discovered out they would have been better off walking from the parsonage as all available parking was taken.

———

Jase was helping with parking at the festival grounds. Any place close was taken by mid-morning, so since 11:00 he had been busy directing people to park in orderly lines in the stubble field at the edge of town. He was disgusted at the driving abilities of the masses of festival-goers. No one seemed to be able or willing to follow directions and park in decent rows. To top it off, it was hot; "hotter'n two goats in a pepper patch," as the other parking attendant put it. He would have to go home and shower before he, Elise, and the kids came back for supper.

———

Just before going off duty, Jase was surprised to see Ray and his Mustang arrive at the overflow parking area — why didn't he just walk? Mizz Bella's wasn't far off the square! Then he realized who Ray's passenger was. Well, well, Miss Kristen couldn't very well be seen walking to the square, right? He thought Ray had been seeing Sarah Jane, so what was he doing with Kristen anyway? Jase laughed a little watching Kristen pick her way across the muddy field. He could just tell Ray was getting an earful!

———

"Would you like to try any of the carnival games?" Ray inquired of Kristen.

"I'm *much* too *clumsy* in this huge *skirt*! But *you* could win a *teddy bear* for me, *couldn't* you?"

"I could sure try!" Ray knew he was out of practice at pitching softballs, but it only cost a dollar with proceeds going to the hospital so he figured it was worth spending some time and money.

Ray eventually won Kristen a modest prize. They sampled the food stands, and laughed over the mayor getting dunked at the fire department's dunk tank. Ray was finding it difficult and exhausting to follow Kristen's petty and disjointed gossiping. He was glad when he could encourage Kristen to meander over toward where the shuffleboard courts were shaded by a line of live oak. "You need to sit down a bit," he said. "You must be getting hot in that get-up!"

As they neared the courts, they saw Sarah Jane standing by herself looking a little forlorn. Ray couldn't help compare the two women. Sarah Jane certainly filled out her costume in a more alluring manner than Kristen. "What's the matter Sarah Jane?" Kristen taunted. "You didn't come all by yourself today, did you?"

"No, Mama roped me into accompanying her, but Amos just claimed her as his partner for mixed doubles in the shuffleboarding! I'll be stuck here the rest of the night!" Sarah Jane was extra irritated to see Kristen clinging to Ray's arm. She thought she had something of an understanding with Ray.

"*What?!* No *man* friend *tonight*, Sarah Jane?" Kristen asked in mock horror. Then she turned to Ray. "Sarah Jane *knows* nearly all the *men* in the *county* I think. *Biblically*, if you get my *drift*! But she *doesn't* have many *girlfriends*!" She laughed nastily.

Sarah Jane gritted her teeth, put on her sweetest saccharine smile, and drawled, "I guess that would be the opposite of *you* then, Kristen. All the little girls follow Kristen, but nary a man in sight!"

"Why you *nasty* piece of *work*!" Kristen was still smiling, but her voice was deadly earnest. "*I'm* here with a *man tonight*, aren't I?"

"Did mommy and daddy bribe him for you? I hear that's how you got a date to the prom back in high school!"

Ray was amused, but decided to step in before two supposedly genteel southern belles started throwing punches — or whatever girls did when they fought.

"Sarah Jane, we're just going to watch a little shuffleboard this evening. How about you join us for a while? Looks like Cora and Amos are getting along pretty well. I think you're off babysitting duty for the night." This earned a dirty look from Kristen but he pretended not to notice.

By 8:00, Ray was beginning to rethink his plan to have Sarah Jane act as a buffer between him and Kristen. He wondered how soon he could take Kristen home although she wanted to see the fireworks. Neither woman seemed very happy and it was obvious that their differences had morphed into open hatred. As the evening wore on, trying to find something neutral to talk about was proving to be difficult. Ray thought perhaps cooking; but it turns out Sarah Jane loved it but Kristen hated to "get her hands dirty." He tried talking about children; Sarah Jane had no experience and Kristen thought she was the expert. Finally, figuring they were both Dixie girls, he asked, "Why do Southerners still have celebrations like this that defend the Civil War? I mean, I'm from Texas, and we have some of our own weird customs, but I would think the south would be embarrassed to celebrate slavery." Maybe politics would work?

"Oh *Ray.*" Kristen drawled condescendingly. "The *war* was *never* about *slavery!* The *South* wouldn't have *had* to fight if the *Yankees* hadn't *invaded* our territory!"

"I thought that kind of thinking went out of style in the 1970's — even in Dixieland," Sarah Jane said dryly. "Who's been filling your pea-brain with that nonsense?"

"You *know* very well, *Sarah Jane*, that *our*, well MINE anyway, great-great *grand*daddy fought *only* to defend the *Southern* way of life! The *slaves* were happy and *well cared* for. There was *no* need for *all* that *emancipation* nonsense. The *Black* people have been *struggling* ever *since*."

"My great-great granddaddy may have left the country during the rebellion of the South, but at least he spoke out against holding another person as property! I suppose you'd like to go back to those days, Kristen? Are you going to buy yourself a slave or two?" Sarah Jane hissed.

"OK, not politics," thought Ray. But it sure explained Kristen's attitude of entitlement. It did seem as if she wanted to live the life of a plantation owner's daughter like Scarlett O'Hara or something.

"I guess that was too serious of a discussion," he said in as charming a manner as he could muster. "Let's get some ice cream before we leave."

"I think I'll meander back toward the shuffleboard courts then," said Sarah Jane. "I'm pretty sure Mama is tired by now."

Kristen barely picked at her ice cream and as it melted into a puddle she said, "Speaking of *serious* discussions, Ray, on my *birthday* last week I gained *control* of some *money* left in a *trust* fund by my *Grandpa* Lile. I was going to use it to *buy* the Lile house *back* for our family — but I *hear* you beat me to it!" She slapped his arm playfully, although her expression didn't match. "*Maybe* you'd like to *help* me *invest* the money instead?"

"Investing can be risky, Kristen," Ray said, although his ears perked up at the mention of her trust fund. "I hope you understand what you'd be getting into."

"But *everyone* is saying *you* know a *great* company that practically *guarantees* fantastic returns! I *think* I can afford to invest at least *$500,000*." Kristen was gratified to see that she finally had Ray's undivided attention.

Ray nearly choked. "Just how much is in this trust fund, anyway?" he sputtered.

"It's been earning *interest* since *before* I was *born*. I *think* it's *nearly* a million *dollars* now."

"I think we'll have to talk," Ray said slowly. "But this is not the time or place."

Just then Ray noticed a furtive movement on the edge of the crowd. His eyes whipped in that direction, but he only caught a glimpse of someone disappearing around the edge of the ice cream stand. "I'll be right back," he whispered and hurried to look around the corner. No one was in sight. "For a minute I thought that was Weasel," he thought to himself. "But why would Weasel be in Alabama? I sure hope he isn't in some kind of trouble."

Ruby was at the "Grits on a Stick" stand next to the ice cream booth. She had been idly watching Ray and Kristen and wondering what kind of hold Will and Kari had over Ray to be able to force him to pay attention to their daughter. It was clear that he could barely drag his eyes off Sarah Jane as she left. Suddenly she saw Ray dart past her to the back of the row of stands. As he passed her table on his return, she asked him what was up. "I thought I saw a drifter stealing a man's wallet!" Ray exclaimed. "But I couldn't see anyone in the shadows and it appears no one is missing their wallet, so I must have been mistaken."

Ray wasn't the only one interested in Kristen's talk of a million dollar inheritance. He was sitting nearby, unremarkable with his appearance changed by heavy glasses and a fake beard. He was actively eavesdropping on Ray.

It had been a difficult journey following the winding back roads that Weasel chose to travel. But, just as he expected, Weasel had led him directly to George. Even in costume, he knew it was George just from the way Weasel was keeping track of him. And from what he was hearing, it seemed that if he played this right he would not only get back what was owed him, but he could see a major profit! How could he get hold of that money? And frankly, he'd like to see ol' George rubbed out in the process.

The next day, Saturday, was the last day of the festival. The biggest crowds came out for the contests, award programs and shows, making it a hectic time. Ray knew the barbershop quartet contest would take place that night and Will had informed him that each group was expected to perform a couple times during the day as well, hoping to pique the interest of the crowds and get them to pay a bit extra for the evening show. He desperately needed to find out if Weasel was really in town. How could he find him without attracting attention? It wouldn't do to advertise that he was looking for his brother. If Weasel was in trouble or needed his help — and Ray felt sure that was the case — advertising that he was here could only complicate the business. He had to hope Weasel would find him soon so they could solve whatever had brought Weasel to Pecan Grove.

Ray had to get his mind off the possibility that Weasel was around so he could really get into the singing. He thought he was doing a pretty good job of it, even ad libbing some dance steps to a couple of the songs. The other guys encouraged him and they talked about making Ray's dancing a part of their evening show. They thought it would impress the judges.

Sarah Jane came by as they were putting on their last afternoon teaser show and he was glad to take a break for some supper with her. "This heat and humidity is wearing me out," he said. "Are there any air-conditioned food vendors?"

"We can just cross the street and go to Betty's Bistro," answered Sarah Jane. "They make a good BLT."

"Sarah Jane, I'm so sorry about last night. I was having an awful time and I thought it would help me put up with Kristen to have you with us, but all I accomplished was making all three of us miserable." Ray wondered how he could make it up to her.

"No worries, Ray," Sarah answered airily. "Kristen's been trying to ruin my life since high school. I think she can't stand it when anyone is happier than she is, so she makes it her business to see that others are uncomfortable. Sometimes I think she has succeeded mainly in making herself miserable. I got over her shenanigans long ago. Now I just avoid her."

After cooling off and occupying a booth for as long as they dared, the couple strolled back toward the amphitheater where the Barbershop Competition would be held. As they moved through a cluster of people waiting in line at the food stands, Ray felt a tug on his pocket. He quickly whirled around with his hand clutching his wallet. He saw a tattooed man slipping through the crowd away from them. He pulled out his wallet to make sure he hadn't been the victim of a pickpocket and saw a slip of paper flutter down. He quickly scooped it up before it blew away. His face paled as he saw Weasel's familiar printing. "Tomorrow morning. Here. 7:00. W."

Chapter Twenty

That Sunday morning was one day Mark would never forget - although he wished he could. He had been enjoying his early morning solitude with nothing more on his mind than getting his newspapers delivered so he could get to church on time. As he pedaled past the city park, he thought he caught a glimpse of someone sleeping near a bench. Well, he wasn't going to bother the guy. Probably a drunk anyway. Dad always said not to mess with anyone who had been drinking because they could be belligerent. So he had pedaled past minding his own business as usual. If only that were all. But on his way home he usually pedaled through the park much closer to that park bench. For some reason, he felt compelled to see if the guy was still sleeping. Just because he never told anyone about what he saw didn't mean he didn't like savoring the feeling that he knew something no one else knew.

So he checked on the guy, surprised to see he was still asleep though the sun was shining right on the patch of ground where he lay. He thought if he made some noise as he pedaled by, the guy would wake up and then Jimmy Fletcher wouldn't put him in jail for being drunk in public. As he came close he noticed the weird way the man was half on and half off the bench — and then... and then, that's when he saw the blood, and he knew the guy wasn't drunk and he wasn't sleeping and he would never wake up again. And Mark started screaming like a girl. And now he couldn't forget.

———

Jimmy Fletcher was excited to be a part of a real investigation. Imagine — a guy brutally murdered right in Pecan Grove! And right at the site of the Harvest Festival too. Too bad Jimmy hadn't been the one to find him. But he *was* first to arrive when the paperboy started screaming. My, what a scene that was. Jimmy would have liked to tell folks about the important role he played in calming Mark, in securing the scene, in the cleanup that followed, but the Chief had warned everyone in the department that if they leaked ONE word about the whole incident he would throw them in jail first and ask questions later, much later. Chief Jones didn't want any gossip traced back to *his* department.

Right now, Jimmy was assigned the boring task of combing the entire park for any scraps of paper or garbage; anything that could be considered evidence. Jimmy didn't really know what was evidence so he was picking up everything. There sure was a lot of trash blowing around after the Heritage Days Festival.

———

Sunday morning Elise had been getting the kids ready for church, but in the back of her mind was a nagging worry that Mark hadn't returned from his paper route yet. Usually he was back, showered and ready to help the little boys with breakfast by 7:00. Then she got the call. The police dispatcher only said that there had been an incident involving Mark and she should pick him up at the police station. Quickly she had called to Megan and told her she was in charge.

"Honey, I have to pick up Mark. They said he's not hurt, but he needs a ride home. If I'm not back by 9:00, see if you can get a ride over to church from Nancy and Chuck. They go right by here on their way in."

Jase was already at the church and Elise knew his phone was off so there was little chance of support from that direction. She worried the whole way to the station and, knowing she should be trusting God with her concerns, she tried to pray. "Oh Lord, you know the thoughts of my heart. Please let whatever 'incident' Mark is involved in be something minor." But something, perhaps the dispatcher's harried tone of voice, made Elise afraid of what she would find.

It was worse than even she imagined. The police station was in chaos. Mark had blood all over his t-shirt and was nearly hysterical. Elise could barely register the word the policeman used: murder. Not Mark! He couldn't be involved in a murder!

After what seemed like hours, she understood that they did not suspect Mark. He had merely *found* a dead man. They were seated in a back room and Detective Jamison was finally free to take Mark's statement. He explained in a calm manner that they needed Mark's cooperation and because he was underage, he needed a parent present. Slowly, interrupted by sobs, questions, and repetitions, the story unfolded.

At every church in Pecan Grove that Sunday morning there were rumors swirling about someone found dead in the park early that morning. No one knew exactly how the guy died. Some said he was murdered! Others said he was a drunk and died in an alcoholic coma, but one thing everyone seemed to agree on was that there hadn't been a more exciting end to the Heritage Days in about forever.

When Ray had swung by the park that morning to meet up with Weasel he had seen all the police activity and steered clear of the area. He knew something bad had gone down and that it wouldn't do for him to get involved. So he was bemused when Ruby asked at the end of service if he knew the deceased man. "I just heard about the death," he replied. "I have no idea who he was. Do they have a name?"

"No, I guess they have no clue, not that anyone has said anyway. I just thought since you are new in town that maybe another stranger would have some connection to you. Guess that's kind of stupid! There were a lot of visitors in town for the festival."

As soon as she realized what was going on, Elise had requested that the police go to the church to get Jase. She sent word that the rest of the children were to go home with Nancy and Chuck. "The main thing, Mark, is the timing." Detective Jamison was saying. "Once again, what time did you first go by the park?"

"I-I have to pass the p-p-park to pick up the papers. I left home at quarter to 5 like always. I-I guess that would take me by the p-p-park about 4:50 or so."

"And you didn't see anyone at that time?"

"N-N-No. It's still pretty dark, and I wasn't looking there anyway. I j-j-just wanted to get started on my r-route." Elise could tell how shook up he was by the fact Mark's stutter was back. He hadn't stuttered for almost five years.

"So what time was it when you DID see something?"

The questions went on and on. Elise could boil it down into five sentences. Why did the detective have to go over it a hundred times, each time phrasing the questions a little differently? Facts: Mark saw something in the park at 5:10. Mark checked on that something at 6:05. Mark started yelling. Mark checked the man to see if he could help — while still yelling. No, Mark never saw anything or anybody else. Period.

Detective Jamison was thorough but seemed a little distracted. Elise couldn't know that he was regretting giving in to his wife's pressure and applying for a job in Dallas. Finally there was action right in Pecan Grove and he was scheduled to leave the department at the beginning of July!

Chapter Twenty-one

Bella was sad to see Ray move out. He had been a model boarder. Never loud, never disrespectful, never flouting the rules. Oh, he and that Sarah Jane had gotten a little "snugly" in the parlor occasionally, but all it took was for Bella to clear her throat as she passed the door and they sprang apart. "Yes," she thought, "if only all renters were as easy as Ray!" And now she was back to worrying about replacing the income from renting his room.

Ray, on the other hand, was eager to put Bella's behind him. He felt that there was always someone looking over his shoulder at the boarding house and too involved in his business. "Probably," he mused to himself, "because there always *was* someone — Bella. She could sneak up on a nervous cat." Today it was Ray who felt nervous as a cat. Too much had happened in the last few days.

There wasn't much to move. He only needed to pack his suitcase, computer and the few things he had bought since arriving in Alabama. Today he was meeting with Leroy Roberts and Mary Ellen Huggens. He had pretty much decided to hire Leroy to do some remodeling at the house — everyone said he was the best at renovating within historic guidelines. First things first though. He hoped Leroy would be able to convert the furnace to gas and put new appliances in the kitchen. That old steam boiler gave him the willies.

He could almost — almost — forget about Weasel for a minute or two. But in the back of his mind the questions repeated over and over: "Why was Weasel here? Who knew his connection to Weasel? Would the police be coming around to question him?" And the nagging fear that HE knew the identity of the body in the park.

Monday morning the Grove Gazette carried a picture of the dead man prominently featured in both the print and digital versions with an announcement that the police were looking for anyone who had seen or talked to the man on Saturday. Herschel Jones, in his capacity as Chief of Police for Pecan Grove, had had to call in help from the county sheriff's department. For the first time in anyone's memory there was to be a press conference. Even the newspapers from Mobile and Montgomery were there trying to get a story!

Jimmy Fletcher had to stay overtime on Monday morning to help with security at the press conference. The mayor stood on the courthouse steps next to Chief Jones, along with the town's only investigator, Detective Jamison. Chief Jones was not a big man but he did have a big voice. He would not have needed the microphones set up in front of him, but with them his voice carried across the square. "I want to reassure the public that this appears to be an isolated incident. There is no danger to any of you. Identification of the victim is ongoing but it is a difficult project since there were so many visitors and carnival workers in town for Heritage Days, but we are making every effort to solve this case."

The reporters started shouting questions. "How did he die? What kind of clues are you following? Did he have any identification? How did he arrive? How do you know there is no ongoing danger?"

The chief's response was uninformative. "There was no wallet or any personal effects found at the scene. The victim's fingerprints have been sent to the national database in Birmingham, but unless he has a record that will not help us. If anyone has any information, or if anyone saw this man at the festival please call the station."

More questions were shouted at the chief.

"No, I will *not* tell you how the man died because the autopsy has not been completed. However, I *will* say that foul play *has not* been ruled out."

The mayor then took the stage and talked about how safe the streets of Pecan Grove were because of their great police department. He stated that he knew the citizenry would support the police and report anything unusual they might have seen or heard. He went on and on until all attending were convinced he just wanted a political speech opportunity.

——— ∼∼∼ ———

Ray seemed troubled when he bought the paper Monday morning at the cafe. Sarah Jane was hard pressed to get her usual smile and greeting from Ray, but he seemed to rally when she teased, "What? No happy, debonair Ray of sunshine for me today?"

"What? Oh, sweetie, it has nothing to do with you! I'm planning to move this week and I was thinking of all I have yet to do."

"Well, those should be happy thoughts! You almost looked sad there when you were buying the paper."

"It is sad. I had come to think of Pecan Grove as a place far removed from the violence of the city. To have the lovely Heritage Days Festival marred by a dead man in the park.... well, it's kind of jarring, you know." Ray was using all his considerable acting ability to conceal the shock and sadness he felt at seeing Weasel's face on the front page of the paper with the headline, "Unknown Drifter Dead."

Ruby also thought she recognized the picture in the paper. She wasn't sure, but it could be the same man that seemed to be watching Ray on Friday night. She wasn't about to talk to Chief Jones, though. He wouldn't be interested in such an uncertain identification.

———

Monday evening Sarah Jane went by the Lile house with a housewarming gift for Ray. She couldn't afford much, but brought him some of the jelly she and her mom had canned along with a fresh berry pie.

"Sarah Jane, I have never been in a real relationship with a woman," Ray confided as they finished their dessert. "I never had a real mom, even. I never knew my grandparents. Once I had a brother, a foster brother, but he's dead now. I had one foster sister a long time ago, but she was older than me, just someone to tease. I've gotten to know you better than I've ever known anyone my whole life! How does a person know if they want to spend the rest of their life with one person? I've never felt like this before, and I never expected that I would, or could!"

Sarah Jane thought for a moment, stunned by the plaintive note in Ray's voice. She had thought he didn't feel things very deeply because he was always laughing, joking and teasing. "I have to confess, Ray, that you and I are more alike than you might think. I've looked for love in all the wrong places. Mama says that my father was never one to face the hard things in life, and telling his wife about a baby with another woman was just too hard. He left Mama high and dry before I was even born. I've tried to find a man who would stay, but so far, none of them have."

"I'm not a good person, Sarah Jane. I can put on a good front, but I'm not really very nice inside. I — well, I'm not sure I can change."

"Ray, I love that you aren't perfect and that you know it. Something in me must resonate with the 'bad boy' inside you. After all, I'm the one with a reputation in town as the loose woman!"

"Maybe we're meant to be together, Sarah Jane. Two partial people would make one whole person, right?" Ray was back to a lighter tone again. "Come on, I'll show you what Mary Ellen and LeRoy want to do with the house!"

The rest of the evening was spent in happy camaraderie. Ray had discovered that he couldn't remove the radiators because of the historic status of the house, but he could convert the furnace to gas power. He planned to gut the kitchen to put in butcherblock counters and a gas stove that was made to look like the old wood burner stoves, as well as a high end refrigerator and dishwasher disguised as cupboards. Sarah Jane chimed in with suggestions for curtains and paint colors.

"Oh! We never got to the garden!", Ray lamented when he was walking Sarah Jane to her car. "I know it's a mess, but you can tell it was once well cared for. I think the brick paths can be salvaged, but plants? I have no idea how to grow even a cactus! I wonder if there's anyone I could hire?"

Sarah Jane vaguely remembered a time when the gardens had been less of a jungle. She had heard talk around town about what a shame it was that the Pearsons didn't keep a gardener. But for the life of her, she couldn't remember who might have been the gardener for the Liles. "I'll ask around, Ray," she said. "Perhaps Mama or Ruby will know someone!"

Later that night, Sarah Jane lay in bed staring sleeplessly at the ceiling. She wondered what a future with Ray would look like. She knew she was falling hard for the charming and debonair man, but there was a niggling voice only heard when everything was quiet and still that asked, "Is Ray too good to be true?" She had felt that evening that Ray was about to divulge more about his past, but then he quickly changed from introspective to irreverent and the moment was lost. As her thoughts meandered over their 'relationship' (was it really a relationship?) she realized that there had been other times when Ray had skirted the issue of his past. All she really knew was that he had been raised in a series of foster homes, had had a foster brother whom he loved, and had been in Minnesota for Bible college. But her heart was entangled so she turned her mind to her own future plans, thinking the issue of Ray's past was probably too painful for him to discuss.

What Sarah Jane really wanted was to open her own dance studio in Pecan Grove. She was saving as much money as she could toward that end, but Mama was always overspending and maxing out her credit card so that Sarah Jane had to bail her out over and over again. "Have *I* ever shared *my* dreams with Ray?" she wondered.

Chapter Twenty-two

~

J ase and Elise were at a loss as to how to help Mark overcome the trauma of finding the dead man. Understandably, he had panicked at the thought of delivering papers on Monday morning so Jase had driven him around his route.

"Honey, that was an awful thing for a twelve-year-old to bear. Maybe we should take him to counseling," Jase commented Elise when he got home with Mark.

"I think it will just take some time for him to put it behind him. We really don't have the funds for counseling, do we?"

"I suppose time will help and the best thing might be if the police solve the case. I think that if he knew how and why the man was killed, it would put everything into perspective for him."

It didn't help that the other kids thought it was kind of cool. "Mark, what did the guy look like?" "How did you know he was dead?" "Did you touch him?" "How did you find him?" the younger boys pestered Mark that morning. Elise sent Mark up to his room while she talked to the younger children.

———

"Boys, if you have questions about what happened yesterday, please come to Dad or me. Mark feels bad about what happened and he really, really doesn't want to talk about it. Now, get at those chores!" Elise tried to be kind, but let the boys know it was a closed subject with Mark. She still caught the whispering among them, and from their guilty looks when she came in, she knew what they were talking about!

Zeke admired Ray. His dad had moved out when he was only six and his mom had remarried when he was eleven. Her new husband and Zeke clashed constantly until Grandmaw Ruby had offered for him to come live with her and go to high school in Pecan Grove. He needed a role model then, but no one really filled that place. Now that he had become friends with Ray, Zeke wanted to model his life after Ray's. Ray was not only fun to be around, he also seemed to have everything figured out in his life - and he didn't mind paying for Zeke's lunch sometimes. Zeke was in awe of the way Ray could find great companies to invest in and thought Ray's manner of making money was about the coolest thing ever. After all, Ray didn't seem to be working that hard. He looked at stuff on his computer, met with people to talk about money and played golf. Zeke figured he could do that!

"What are you going to do today?" Ruby had asked her grandson that morning. "I hope you're planning to look for a job!"

"I've got a website and logo to plan for Ray. He wants me to bring him some ideas tomorrow. Maybe I'll stop in and help him at his new house."

"Sure hope you're getting paid for this one!" Ruby muttered.

Zeke was hoping that *Ruby* would be the one getting paid after he invested her money with Ray.

Herschel Jones was in a difficult position. The chief of police was appointed by the mayor of Pecan Grove and he had never worried about being reappointed because he and Mayor Clemons had always seen eye to eye. However, just a couple weeks ago, Stan Bigelow had filed to run against Mayor Clemons in the November election. He had been an outspoken critic of town politics and two years ago he had managed to land a seat on the town council. He felt that Pecan Grove needed to focus more of its time and resources on the newer areas of town instead of the historic areas. He was proposing the downtown buildings be razed for a shopping mall, of all things! Stan also wanted a younger police force and if he were elected Herschel would be out so fast it would make your head swim.

There were few clues for him to go on in solving the biggest case ever likely to come to a town like Pecan Grove. Yet he knew it would help Mayor Clemons win re-election if he could solve this. It wasn't like the death of old widow McNeely. People had spread rumors that there had been foul play in her death, but after a brief investigation it was obvious that no one had profited. It was pretty much a given that in her advancing dementia she had mistakenly taken an overdose of morphine and died. But this fella in the park was another story. He had been stabbed, the knife slashing his carotid artery. However, there didn't seem to be much force behind the thrust which made Herschel wonder if the wound had occurred accidentally during a struggle. The only fingerprints on the knife were the victim's own, and the victim was wearing a knife sheath on his leg. The weapon itself was left at the scene. It was the kind of Army knife carried by thousands of street people and former Army men across the country and available at any Army surplus store for around $15.00. Could the wound have been self-inflicted? Kind of an unusual way to commit suicide, but stranger things had happened. But then, why were his pockets emptied? Had that been done after the man was dead? And what about the marks in the grass that could have been from a small scuffle? The distinctive heel print that the crime scene guys photographed could have been made anytime during the festival. The chief didn't want the manner of death leaked to the public. Maybe another call on young Mark Griffiths was in order.

He was impatiently waiting for the fingerprint analysis to come back. He had assigned the overnight flunky... what's his name?... oh yeah, Jimmy Fletcher, to sort through the park garbage bins for anything that couldn't be accounted for as part of the festival trash. He hoped the kid would recognize something that wasn't ordinary, but he seemed like the conscientious type who would keep more garbage than he threw away. The sheriff's office was handling questioning of the carneys since the carnival had moved to a town outside his jurisdiction and the sheriff had working relationships with neighboring counties. Personally, he was sure that was the key. The guy was most likely with the carnival and had some kind of altercation with another carney. At least the out-of-town press had basically lost interest when they realized the man was likely just someone passing through with the carnival. He hoped the town forgot just as quickly that the murder was unsolved.

"Jimmy!" Chief bellowed, walking into the evidence room. "What kind of success have you had with that trash?"

———

Zeke was excited to see inside the Lile house. His ma and grandmaw had talked for years about the grandeur of the rooms and the lavish parties Geraldine Lile had thrown. Grandmaw Ruby had been part of the catering staff when she was young and was enthralled with the way the people dressed and behaved on "the other side of the tracks." Not too many people had been in the house since it was sold to the Pearsons and now, because of his friendship with Ray, he would be able to tell Grandmaw Ruby all about it.

He knocked on the imposing front door hoping Ray wasn't on the golf course this morning. He was excited about the logo and website graphics he had designed for Ray's investment business and figured that was a good excuse to stop by. Then he would casually ask about investing Ruby's money. Ray was on the phone and seemed distracted when he answered the door. He motioned Zeke into the parlor area where he had a desk set up looking over the wide front lawn. "I'll be right with you Zeke," he murmured.

Zeke wandered around the room while Ray's call went on and on. He tried to ignore Ray's laptop on the desk; he *really* did! But the computer drew him like a magnet. He could tell Ray had been working on something because the screen saver had a little flashing icon in the lower left. He figured he could wake the computer just to see what kind of work was involved in investing and no one would ever know he had snooped.

At first Zeke was confused by the information that came up on the screen. Then he began to wonder why Ray would record all that stuff. Was it a kind of diary, maybe?

Chapter Twenty-three

W ill couldn't wait to share with Kari the news Ray had given him on the phone that morning. When he finished his office work he practically bounded over to the parsonage for lunch. "Kari, guess what!?" He grabbed her around the waist and twirled her about the room. "I invested some money with Ray! He says it's earned nearly 50% of its value back in under two months! I decided to reinvest the interest instead of cashing it out - we'll be able to afford a vacation in Hawaii like you've always dreamed! And we'll still be able to afford a wedding should Kristen ever settle down!"

Kari was breathless. "REALLY?!?" she squealed. "But of course, Kristen has her own money for a wedding now!"

Will had forgotten about the trust fund. Mainly because he'd never approved of it in the first place. It always seemed to him that there were families who had lost their livelihood when Kari's father declared bankruptcy, and yet he had protected a large sum of money by starting that trust fund. Shouldn't that money have helped to repay those he had borrowed from? Illicit gains and easy money couldn't be a good thing for Kristen.

"But if this continues, and Ray says it should be good for years yet, we won't need to use Kristen's money. She can just give it away."

"Oh, Will," Kari sighed. "You are too kind! You know that, don't you? I wonder what Kristen would think about that?"

———

Ray had also advised Kent Kirkland to keep his dividends to let the stock market keep earning for him. He was inclined to follow Ray's advice although he talked it over with his wife first. "Gina, I know you supported my investing with Ray and now we have the opportunity to cash out some of the dividends we've earned. Or we can reinvest it to have more money earning for us. What do you think?"

Gina was more than ready to have more money now. "If we cash out part of the dividends, we could lease that sweet Lexus SUV over at Main Motors, couldn't we? And then I'd have a car I can be proud to be seen in. By spring we can still buy the bigger RV that we really wanted. And if it keeps growing at this pace, maybe I can quit teaching and stay home with the kids."

"I wouldn't count all those chickens before they hatch, dear. But I suppose you're right. No sense driving that junk heap when we can afford luxury."

———

He hadn't counted on Weasel's death, although the guy was just another low-life petty crook in his eyes. Still, it complicated matters. He wasn't able to stay in Pecan Grove when any stranger in town would be linked to the killing. He daren't show his face around George, 'Ray,' either. He thought about that Saturday night, well, actually early Sunday morning. Weasel had spotted him and cornered him, demanding to know why he had been followed in Minnesota and all the way to Alabama. "I saw you lurking around the bar in Minneapolis! What are you doing here?" Weasel's voice had been quiet but threatening.

He thought he could just walk away, but then Weasel had pulled a knife. The fool thought his Army training would be enough, but he didn't know who he was dealing with. He had learned to fight hard and dirty when he was still addicted to meth. Still, he had been shocked when in the struggle the knife jabbed Weasel's neck. But there was no way of connecting the death to him; he had only grabbed the hand that was holding the knife. No stranger to killing, the death only bothered him because it made things difficult.

"Mom, you'll never believe what happened this morning," Lisa gushed as she juggled the phone, a fussy toddler and the breakfast dishes concurrently. "Daryl sold *another* house! That makes the third one since the Lile house."

"Well! I never thought he had it in him." Laura was suitably impressed. "What do you suppose got into that boy?"

"You know, I think he just needed a boost in his confidence. Maybe we were wrong, maybe it isn't real estate that is a bad fit for Daryl, maybe it was the job as a surgical tech that caused his problems. And you know, our relationship is better too. It's almost like we're newlyweds again. He's so thoughtful and considerate."

"TMI!" Laura laughed. "Do you want to hear what I heard about that dead guy? The women at Bible Fellowship are saying he was dealing drugs and came to town to get the kids all hooked on drugs!"

"Oh, Mom! Not that again! Every stranger that shows up in Pecan Grove is reputed to be a drug pusher! You might as well accuse Ray Jacobs of drug dealing. He's new in town too."

"I guess we know *that* isn't true, don't we? You know your Daddy decided to put the kids' college fund into investments with

Ray. He didn't want to be left out of all the wealth that is coming to Pecan Grove. I'm glad, too. The kids will have *so* much more money for college now."

———

Jimmy had spent nearly all of his last shift sorting through the garbage he had picked up in the park. There were innumerable greasy food wrappers, tons of sticks from pronto pups and everything else sold on a stick, as well as plastic cups and bottles galore. Man, what kind of slobs came to that festival anyway? Only a few things seemed out of place to him so he had set them aside. There was a grocery list, a receipt for gas from Missouri, a pen from a car dealership he'd never heard of, a scrap from a matchbook with an unusual logo and two beer bottles from some weird brewery called Leinenkugel's.

The chief looked the items over, grunted something that sounded like approval, and told him to go home. Tonight he was assigned the thankless task of tracking down the brewery, the dealership and the matchbook. Boring computer work and probably fruitless, he thought.

———

Kristen met with Ray later in the week. Her dreams had been populated with great plans for the things she could buy when the money started rolling in. She was just sensible enough to realize she shouldn't outright spend the money she was inheriting, but figured any return on her investment was fair game.

Ray followed his plan to keep this all about what God wanted to do, not just about making money. "You know, Kristen, I'm convinced that part of the success of these investments is rooted in our motives. I know I wasn't successful in getting rich until I trusted God with the money he had given me. It seems God has given you a great deal of money that you didn't have to work for. What is your motivation in making even *more* money?"

Kristen was flummoxed for a moment. But she didn't grow up in church without learning the proper religious lingo. "I *just* want to be *able* to serve *God* with my *money.*" she said piously. "I *thought* I could do *that* by buying *this* house back, but I *see* that maybe *God* wants me to have something *bigger.* If I bought a *country estate* I could start a *home* for… for…well, for abused *women* or…or… something!" She thought that was pretty good thinking for being put on the spot.

Ray didn't really care what she planned to do with any profits she garnered. He just wanted to make sure she was going to blame any losses on God, not on Ray. If there was one thing Ray had gained from studying church people over the years, it was that they accepted almost any reversal of fortune with equanimity if they believed it was from the hand of God or if they were convinced it was because of their own lack of faith. All he had to do was plant the seeds.

By the end of their meeting, Kristen had trusted Ray to invest $750,000 in the cyber security stock. She said she wanted to be ready with enough money when the next great property became available. Ray wondered if Will knew what she was up to. Oh well, not his lookout. She was an adult, right?

———

Chief Jones had settled at his desk to read reports from the various lines of inquiry he had set in motion. He looked over the sheriff's department report and, as he expected, none of the carneys would admit to knowing *anything.* He wondered what kind of motivation would make them talk. Was there anyone willing to put up a reward for information about the death of a drifter?

Jimmy Fletcher had been excited about the results of his computer searches so the Chief picked that up next. Ok, so Leinenkugel's beer was popular in Wisconsin and Minnesota. But it was a stretch for Jimmy to connect that with Ray Jacobs having moved here from Minnesota. Especially since a side note admitted that Leinenkugel's had expanded their distribution to Atlanta and Austin in 2006. He wondered if there were any stores in Mobile selling the stuff.

And a pen from a car dealership that had been traced to Iowa and a receipt from Missouri were pretty much dead ends — after all, people had come from all over for Heritage Days. But the matchbook logo... Jimmy had done some good work in matching that partial logo with Sven and Ole's bar in Minneapolis. Maybe he *should* go talk to Ray Jacobs.

His thoughts were interrupted by the dispatcher informing him that the crime lab was on the line with fingerprint results. Now this could be a solid lead.

Zeke got through his session with Ray, although he couldn't remember a single thing about the Lile house to tell Ruby later. He wondered if Ray caught on to his nervousness, although he had lied to cover it, saying he had a job interview later that morning. At least the funds were invested with minimal fuss. He wished he had been able to focus on just what Ray was doing with them, though. What should he do about what he had seen? Ray was his hero, and nearly everybody in town thought he was wonderful. On the other hand, they all looked at Zeke as a lazy bum. Who would take his word against Ray's?

Maybe there was a logical explanation. Maybe Ray had a reason for keeping information, very *detailed* information, about the business, financial and family life of everyone in Pecan Grove. Zeke knew some of the names on that list hadn't invested with Ray because he saw Grandmaw Ruby on that list! And it called Zeke a liability to Ruby! He saw Daryl on the list, too, with the notation 'easy mark.' Zeke thought Daryl was making money and helping advertise Ray's investment business all over town! Why was he an 'easy mark'?

What to do, what to do. If he told Grandmaw she would chide him for snooping and for believing the worst about someone. The police were too busy with the dead man in the park and all that entailed to care about someone's journal. And he didn't want to spread rumors. He wasn't sure but he thought God looked down on that.

———

Jase wasn't sure who he could ask for advice either. He knew Bob Huggens wasn't a fan of Ray's, but he was pretty sure Bob wasn't too computer savvy. So when he saw Bob in town late in the week he wondered what to tell him. But it was Bob who had news this time.

"Hey there Pastor Jase," Bob greeted him. "I got me a new job in town!" His chuckle almost sounded fiendish. "Ya know that there Ray Jacobs is fixin' up the Lile place - wa'll, MaryEllen and her Leroy are helpin'. He wanted a gard'ner, so guess who's a-gunna do it?" He grinned hugely.

"That's great Bob!" Jase enthused. You can keep an eye on things better when you're close to his home and office like that." Jase was talking quietly, being cautious in case anyone nearby was interested in their conversation. "I was trying to do some computer research on Ray, but I'm not too well versed in all that computer jazz. I didn't find anything yet.

He was headed back to Minnesota.. He planned to return to his job for a month or so before checking on George Ray again. He figured since 'Ray' had bought a house, was raking in cash left and right, and was well liked in town that there was plenty of time before he was likely to close up his operation in Pecan Grove. All the money Ray could amass would belong to him in the end. Let him make more!

He thought it highly unlikely that there was anything to connect the killing to him. He had taken all Weasel's personal items and the cash he was carrying. He had driven the car into a deeply wooded sinkhole and hiked back to town. There was no clue — he was sure there was no clue — but still he worried.

———

Kristen had spent an uneasy week after her session with Ray. Whatever had possessed her to blurt out that nonsense about a women's shelter? She knew nothing about abused women. Nothing! Had she ever even seen an abused woman? No, surely not. What did they look like, anyway? She imagined women with broken, bloodied bodies running screaming away from monster men in black leather jackets.

But then she thought about Tara Knight. Tara came to church every Sunday with her three kids. Her husband was a trainer at the health club and he was so buff and handsome! One time Tara and the kids had stayed for a fellowship dinner after church. Tara was laughing and talking until her husband walked in. He spotted her, barked "time to get on home" and turned away. Tara's face had blanched, her eyes grew wide and her cheerful demeanor fled. She gathered up the kids without a word and left. The next Sunday Tara had a broken arm. She said she had tripped over the kids' toys. Now Kristen wondered.

Then there was Mrs. Hughes. She never smiled, never initiated a conversation. She seemed afraid of her own shadow. Kristen and her girlfriends had laughed at her and called her Mrs. Scaredy-cat to her face. But could she be abused?

There were others and they were haunting Kristen's thoughts and her dreams. How had she become so insensitive to the people around her? And now that her eyes were open, she somehow knew she could never just return to her carefree life where the biggest problem was what to wear.

That week, Kristen spent her break time at the library looking up domestic violence. She was shocked at some of the statistics. Could it be true that one in three women were physically assaulted at some time in their lives? That *twenty* people *per minute* are physically abused by a *partner?!* But why was no one saying anything? Who *were* all these people? She was left feeling even more unsettled.

Chapter Twenty-four

~

C hief Jones took the call from the crime bureau hoping there was an identification for the body in his morgue.

"This is Chief Jones."

"Hey Chief!" he was greeted by the voice of Tony Morales, his longtime friend from the police academy. "Hear there's been a spot of excitement in your sleepy corner of the woods!"

"Hey Tony, how're ya doing? How's the wife and kids? Aw, you big city dudes are used to stuff like this, huh? But this killing has thrown Pecan Grove for a loop, that's for sure!"

"Well, Carolina and the kids are great. Judson just graduated from SMU, you know. That's finally the end of college tuition for our family. But I might just be able to help you a bit with *your* problems since we got a match on the fingerprints."

"No kidding? I thought after waiting over a week that the news wouldn't be good." Chief Jones couldn't resist a little dig. "So who do we have?"

"So sorry," Tony replied breezily. "Place has been swamped. Guess your request got buried under the avalanche. Anyway, we matched him up through military records. Guy by the name of Wayne Simonson. Turns out he was an Army Specialist. Codes and encrypted communications were his responsibility. Honorable discharge five, almost six years ago after three tours in Afghanistan."

"Wow! He sure didn't look the part of a successful fella when we got him. Looked the part of the classic drifter or carney."

"Course, he coulda been both," Tony countered. "Hear of a lot of these soldiers going off the deep end when they get back. I'll fax the information on his record and next of kin for ya."

"So what's your family up to?" Tony enquired.

"Walker is on the force over in Jackson, as you know. He's up for promotion in the spring and it's a good thing, too. His boys are growing and eating him out of house and home." After a few more pleasantries, the men signed off. Chief went to the fax machine immediately thinking surely they'd get some answers when he contacted the family.

<center>~~~</center>

When Elise answered the door she was surprised to see the Chief of Police on the other side. "Chief! What can I do for you? I hope you're not here for Mark again. I think he's finally beginning to heal from the initial trauma. At least he hasn't had nightmares for a couple nights now."

"I just wanted to talk with Mark one more time if I could. I was hoping he might have remembered something else and I also wanted to caution him about what he could say to his friends or others who might be asking questions. You know, just to tie up some loose ends."

"I suppose you're just doing your job. I hate to see him get stirred up again though."

"I'll be gentle, Mrs. Griffiths. I know how worried you've been. By the way, we finally have a name to attach to the poor fella. Can't make it public, though, until I talk to the family. I have a call in for a sister right now."

When Mark came into the room he noticeably shrank from the police chief. Elise encouraged him to relax, reassuring him that it was all routine procedure.

"Mark, I want you to know the police are going to solve this crime," the Chief began. "There is still a bit of uncertainty about what exactly happened in the park, but, as you know, the victim was stabbed, apparently with his own knife. All this is information that we haven't made public. I know we told you right away that you shouldn't talk about what you saw, but I want to remind you that it is still vitally important for you to keep everything about the crime scene quiet. You see, there's often information at a crime scene that only someone who was there, like the criminal, would know. If and when we are questioning a suspect he might reveal something that only someone who was there should know. Do you understand?"

Mark nodded. "I like to read the Hardy Boys mysteries. Sometimes in those books they catch the guy because he knows too much."

"Perfect!" the chief beamed. "I was sure I could count on you. Are you doing ok otherwise?"

"Yeah, I guess so." Mark straightened his shoulders. "Mom and Dad are helping me not to think about it too much. I mean, people die everyday and someone has to find them. Why *shouldn't* it be me?"

The chief was impressed with Mark's maturity and resolve. "Now, just one more time. Start from the beginning and tell me what happened that Sunday morning…"

Elise stepped out on the porch with Chief Jones as she showed him out. "I hope you weren't shocked by Mark's comments, Chief," she began. "Jase has been teaching the kids about pride and how not to expect the world to treat you better than anyone else. He thinks too many young people feel entitled to special treatment these days."

"I think that's a wise life lesson, Mrs. Griffiths. You tell young Mark he can come work for me when he's all grown up. I like his attitude."

———

"So, Will, I think I'll try a long iron on this par three. How are you going to play it?" Doc asked halfway through their round of golf.

"I think I'll use my four iron this time — and pray," Will replied.

After Doc hit his ball up on the green, Will stepped up for his shot. Unfortunately he topped the ball and watched it dribble a few yards out.

Ray watched the two men and shook his head sadly. "Will, I don't know much about Baptists, but when I pray, I usually keep my head down!"

Doc and Rob cracked up. It took Will a minute to catch the joke, then he laughed too. "Ray, after we golfed with my wife and daughter they said you weren't funny at all. Why couldn't you have been more entertaining when they were with us — maybe take some of the focus off Kristen's troubles?"

"Kind of afraid to be, Will. Seems like they've both got me pegged as your future son-in-law.

"Aww, sorry about that. Kristen would get over her crush quickly, like she always does, if you hadn't bought her granddaddy's house. Me? I don't get the obsession Geraldine had with that house and it's an obsession she's passed down to Kari and Kristen. I mean it's just a place to live like any other."

"I never even realized the connection until after I bought it, Will. But there weren't any other houses available that fit my criteria and the Lile house is perfect for me. I hope they come to terms with it sooner rather than later. I don't want to give up our friendship."

"Good thing I don't have any eligible daughters, Ray, or maybe you'd have to fend off Rasmussen women too!" Doc laughed.

"Maybe you'd be willing to wait for one of my daughters, Ray," Rob chimed in. "But, hey, if things don't work out with that beautiful hostess down at the Garden Cafe maybe you'd like to start courting my Olivia. She's beautiful, talented and has a corker of a personality! She just turned five... that's only what? Twenty-six years too young?" Rob's outrageous proposition had the men chuckling all the way to the clubhouse.

The Lexus in the parsonage driveway was a source of constant comment at Bethel Bible Church. While a few were skeptical and called it a showy indulgence, there were many more who quizzed their pastor on how they could get on the gravy train, too. Pastor Kent Kirkland was never one to let a good opportunity slip by so the next time he ran into Ray at "Book 'n' Brew" he said, "I've been studying up on your retreat topic of God's blessing and I'm wondering if it wouldn't make a good Sunday evening sermon series. What do you think?"

"Pastor, I think you need to follow God's leading on your sermon topics, not mine," Ray replied humbly. "But I'm sure your people would benefit from an infusion of trusting God for His blessings."

Kent was glad Ray didn't object. He was always happy when he could increase his importance by passing a popular subject off as his own idea. And if more people got involved with investing that would mean more money coming into the church. More money would mean they could start that building project he wanted. It irked him that Jase wouldn't support him to drum up interest in adding a new auditorium. Sure they had enough room for right now, but the rich members of his church were getting older and Kent wanted to secure his legacy while they were still around to give.

———

The hot summer evenings were perfect for sitting on the wide verandas of the Lile house and watching across the back lawn as the deer and other wildlife ventured out of the fringe of forest by the creek. Ray and Sarah Jane often sat there in the evenings snuggled in the porch swing Ray had installed or sprawled in the comfortable lounge chairs. Ray had started a game he called 'Where In The World Am I?' He would begin by describing a place; sometimes one he had visited but just as often a place he wanted to see. Sarah Jane would try to guess where he was describing. His vivid descriptions made the exotic, faraway places seem so real she began to yearn to travel.

"I'm thinking of a place where the sun is always shining," Ray began one night.

"Oh, Ray! That one's too easy. Pick somewhere else."

"What do you mean, 'too easy?' I haven't hardly started!" Ray said indignantly.

"Everyone knows that the only place the sun is always shining is wherever *you* are, Ray. You're the Ray of sunshine."

"So that's how you're thinking, huh? Well, then, you're only half right."

"Half right?" she giggled. "I guess that's closer than usual."

"Yes, half right. Because the sun only shines for me when we're together," he murmured into her hair.

———

Doc Rasmussen had heard enough from Will about his gains after investing in cyber security stock. Will was pretty vague about the specific stock Ray invested in, saying that Ray didn't want to divulge that information or the market would get flooded. Doc decided perhaps his own portfolio could use a little boost from some higher risk, higher potential stock. He checked on his computer for the latest information and what he found convinced him that he had to move on this fast. The press releases for various cyber security companies were pretty impressive. Why, one company called CySec was bringing out their "checkpoint infinity software that could manage cloud, mobile and business protection including ransomware and cyber extortion as well as poisoned Wi-Fi networks and phishing schemes." It sounded like multiple businesses as well as the government would be interested in this product — the stock prices would skyrocket just as Will was saying.

He picked up his phone and called Ray for an appointment that same afternoon. He was so pumped that when he ran into his colleague, Dr. Swanson, he told him all about it.

Carefully looking over the report from the Crime Bureau, Chief Jones waited for a return call from Wayne Simonson's sister. Having a name wasn't enough, he realized. He needed information on where Mr. Simonson had been since he was discharged from the Army nearly 6 years ago. The report made it sound like the 34-year-old specialist had behaved in a heroic manner during his last tour of duty in Afghanistan. He wondered what the dickens had turned him into the scruffy-looking body in the park.

Just then his secretary announced a call from Wendy Parker — finally! He eagerly picked up the phone.

"Chief Jones speaking," he answered. "Yes, I did call you. I'm wondering if you're acquainted with a man named Wayne Simonson."

The quiet, reserved Midwestern voice on the other end of the line took on a more enthusiastic tone. "Oh do you have news about Wayne? I haven't heard from him since he was discharged from the Army!"

The chief's expectations fell along with his countenance. "I'm afraid the news isn't good," he began.

After her initial dismay, a distraught Mrs. Parker was able to fill in some gaps. "Oh, I have been so worried that something would happen to him. He called me after he returned from his last deployment. He said he had seen too much violence and inhumanity and that now he was going to see parts of America that he had never seen. After that, nothing.

"I told him he was always welcome to stay with us when he got tired of seeing the country, but I'm afraid he and my husband never did see eye to eye. I wanted Wayne to come live with us when mom died during Wayne's last year of high school. But he wanted to finish school in Oklahoma. I had moved to Kansas City when I married and he felt he needed to keep an eye on Dad. I'm afraid that last year at home was rough on him, though. Dad had started drinking when Mom got sick and he was a nasty drunk. Then Mom died and Dad started carrying on with that young bartender, and I guess Wayne had had enough. As soon as he graduated from high school he joined the Army. And now he's dead. I always wondered if he had that syndrome... what's it called? PTSD or something," her voice trailed off amid a quiet sob.

"Thank you for your time and help, Mrs. Parker. If it's ok with you, I'll call back in a couple days. Maybe you'll have remembered more about your brother's friends or anything else that might help our investigation." Chief Jones was as gentle as he could be.

"Farp!" he exclaimed as soon as he was off the phone. "I sure as Shitzu was hoping for more." If the guy had undiagnosed post traumatic stress disorder it was looking more and more likely he had run with a rough crowd. Probably going to be one of those unsolved murders. But he wondered… if the press got wind of the man's identity, would they find more information?

His secretary overheard him and chuckled. The chief tried hard to stick with his New Year's resolution to quit swearing and it sure made for some interesting oaths.

Chapter Twenty-five

The area around Pecan Grove had an abundance of cheap labor due in part to the fact that most of the textile mills had moved to foreign countries. A couple of years ago there had been a scare that the Grove City mill would move to Honduras, but the county and state worked together to negotiate some hefty tax incentives to keep them in Alabama. Jobs at the mill were steady, but the pay wasn't enough to fuel the dreams of the young people in town. So Leroy had no trouble hiring workers to help with the renovations at the Lile house. Besides the carpenters working on repairing the drywall in an upstairs bedroom, he had a team of men working on a new slate roof and another fellow sanding the wood floors in the kitchen, dining room and parlor, making for noise and mess.

In addition, Ray had hired old Bob Huggens to spruce up the garden. He had heard that Bob had always been gardener for the Liles so he would know how the garden was meant to look. Bob had brought in his cousin's grandson to help him prune the bushes and trees, and that made for disruption outside as well. Ray wanted to live in the house, but it sure would have been easier on everyone if he wasn't trying to meet with clients in his front parlor/office while rushing the renovations.

"Sorry about the noise, Doc," Ray apologized. "Someone told me that remodeling a house is like being in a war zone. You just have to get through it and hope you're alive at the end."

"Looks like you're tackling everything at once. What's the rush?"

"Oh, I'm hoping to do some entertaining come fall. Also, I think I'll enjoy living here more if everything is fixed up right away."

"I remember when I was a kid and the Liles used to live here. There were parties all the time and the gardens were spectacular."

"That's the kind of reputation I'm aiming for. Old Bob says the gardens just need some trimming and sprucing seeing as most of the old plantings are still there and the layout hasn't been altered." Ray was eager to get down to business. "Let's just step into my office and close the door here."

Dr. Rasmussen was ready with the information he had dug up on the internet. "So, Ray, do you think this CySec is a good company for me to invest in?"

"You've really picked a winner here, Doc. There's only one reason I rarely recommend that stock. You see, they cater more to businesses and government so it takes a hefty amount to meet their minimum investment threshold. Not everyone has that kind of money to put in one place. But there's another company that I've been using that has just as good or better results. They require a hefty startup investment too, but not so much as CySec."

"Hmmm. How much are we talking, Ray?"

"Well, I've recently had a commission to invest $750,000 for a client. If you're willing to match that, I could put the two of you together and we'd meet the minimum." Ray was earnestly persuasive. "I was really hoping to see God do something spectacular for this particular client. I think her faith needs a boost and I'm sure this stock will outperform the others I use."

"Oh, that's not so bad. I'm sure I can juggle some other securities and come up with that much by next week or so. I'm *so* glad I didn't try to run this through my usual broker. He's so *very* conservative that I feel like I'm getting nowhere with my investments."

Ray felt he needed to make sure that Doc understood the challenge to his faith that was implicit in high risk investments. "Just a word of caution, Doc. I always remind my clients that the success or failure of any investment rests solely with God. I know you're a man of faith; you wouldn't mind praying with me that God would bless your faith before you make a final decision, would you?"

After the men prayed, Ray took Doc on a brief tour of the rooms he was having remodeled and then the doctor was on his way. "Would it be alright if I tell Dr. Swanson about this company? I know he's raising money for a new clinic he'd like to open in Pecan Grove. I think he's hoping to get in before the big HMOs discover our town and price him out of the field. He's got a couple mil raised but it would be wonderful if he could put the money he's raised to good use like this."

"Sure, send him over. We can at least talk about it."

<hr>

Bob was taking a break for some of the fresh-squeezed lemonade Mae had sent in his thermos when he saw Doc leaving the house with a spring in his step. "Hey, Doc!" he called. "What's got you so all happied up?"

"Hi, Bob. I *am* pretty excited about the investments we discussed today. I researched a great company online and Ray is willing to get me in on some stock in a similar company. My regular broker has me in such boring funds. I figure at his rate I'd be ninety-three before I could retire with enough money to travel."

The next morning the Grove Gazette carried a full front page story on the man found dead in the park. "IDENTITY REVEALED," was the headline, with a picture of Wayne Simonson in Army dress blues. The story contained all the information that Wendy had shared with Chief Jones plus some additional tidbits from Wayne's commanding officers and the buddies he served with overseas. All remembered Wayne "the Weasel" Simonson with affection and admiration. One colleague remembered that, "Weasel was always up for anything. It's what made him a hero: he was never afraid to try -- at least once!"

The article closed with a statement from the police department. "We have still been unable to discover the reason Mr. Simonson was in Pecan Grove at the time of his demise. Although it is suspected that there was an altercation with one of the carnival workers, Mr. Simonson does not appear to have been employed by the carnival. If anyone has any further information about Wayne Simonson, please contact the police. The case is still considered open."

The information about the Army hero who died under suspicious circumstances was picked up by the AP and reprinted with varying degrees of prominence in papers across the country. Chief Jones was hoping that someone would turn up more information about where Wayne had been since his discharge from the Army.

As was his habit, Ray bought a paper as he entered the Garden Cafe. He was so engrossed in the article about Weasel that he barely acknowledged Ruby and her coffee pot. He was totally unaware that both Ruby and Sarah Jane saw a few tears slide unheeded down his cheeks.

"I wonder what makes him so emotional over that drifter?" Ruby whispered to Sarah Jane.

"Might be because he heard the other day that his foster brother died in Afghanistan." Sarah Jane whispered back.

But if anyone had been seated close enough to Ray, they might have heard him murmur, *"Rest in peace, Weasel, my brother."*

———

He congratulated himself. He had done the right thing by getting the Grove Gazette online subscription. When he saw the article identifying Wayne Simonson, he knew he had done the right thing by getting out of Alabama too. He wished there was a way to influence the police to drop the investigation in favor of a verdict of "death by persons unknown," but that was too much to hope for, he supposed.

———

Elise stopped in at the pharmacy for something for her headache. She usually just used peppermint oil, but this was one headache that wasn't responding and she felt the need for something stronger. She decided to buy some face cream as well although she usually bought it at the discount store. It would save time if she picked it up while she was here.

Cora Windham had been working the cosmetics counter at City Center Pharmacy for over twenty years. When she was hired she was a fresh faced 30-year- old with startling blue eyes and a flawless complexion. The years had not been kind to Cora's face. The blue eyes were still startling, but years of smoking had etched deep lines around her mouth. Too much exposure to the southern sun had turned the once flawless skin to something resembling shoe leather. Although she had access to and knowledge of the best cosmetic products available to slow and/or reverse the ravages of time, she had rarely had the money to buy them. Unfortunately, for her, cigarettes came first.

The pharmacy was looking for a way to ease Cora out, recognizing that their younger, wealthy clientele wasn't eager to buy cosmetics from an older woman with wrinkles. But the owners had lived in Pecan Grove forever, and they knew that such a move could backfire with their long term clientele, since they considered Cora and the pharmacy as inseparable. She knew all the regulars at the counter as well as their preferred products. Cora was ready for a change as well but how did a 50+ year-old without much education find a different job? This one covered the rent, albeit with Sarah Jane pitching in, but so help her, she was sick of snotty young women looking at her like she'd crawled out from under a rock when she recommended beauty products to them.

She hadn't ever seen Elise come in before, but she knew who she was. Pecan Grove just wasn't that big. "Hello, Mrs. Griffiths," she greeted Elise with a smile. "What can I get for you today?"

Elise told her the name of the cream she'd been using. "Oh, we don't carry that brand. Maybe you'd like to try this one instead? I assure you it's an upgrade from what you've been using. And really not much difference in price."

It wasn't hard for Elise to get Cora chatting about Sarah Jane and Ray. She practically gushed when Elise asked how her daughter was doing. "I just *love* that Ray! He is *so* good to my Sarah Jane. Why the other night there were a dozen roses waiting for her when she got off work. Do you know how much it costs to order roses?"

"How nice," Elise murmured. "I wonder how he ended up here in Pecan Grove?"

"I think he was just looking for a small, friendly town to settle down in. He can run his business from anywhere, you know."

"I suppose so," Elise agreed. "But I wonder how he escaped from wherever he was living without a wife and kids in tow. Everyone says he's such a charming man."

"I guess that's Sarah Jane's good fortune then," laughed Cora.

Elise walked out with more products than she ever thought she could use. "I'm going to have trouble explaining this one to Jase," she thought. "But somehow, I just felt sorry for her. She probably makes a commission on what she sells and it has to be hard to sell beauty products when your face has failed to keep up with the societal image of beauty."

When Chief Jones was able to talk to Wendy Parker again she was in a talkative mood. "You know, I'm not sure what I can tell you that will help your investigation, Chief," she began. "Wayne was quite a bit younger than me and I don't feel I ever really knew the adult version."

"Just tell me about your growing up years, then. You never know what will help."

"When Wayne was little we spent a fair amount of time together. I babysat him after school and he was so bright and happy. When he went to school, though, it seemed his personality changed. His first teacher was super strict and almost seemed to pick on Wayne. He withdrew into his books, legos, and later, computers to the point you could hardly get him to interact at all

"Then about the time I went to high school, Mom got the bright idea to take in a foster child. She thought it would be nice for Wayne to have a brother. I was busy with school and boyfriends, but those two became inseparable. And tease! They were like to drive me crazy some days. Wayne idolized George but George had a wild streak and they got into plenty of trouble.

"It all came to an end when George hatched a plan to steal bicycles and the two would repaint them and resell them. George insisted it was all his idea and that got him some time in Juvenile Detention. I don't know why Mom and Dad decided to move to Oklahoma at the end of the school year — maybe they thought it was too risky for Wayne's future to have any more contact with George. Maybe it had more to do with Mom's cancer diagnosis and access to better health care. That was my senior year and, as wrapped up in myself as I was, I still remember some epic scenes between Wayne and my parents. He accused them of throwing their son away, said they didn't love him either and they were trying to ruin his life.

"After that Wayne became sullen and uncommunicative again. He tried to run away a couple times to find George. Looking back, I think Mom was already sick with the cancer that eventually killed her and moving to Oklahoma got her closer to good medical care. But Wayne never did recover his happy outlook and it was worse after Mom died. It was almost a relief when he joined the army. He once told me he was going to get a tattoo for every bad memory from childhood — and as you know, he had a lot of tattoos!"

Renovations were moving along quickly at the Lile house. Bob was getting the gardens ready for fall blooming with an abundance of asters and mums in addition to the roses that proliferated under his green thumb. He had an eye for color and fall plantings were his specialty. In the past he had been hired to prepare a couple of grand homes for the Home and Garden tour and it had been a lucrative side business for him. But when the big nursery moved in at the edge of town, most of the wealthy folks went with them. Still, the homes where he had gardened had always done well in the competition. He wondered if there was any chance Ray would be interested in having the tour stop at his house. Back in the day the Liles had nearly always been featured on the tour. Why once they even had a closing dance and celebration in that huge third floor ballroom. Well, Ray was a mover and a shaker so perhaps he would be interested.

"Hey there young Leroy!" he hailed the carpenter. "How're you 'n' MaryEllen doing on the insides there?"

"Hey Bob. We're getting along pretty good. Sure helps a project move when the owner isn't afraid to spend some money on it. Mr. Jacobs usually says to 'hang the cost, just get it done,' so we've been able to have the furniture reupholstered on a rush order and the same with getting the wallpaper we decided on. I think he's aiming for a big party sometime this fall."

"Ya know, that's what I wanted to talk to you about. Do ya think Ray might be in'erested in the Home and Garden tour this fall?"

"You and MaryEllen think alike," Leroy laughed. "She's been after me to ask him about that. It sure wouldn't hurt my reputation if people would see what we've done here."

When Leroy had a chance to mention the upcoming tour, Ray was *very* interested. Privately he thought it was fortunate that the town had seemed to lose interest after Weasel's body was identified. But he also thought it would be great for people to focus attention on Ray as a part of the prestigious Home and Garden Tour. Ray wasted no time in getting the Lile house nominated.

Sarah Jane was as excited as Ray when he told her his house would be part of the Home and Garden tour. She began chattering about all the great parties that were rumored to have taken place there in the past. "Wouldn't it be fantastic if we revived the tradition of having a big dance at the end of the Home and Garden tour?" Sarah Jane asked. "But I suppose the ballroom hasn't been too much of a priority yet."

"Leroy says it's in pretty good shape. I bet he could have that ballroom floor refinished quickly and the curtains just need a good cleaning, I guess."

"Oh Ray! Doesn't that sound like *fun* — you'd be the town hero!"

"Do you know a good band? One that could play the oldies as well as some more modern tunes?"

"I think the 'Willie Nillies' play that kind of music," Sarah Jane mused. "Want me to check availability?"

"Why don't we find out where they're playing right now and go check them out? We'd get a night of dancing in the bargain."

Sarah Jane flew into his arms with a squeal of delight. The kiss that ensued nearly derailed their plans to go dancing. Not that Ray would have minded exactly. But something was holding him back from making their relationship physical. He sensed that Sarah Jane was willing, but he thought most of the men she had dated never saw the real person behind her Barbie doll looks and figure. His better self wanted to be the one man who treated her differently.

Sarah Jane insisted that Ray take her by her house so she could get dressed properly for dancing. She ran in and quickly stripped out of her tight jeans and tee shirt and slipped on a flowing, flowery skirt and lacy white tank top. She hesitated for a moment: would she be out of place if she wore dancing slippers? She decided she'd rather be comfortable than fashionable and slipped on her white ballet flats.

Ray hadn't realized just how much Sarah Jane loved to dance. In the car on their way to Jackson she was so excited she was tripping over her words. "I haven't been to a dance with a willing partner in just ages. I was on the dance team in high school, you know.

I've studied dance and taken some on-line business classes, but there's never been enough money for me to launch my own dance studio. As a kid I could only take lessons when mama was dating a generous man, but it was enough to get me hooked. I sure hope you're as good at dancing as I suspect you are, my darling Ray."

"Oh, I'm adequate," Ray said modestly. "I learned long ago that most women want to dance, and most men don't think *they* want to. So, to please the ladies, I learned the basics and along the way I found out I enjoy it too." He winked at Sarah Jane. "Here we are. Ready to put on a show?"

Jase just knew there was something, somewhere that would show that Ray's investment business was offering returns that were just too high. He was a firm believer in the saying 'that if something seems too good to be true, it probably is.' Every chance he got he searched the internet; there were plenty of ads for companies offering high end solutions to cyber crime. Some of them had press releases announcing that they had taken their company public and stock was available. Some even cited great returns, although nothing quite so grand as what he had heard Ray was quoting. He just couldn't *prove* it! Ray had his own business so it wasn't as though he was held responsible to a brokerage firm or anything, either. Maybe he should check again on the names of the companies Ray was recommending. There might be something there, although he felt it was a long shot.

One afternoon after another frustrating half hour surfing, Mark stopped by his desk. "Whatcha working on Dad? You look hot and bothered."

"It just bugs me that all these people are investing with that Ray Jacobs guy. I think they're in for a rude awakening although it really is none of my business, I guess." Why he was confiding in his twelve-year-old son, Jase couldn't have explained. "I'm just not good enough at the computer to separate truth from fiction."

"Why don't you ask your friend Zeke to help you? I've heard he's a computer whiz."

"Really? Where did you learn that? I know he dropped out of technical school - thought maybe he flunked his classes."

"Naw. All the kids say he's fantastic. They joke that they want to be able to hack like Zeke."

"Maybe I will...

It was frustrating being stuck in Minnesota in a dead end job. His desire for revenge, his lust for Ray's money, his thoughts of justice were consuming him. Killing that Weasel only whetted his appetite for the death of Ray. He was glad, glad, glad that Ray would suffer, knowing that somehow he had caused his brother's death!

His live-in girlfriend knew nothing about his trip and it was best to keep it that way. Maybe it was time to cut his ties here and get closer to the action. He could just leave... after he tied up a couple of loose ends.

Chapter Twenty-six

While Heritage Days focused on the glitz, the Home and Garden Tour was all about the glamour. The lifestyles of the wealthy plantation owners were stylized and sterilized until they had little resemblance to history. But the tourists loved it and most of the town believed it, too. Ray found out that each home selected to be a part of the tour was required to put together a group of amateur actors and actresses to portray a historical event — one associated with the Civil War period and relevant to Pecan Grove. However, in more recent years the skits had evolved into entertainment only somewhat connected to town history.

Ray and Sarah Jane were hard pressed to come up with a plot for the vignette at the Lile house that was not trite, far-fetched or overused. Pouring over history books had never been Ray's forte, but he found himself trying to imagine the dry old texts coming to life in living color. Trouble was, Sarah Jane shot down most of his best ideas.

"Why don't we erect the old fort that was here during the days when the Creek Indians lived in this area? We could have warriors and…." he broke off at the horrified look Sarah Jane shot his way. "Well, why not?"

"Two words." Sarah Jane replied succinctly. "Civil War."

"Oh yeah." He went back to reading the old history text.

"Here's something," Sarah Jane mused. "Perhaps it would work to do the Ghost of Skeetoe's Hole. It's Civil War, and I don't recall anyone trying to reenact that story!"

"I've never heard the story," said Ray. "but I've always liked ghost stories. What does it have to do with history?"

"It actually happened a couple counties over from here, but I think we could stretch things to have it occur in our area. See, Bill Skeetoe was drafted into the Confederate army. Some accounts say he went but returned home when he heard his wife was sick. Anyway, the local guard came to arrest him and charge him with either desertion or draft dodging or whatever. They tried him, convicted him and sentenced him to hang."

"That's awful!" Ray interrupted.

"I suppose it wasn't much worse than all the other stuff going on at that time, but, anyway, let me finish. They marched Bill down to the riverside and prepared to hang him on an old oak tree there. Trouble was, Bill was a tall man and they hadn't taken his height into account. So when they went to string him up they found, to their horror, that his feet still just touched the ground."

"They couldn't hang him then, right? Because that would be double jeopardy or something?"

"I'm not sure that applies to executions. Guess they didn't care too much about the finer legal points anyway. One of his executioners used his cane — he had been wounded in the war — and scraped out the dirt under Skeetoe's feet and, unfortunately, old Bill was hung and he died."

Sarah Jane paused in her story telling. Her voice slowed, "The weird part came later, otherwise we probably wouldn't have ever heard about Bill Skeetoe. See, that hole they dug could never be filled in. You could fill it with dirt, trash, whatever, but by the next morning the hole would be back. People got to saying it was Bill Skeetoe's toes hanging there kicking the dirt out of the hole..."

Ray shivered involuntarily. "Sounds like a perfectly haunting skit for an autumn evening... I wonder why no one ever used it before this?"

"Well, it says here that in the 1960's heavy spring rains were threatening to wash out the nearby highway bridge. They dumped a huge pile of gravel and cement in that hole to fix it. Guess old Bill's ghost couldn't overcome that! I suppose people just forgot the story then."

———

Often, the young adult sector of a church is ignored which causes many twenty-somethings to leave looking for their fellowship and excitement elsewhere. Jase was trying to combat that at Bethel by arranging a special Saturday night Bible study followed by snacks and games that would appeal to the college kids and young 20-somethings. He had finally convinced Zeke to give it a try. Zeke wasn't sure about this. He figured he'd be out of his element, that the others would probably all be college grads with great jobs. Although he had attended the local high school, he had kept mostly to himself because all the other guys had pretty much grown up together. He was secretly pleased when he was greeted warmly by a few of the guys and several girls. After introductions he recognized some of the names as kids in his class, or a few years ahead of him. He was surprised to realize that there were quite a few young people that had not fled from Pecan Grove.

The Bible study centered on finding God's will for your life and Zeke listened intently as Pastor Jase gave some simple and some not-so-simple ways to determine what God wanted you to do. Zeke had never thought about God being interested in *his* life.

God was just there tending to the big things like earthquakes and hurricanes.

Afterwards the competition was fierce over sand volleyball and Zeke found himself having more fun than he thought possible in the backwater that was Pecan Grove. Lingering over pizza, Pastor Jase asked him about his relationship with Ray. "So is Ray Jacobs someone you've known for a long time Zeke?"

"Naw. I think it's just that I came back to town about the same time Ray arrived in Pecan Grove. I've been at loose ends and he doesn't work, at least he doesn't keep regular hours, so I see him around town quite a bit, and he asked me to help design a website for his business."

"Has he talked to you at all about that? His business, I mean?" Jase knew he was probing and hoped the younger man wouldn't take offense. "I heard his talks at the men's retreat last spring and I wondered if people were still coming to him for investment advice."

"He don't say much. But I'm there quite a bit while working on his website and I've seen some pretty rich guys come and go from his office."

"Well, I could use someone savvy about computers to help me do some research. I'm not good with this technical stuff. Do you think you'd be able to work with me a bit?"

"Sure!" Zeke was thrilled that the pastor would single him out for special attention.

———

"It was puzzlin' sometimes," Bob thought as he worked. "You could have your mind all set one way and somethin'd come along and make ya do a 180." He had been working in the gardens at the Lile house for a few weeks now and he couldn't for the life of him find anything sleazy or underhanded about Ray. He paid well and on time, often springing for a lunch. He was courteous to all the workers. He would stop by to chat, and was always funny and charming. He even saw Ray pray with his clients. Moreover, he treated Sarah Jane better'n anybody ever had. "Gonna have to tell Jase we might be barkin' up the wrong tree. He seems to be doing everythin' he preached at that there retreat!"

It was probably silly but once she thought of it, the idea wouldn't go away. Kristen called Beth. "Want to take a trip to Montgomery next Monday?"

"Montgomery? I don't think Mom would let me drive there - and you hate to drive in Montgomery! What's up?"

"Oh, I'm *sick* of the stores in *Jackson*. They *never* carry the *fashions* I see in the current magazines. I thought we could check out that sweet new boutique I heard about last month... 'A-Dora-Bull' Isn't that just a riot?"

Beth laughed. "Well, as long as you're driving, I'll be ready to be the navigator."

What Kristen failed to mention was that there was a women's shelter in the same neighborhood. She planned to inveigle Beth into helping her check it out.

Zeke was more than surprised to get a call from one of the guys he had met Saturday night. "Hey Zeke! This is Mike Sheffield — remember me? We met Saturday night at the church."

"Yeah, sure. Tall, red hair?"

"That's me! We were wondering if you'd be at all interested in joining our sand volleyball team? I mean, you're really good and we're short a couple of players. Rick got married and Sam went off to grad school. Anyway, what do you think?"

Even Zeke could tell Mike was a little nervous. He wondered why. "Gee, that sounds like a blast! When do you play?"

"That's the thing. We practice Monday and Thursday and games are usually Friday and Saturday with an occasional makeup game on Tuesday. So it's kind of a big commitment... .of course if you need a night off you can usually get a sub... but it's probably too much...." his voice trailed off.

Zeke wondered how many guys had turned him down. But, still, it sounded like fun. And what else was he doing with his evenings? "You know, I think I'd like to give it a try if you think I'll be good enough."

"Great! Wonderful! Aw man, I'm so glad!" Mike was clearly relieved. "Can you come for practice tonight?"

As sometimes happens, the investigation into Wayne Simonson's death stalled. There seemed to be nothing more to go on. All the carnival workers had been interviewed and their stories checked out. So did their alibis. No one had ever seen the boots with the distinctive heel pattern either, if people were telling the truth!

Chief Jones had tried finding where Wayne had spent time since being discharged from the Army. There was no record that he had ever sought medical treatment at any VA hospital or clinic; he was not disabled so there were no checks for him to collect. It was like the man had dropped off the face of the earth and only resurfaced to die in their park.

The chief was frustrated whenever he thought about it, which wasn't often enough, he admitted. The mayor was after him to help with the election campaign coming up and that distracted him. Also, there had been a couple of accidents in the fog and it was a lot of work clearing those up. It didn't help that his detective up and quit when he got a job in Dallas. "No excuse," he thought, "before I was chief, I was Pecan Grove's detective for half my career at least. Solving this case would do more to put Mayor Clemmons ahead in the polls than any amount of speeches and handshaking!"

He pulled out his notes and went over them again. What was this paper? He had forgotten about Jimmy's research on the items found at the scene! What if they sent a picture of Simonson up to Minneapolis? Would they get a hit at that bar with the weird name? Sven and Ollie's or something?

On a hot and humid evening in early August, Chuck and Nancy had invited some of the church folk out to their property for a big pulled pork barbecue. Elise was looking forward to the break in routine. In the month since the Heritage festival,she had been kept busy canning the first batch of vegetables, ordering school books for the fall, and supervising the little boys in the backyard pool. Seemed she didn't have time to turn around. Already it was time to think about planting some fall crops and Chuck had already tilled the garden for a second planting of beans, broccoli and some winter squash. Thankfully Mark was doing better and was handling his paper route without help anymore!

After a delicious dinner, the kids started a game of kick-the-can and the men were gathered around the picnic table chewing the fat.

"Ain't somethin' the way that there Lile place is gettin' spruced up so fast?' Art Vance said. "You'd think there was some hurry to get the place flipped or somethin.'"

"Naw, don't think so. Says he just wants to make it nice so's he can entertain. Who does he think is coming? The Queen of England?"

"Personally, I think the guy just likes to show off his newfound wealth!"

"I don't know what his motivations are, but the house looks great and he sure is making me a lot of money!" inserted Pastor Kirkland. "Fact is I'm going to preach a series on Sunday evenings about how God can use our little to make more! I think I'll call it, 'Little is Much With God.'"

"Do you think that's wise, Pastor?" Chuck asked. "I mean, it would be so easy for people to get the message that their materialism is blessed by God."

"But that's just it! It's only blessed by God if we plan to use the wealth for His glory! I've been studying this and in James it says that if we ask with wrong motives we won't receive anything! It's so simple!"

Jase privately (and snarkily) wondered what Kent's godly motives were in leasing the new Lexus.

In the house, the women were chattering while cleaning up the kitchen. "Can I get your recipe for that broccoli salad?" "Did you use your own barbecue sauce recipe, Nancy?" "I always liked Ken's when we lived up north, but you can't get that here." "You know who makes the best barbecue sauce — Cora Windham."

There was a sudden lull in the conversation. "Really?" Elise was surprised. "I would never have guessed."

"Oh, yes!" Nancy concurred. "She used to take classes toward becoming a chef, but when Sarah Jane came along and she was left alone, well, she was forced to take a different kind of job. The internship process was just too grueling with a small child. It's really too bad."

"Do you think Sarah Jane and Ray Jacobs are really serious?" Gina Kirkland asked.

"Hard to tell with either of them. Sarah Jane has something of a 'reputation.' And I don't know Ray well enough to say."

"Cora would sure be thrilled if they are." They all laughed.

"Is Kristen Stewart still mooning over Ray?" asked Mae Huggens. "That's one girl who needs a focus in her life — other than dreaming about every eligible guy who crosses her path." Once again, the group chuckled. The conversation drifted to different topics.

———

There were only so many restaurants in Pecan Grove. And there were days when it just seemed too much effort to get cleaned up and dressed up to go out. Ray felt he had a reputation to uphold around town and he didn't like to just go grubby like so many people did. Of course, you could always get pizza delivery, but unless you're 17 that gets tiring after awhile too. Ray found himself wishing for a good old anonymous drive-through, like Boston Market or Eddingtons, where he could get something that resembled home cooking without being judged for his lack of a sophisticated palate. It was nice when Sarah Jane cooked for him, but she would never let him buy the groceries and he had no idea what to keep in stock at the house. Maybe he should hire a cook and housekeeper. He wondered who he could trust to be in the house that often and that intimately.

He figured that in the old days a house as grand as the Lile house would have had a full staff of servants. There would have been a maid, a butler, a cook and a chauffeur. Ray didn't know, but he had a feeling that back then, with its rigid caste system, the help wouldn't dare talk about the things that happened in the master's house. Or if they did, they would never get a job again. There were advantages to that, he supposed. But if he lived back then, he would probably *be* one of the servants: forever destined to chauffeur the master or muck the stables.

When he saw Sarah Jane the following afternoon, Ray took her into the park for a quiet stroll. It was too hot to enjoy much outdoor activity in the afternoon, but the deep shade under the live oak trees kept the park a bit cooler. "Your mama likes to cook, right sweetie?"

"Yes, but what brought that up? Here I was looking forward to some sweet talk and you're thinking about your stomach!" Sarah Jane teased.

"It's never far from my mind! Unless, of course, I'm kissing you!" and he suited action to words.

A few breathless moments later Sarah Jane murmured, "Well, that's more my style! But I'm still curious. Why did you ask about Mama?"

"Thing is, I was looking at the nice little housekeeper's apartment at my house. You've seen it; two bedrooms, sitting room and private bath right off the kitchen. And I thought how nice it would be to have a housekeeper living there who could do some cooking for me too."

"I'm not sure I'd like having some woman living in your house with you, Ray. I might find out I'm being replaced in your affections!"

"I have no intention of replacing you, honey pie. I was *talking* about your *mother*!" he chuckled. "And furthermore, I thought perhaps you'd like to use the second bedroom in the apartment?"

"Ray, sometimes you are brilliant! That would solve a host of problems. Mama hasn't been happy at the drugstore for a while now. And our landlord is threatening to raise the rent on that dump we live in. Only thing…" She hesitated. "It's just that, even though she's never raised me to think I'm better than anyone else, I wonder if Mama would feel like she's too good to be 'just a housekeeper.'"

Ray waggled his eyebrows and winked at Sarah Jane. "We could tell her she's chaperoning our 'getting to know you better' phase. Then she might feel it's her *duty* to take the job!"

Sarah Jane giggled. "If anyone can convince her it will be you, Ray!" She thought for a moment. "If she thinks it's all her idea, it will go over better. Come for supper tonight, say about 6:30. I'll cook and get her talking about how superior her cooking is!"

Chapter Twenty-seven

The Twin Cities of Minneapolis and St. Paul are situated on either side of the Mississippi River as it meanders from its source at Lake Itasca in northern Minnesota down through the heart of the state until it is joined by the Minnesota River and then the St. Croix River at the border between Minnesota and Wisconsin. Although they are known as the twins, the cities are quite different in character and anyone who has lived for any time in one or the other will have fierce loyalty to his or her chosen city. This rivalry began in the 1800's, and for most residents the causes have faded into legend and it is now only a mild, joking matter. Others, more knowledgeable perhaps, recognize the history and understand where the resentment originated. And for a few, the feud is as new and real as today's paper.

No city department held more active haters of St. Paul than the Minneapolis Police Department. It started in the 1920's and 30's when St. Paul became known as a refuge for the mobsters generally headquartered in Chicago. Al Capone, John Dillinger, and Bonnie and Clyde were only a few of the notorious gangsters who spent time in St. Paul. Aided by corrupt politicians and an unofficial contract with the St. Paul chief of police, the gangsters were protected from the FBI by tip-offs while the police turned a blind eye to their illegal activities. Why? Well, the mob was required to check in with the police department when in town. They were expected to contribute part of their gains to the police pension fund. And they were to commit no crimes within St. Paul city limits... but Minneapolis was fair game!

Ken Johnson was one of those police officers for whom contempt of St. Paul was as natural as breathing. His granddaddy had been on the force in the 1920's and had told young Ken countless stories about risking his life while pursuing bank robbers as far as the St. Paul bridge and then getting no help from the St. Paul police in apprehending them.

So when Chief Jones sent a fax with Wayne Simonson's picture to the Minneapolis police department, it was his misfortune to have it end up on the desk of investigator Ken Johnson. The Chief detailed the items found at the scene, including a picture of the distinctive heel imprint (who knew?), and asked whether they could spare someone to ask a few questions at Sven and Ole's bar. Unfortunately for his investigation, Sven and Ole's was located on the St. Paul side of the river. Ken was immediately irked at the ignorance of poor Chief Jones who didn't know the difference between Minneapolis and St. Paul! So he figured he'd get around to sending the information over to St. Paul when he had a minute. Whenever that would be!

The fax could have been ignored forever, as low as it was on Ken's priority list. But, as chance would have it, Ken was watching a petty drug runner; finding him useful in supplying information on those higher in the supply chain. The kid thought he could branch out to the St. Paul side of the river and Ken decided that, although he had been useful, it was time to arrest the punk. The fella had been said to be hanging out at Sven and Ole's. So, although it took awhile, he eventually got around to calling his St. Paul counterpart and using the fax as an excuse, arranged to meet the St. Paul detective at the bar.

He was taking longer to wrap up his Minnesota dealings than he wanted because he couldn't leave his job until that last shipment of drugs had been delivered. It just wouldn't do for anyone to suspect that the friendly janitor who always signed for the late packages was actually receiving some special packages for himself! He congratulated himself on how diabolically clever it had been to set up a drug delivery system right under the noses of those high and mighty FBI agents! Oh well, there would be a better opportunity after he had all that lovely money. He figured another week would clear the last of the packages.

Kristen made sure to park in a public lot a few blocks from the A-Dora-Bull Boutique. As she and Beth strolled casually down the block she took note of the storefronts they passed. Ah, and right across the street from the boutique she spied the shelter she wanted to visit: 'Aunt Violet's House'. The two young women found the new boutique to be everything they had expected. All the merchandise was unique, from the sassy logo of a bull with a feather boa and a jeweled ring in his nose to the proprietor, petite Dora Eldridge. Dora shared a sense of style with her sassy logo. Feminine to the extreme, but with a quirky humor, she was quick to show Kristen and Beth the *best* and *latest* (and most *expensive*) clothing choices.

Kristen had a hard time concentrating or behaving in her usual flippant manner. Her thoughts weren't with shopping at all and she found her mind wandering at inappropriate moments. "Hmm? Oh sure, of *course* I want the *turquoise* pendant with the *paisley* top." What? Luckily her extensive wardrobe and generous allowance would cover these errors in judgment.

Beth was chattering happily about their purchases as they returned toward the car when Kristen abruptly stopped in front of Aunt Violet's House. "We have an appointment here," she announced.

"Is this another boutique?" Beth squealed. "Or is Aunt Violet a private dressmaker? That would be soooo cool! Ordering your *own style* to be created for you."

"No," said Kristen flatly. "This is a *shelter* for battered and abused *women*. A *safe* house, if you *will*. And no, I am not *abused* or *battered*! I am just *interested* in how a *place* like this is run and what the *possibilities* are of *opening* one *closer* to Pecan Grove. And *close* your *mouth*, Beth. You *look* like a *fish*!"

It was a quiet ride home to Pecan Grove for the two young women. Both were lost in contemplation, with impressions from their afternoon visit swirling in their minds. As they neared home, Beth turned to Kristen and said, "You know, the thing that bothers me the most is that those women, well, they all wanted the same things that we want. A handsome husband and a nice home. How can a person keep from making the kind of wrong choice that will land them in an abusive situation?"

Spaghetti and meatballs. That would taste delicious even though she did her best to make it less than perfect. Sarah Jane set to work in the kitchen as soon as she got home from the cafe. It would take concentration to make this meal turn out the way she planned!

"Are we having company?" Cora inquired the minute she stepped in the door. "Who's coming to dinner? Ray? Shouldn't we take him somewhere? This house is too small!"

"Hi, Mama," Sarah Jane answered sweetly. "It's just Ray. No need to get in a tither."

"But Ray? Coming here? He's got that big fancy house! We have nothing! And all you're making is spaghetti?"

"Mama, calm down. Ray likes spaghetti and I used your special meatball recipe! He gets tired of eating out all the time and I thought it would be nice to cook where you can join us—though I love to cook in his new kitchen with all the super appliances."

Cora moved over to inspect the pan of meatballs. "Sarah Jane! You've let the meatballs get flat on the sides! How many times have I told you to keep them rolling while they brown so they'll be perfectly round?"

"Mama, it's fine. They'll taste the same. Now go change clothes and put your feet up for a minute. I'll bring you something to drink." Inwardly Sarah Jane was gloating. Mama's response was just what she expected and hoped for.

—⁓—

By the time Ray arrived, Cora had smoked a couple cigarettes and had a glass of her favorite wine. She was feeling more relaxed and started immediately with her brand of teasing. "I suppose you came to see how the other half lives, huh Ray? Are you sure you'll still be welcome to play golf with the high and mighty Reverend Stewart if you eat here with us sinners?"

"Cora, you know I think the world of Sarah Jane and I don't care where she lives. People are way too concerned with how much money a person has. I say, it's more important how much faith they have. With faith you can always make money!"

"Maybe," Cora wasn't willing to give up feeling sorry for herself. "But it always seems to me that you have to have *some* money to make *more* money!"

"Supper is ready," Sarah Jane interrupted them. "Come while everything is hot."

Cora found fault with nearly everything Sarah Jane served. The meatballs were lumpy, the pasta was over cooked, the salad greens were slightly wilted. "If only I could get home from work earlier, I'd serve a properly cooked dinner!" she lamented.

Sarah Jane winked at Ray. It was time for him to step in.

"I heard you were on track to become a famous chef, Cora. Did you ever consider being a private chef instead?"

"Once upon a time, I might have thought someone would hire me. But I was rejected at a couple places because I wasn't willing to leave Sarah Jane with babysitters for that long. Now I've been away from it for too long."

"I wonder," Ray appeared to be in deep thought. "Well, I'll be having parties and client dinners and could use someone….but Sarah Jane will probably cook for me, won't you sweetie?"

"Oh, Ray I love to cook. But…"

"Nonsense! Sarah Jane isn't careful enough! You can see how she made *square* meatballs instead of round ones! You need a professional. I'd think about it, but then I'd have to get a better car. I can walk to work at the drugstore, but your house is too far." Cora was eager and trying not to show it. "Probably you'll have to find someone else."

"But that's just it, Cora! There's an apartment built onto the kitchen! Two bedrooms, sitting room, full bath. You and Sarah Jane could live right there! Why didn't I think of that before?"

Later, Ray and Sarah Jane laughed about how easy it was to convince Cora to take the job. Of the three, it was hard to decide who was the most excited.

In the late summer the gardens in Pecan Grove began to take on an almost surreal beauty. Luckily for the whole state, rain had been frequent enough without any damaging storms and everything was lush and green. No matter if a person lived in the simplest bungalow or the grandest mansion, the fact that their town was host to a Home and Garden Tour that brought in visitors from far and near was enough to make them do their best to have a lovely display of color. The expensive displays of roses and showy asters and mums were rivaled by the more humble but vibrant colors of marigolds and sunflowers. The trick was to have them at peak bloom in mid-September. If one got the timing wrong, all their garden would showcase was dead flower heads during that all-important weekend.

Having decided to open the Lile house for the tour rather late in the game, Ray had given Bob Huggens free rein to beautify the gardens as best he could. Bob had been masterful at creating a display that was just beginning to hint at the glory it would exhibit in mid-September.

Meanwhile, Ray had to scramble for actors willing to play in the skit he planned. Most of those who volunteered for the local community theater were scooped up early in the year and were already committed elsewhere. Ray figured they needed a narrator, several Confederate soldiers, a weeping Mrs. Skeetoe and, of course, Bill himself.

Zeke had taken to stopping in at Ray's house "just to talk." He had sort of put Ray's computer list to the back of his mind, but he was still more watchful with Ray than he had been before. Especially since Ray was now guardian of a sizable portion of Ruby's savings.

Today Ray brought up the subject of the upcoming skit. "You ever done any acting, Zeke?" he asked.

"Not since I had to be the gingerbread man in our first grade Christmas program! And I'm not starting now!"

"Aw come on! You can be one of the soldiers. You'd hardly have to say a word!"

"Um, Ray....did you ever notice I'm kinda the wrong color for a Confederate soldier?"

Ray started to laugh and couldn't stop. "Never once have I thought of that!" he finally choked out. "But it doesn't matter. It'll be dark, and didn't they use black people for some of the dirty work anyway?"

"How about I just run your stage crew?" Zeke suggested. "I'm better at the tech stuff anyway!"

"Well," Ray conceded, "I do need a lot of special effects. So you got any buddies to play the soldiers? And maybe the judge?"

———

While out golfing, Ray decided to see if he could recruit his fellow golfers for actors or to help with the technical crew.

"So Will, what would you think of helping out with my Civil War skit?"

"No can do, buddy. Kari's got me playing old Dr. Hefflefinger."

"Too bad! I thought you'd make a great hanging judge."

"Hanging judge? What are you portraying, anyway?" Rob chimed in. "I'd like to be a hanging judge."

"We finally decided on the Ghost of Skeetoe's Hole," Ray answered. "But we're supposed to keep it sorta under wraps so you didn't hear it from me."

Rob was enthusiastic about the skit idea and immediately volunteered. "I really would love to be a part of that, Ray. I've been left out of all the fun of your investments because my soon to be ex-wife has all my money tied up in court. Count me in!"

"I used to act in those skits, but I got out of practice when the kids were smaller. Who can I be?" Doc wanted to be included too.

"Man, that sounds like more fun than Dr. Hefflefinger!" Will had a jealous note to his voice.

"Too bad, Will. But, Doc, how about you play the soldier with the cane who digs out the hole? I can't think of his name right now but he's supposed to be shorter than old Bill and you'd fit the part."

"Sure! Who's playing Bill?"

"I thought I would take that part. I'm fairly tall and since Zeke is working on a way to make the hanging look real I'll be able to practice with him," Ray explained.

With the guys Zeke had recruited from the church group he had been going to, that made up the cast. Now they just needed the narrator; someone with a good speaking voice. He thought he'd ask Reverend Findley. He hoped no one had tapped him yet.

Dr. Swanson left Ray's parlor office with a satisfied smile. He was sure he was doing the right thing by investing the money he had raised for the new clinic. After all, the results Dr. Rasmussen quoted and the prospectus that Ray showed him would give him returns far above what the money was earning now. He needed to get that clinic underway soon or one of the big HMO's would build in Pecan Grove, and the town just wasn't big enough to support two clinics. If he could just open his facility first they wouldn't be likely to try to compete. He figured he needed at least $6 million on hand to break ground so he had just invested the $2.5 million he had raised to this point. He tried to figure out in his head how long it would take to multiply that money... Forget it. That's why he hired an accountant.

After the doctor left, Ray worked in his office for several hours. He calculated how much money had been entrusted to him, where the investments were, and what he would need to do with the money he had yet to invest. He sensed that his business was turning serious with the huge amounts of money people were investing with him. It had been fun watching the money pour into his accounts. Watching the excitement as people began seeing returns on their investments was fun too, in a different way. Not for the first time, Ray wondered if he could make a go of living honestly in Pecan Grove. He knew he would have to back-pedal.

He had paid out the first investors with some of his own money. Daryl, Kent and others had done a good job of promoting the company and he was able to pay out great dividends with the money coming in from the investors they had sent his way. He had invested some of the money, and the websites and reports that Zeke had set up for him were convincing enough that no one questioned him about their returns. But most of the money was in his personal accounts in the Cayman Islands. He would have to actually invest that money, pray for continued market performance, and gradually let the returns drop to a normal level. Or, pretty soon he would have to leave town.

His original plan to take what he could get and get out no longer felt like the best option, since that would mean leaving Sarah Jane. It had also occurred to him that some of the people who trusted him with their money were his friends.

He shook off his mood. Weasel's death must be messing with his mind. He had never been one to get maudlin! Let tomorrow take care of itself had always been his motto.

By summer's end, the Book 'n' Brews group had progressed to discussing Bible words starting with "F." Ray had missed the first week, but some of the guys said they had learned a lot while talking about Faith. Tonight Reverend Findlay suggested the topic of Forgiveness. As he listened, Ray wondered if there really was such a thing as forgiveness for someone like himself. Pastor Jase said that forgiveness is the same to God as forgetfulness, because God promises to forget our sins once we are forgiven. Ray didn't think that could be right. Even when he was small and did something wrong, no matter how sincere he had been in saying he was sorry, the infraction seemed to go into a "big book of bad stuff," and when the chapter was full, little George had to leave that foster home.

Some of the guys thought you had to *do* something to get forgiveness. Others thought you had to do something *after* you had asked forgiveness to be fully forgiven. Ray figured doing something *before* would be like a prison term and doing something *after* would be like restitution. He could understand that. But the idea that what you had done could be forgotten? That was too wild! Everyone knew that even though you may have paid your debt, you still had a record.

Ray had wanted to talk to Jase about the forgetting thing, but something about the man still made him uneasy. He sensed that Jase was one of those truly good people, the kind Ray always felt could see right through him. That night, however, as he was lying in bed, the verse Pastor Jase had referred to was going through his head. "For I will forgive their iniquity, and I will remember their sin no more."

Jase came home from the Book 'n' Brews session feeling dissatisfied. Kent had encouraged him to show up there once in a while, supposedly to minister to the men where they were. So far he hadn't seen that anyone was really interested in truth, they just wanted to give their opinions. In his mind, it really didn't matter what a person *thought* about something, what mattered is what God *said* about it. Tonight he thought Ray had looked pensive when they talked about God forgetting sins, and he wished he'd had some one-on-one time with the man. Before he could follow up on the topic, one of the rowdier guys told a stupid joke about getting his wife to forgive him and the mood was broken.

As he showered away the smell of smoke and beer he decided the Book 'n' Brew sessions didn't fit with his idea of ministry. But maybe he should continue his investigation of Ray by getting to know him personally. That would give him a better chance to minister and ultimately, that was what he was called to do.

———

He'd planned that Friday night would be his last night hanging out at the bar. He had put a letter on his boss's desk resigning "effective immediately." He had found an obscure website that advertised private cabins available for rent and luckily there was one place near Pecan Grove that would suit his needs. It had been listed for months with no activity. He didn't figure on actually renting it - he was just planning to borrow it for a time.

He was shocked when the cop started showing Weasel's picture around that very same night. Luckily they were calling him Wayne and the picture was of a military guy in dress uniform. No one admitted to recognizing Weasel. He knew then that he had to leave town immediately. He decided not to even wait until morning.

Chapter Twenty-eight

The Home and Garden Tour lasted for three days. People were attracted to town for the quilting festival, the historical society specials and especially the home tours. Many of the historical homes had vendors begging for space on their lawns, rightly expecting that most of the tourist action would be concentrated there. The city council had strict rules about what type of vendors would be allowed at this festival so they could preserve the historical character of the event.

At the Lile house, they had allowed a candle maker to demonstrate and sell homemade beeswax candles, a kettle corn stand, which would pop and season the corn over an open fire, and a weaver who set up her loom and sold her hand woven rugs.

Each home was scheduled to put on their skit twice a day: once in mid-afternoon, and again in the evening. The schedule was staggered so that over the three days, determined visitors could manage to see all the skits.

Ray wanted the Lile house to be the star of the tour. He wanted the gardens to look nice, but his real interest was in the house and the skit. He and Zeke spent numerous hours perfecting their plan to make Bill Skeetoe's hanging look realistic. They had fashioned a leather harness that looked like suspenders for Ray to wear. When the hanging rope was being put over his head a black rope would be affixed to the harness. The black color would assure its near-invisibility. Then, when the hanging rope was raised, the other rope would support his body so no weight was actually on the rope around his neck. It was simple and ingenious and they practiced until they had it perfectly timed. But it still made Sarah Jane nervous.

———

Chief Jones had finally heard from the Minnesota Police. His error in sending his request to Minneapolis instead of St. Paul was detailed along with some insincere apology for the delay in getting back to him. Apparently Wayne Simonson had a small computer repair shop in St. Paul called Sim's. He had closed up shop shortly before his death, telling his assistant that he was planning to do a little traveling and would let him know when he returned. According to the assistant, this was not the first time he had just up and left for a week or month or more. Interesting information, but not exactly what the Chief was looking for.

Also, there was no one at Sven and Ole's who would admit to knowing Wayne. Some looked a little uneasy when questioned, but that was all. The boot print - now that *was* a Minnesota thing. Turns out everyone up there recognized it as being from the Red Wing boot company. It was not as common as a cowboy boot, but generic in a work boot--still, it was another Minnesota connection, however tenuous. Aw, shoot. Nothing much to build a case with. But still, nearly two months had passed and he hadn't even talked to that Ray Jacobs fellow. It was time to do that, seeing as he was yet another Minnesota connection.

———

"So, Zeke, how do you go about tracing someone on the internet?" Jase asked before the Friday Bible study.

"You can just google them. If they've ever done anything noteworthy, they'll be there."

"What if you look at all the people with that name and nothing seems remotely familiar to the person you're looking for?" The frustration Jase felt from hours of reading Ray Jacobs profiles crept into his voice.

Zeke shrugged. "There are other places to check. Did you try LinkedIn? Facebook? Tumblr?"

"Whoa! Too much, too fast. I did try Facebook and found nothing I didn't already know. Part of the trouble is that I don't really know *what* I'm looking for, just a feeling that there's *something* to find. I'm thinking I'll know it when I see it."

"Mind if I ask who you're investigating? I mean, it's none of my business, but maybe I can help."

Jase lowered his voice. "I don't want you to get upset because he's a friend of yours, but I can't get over the feeling that there's something about Ray Jacobs that just doesn't add up. He's a really nice guy — on the surface. But I want to know what makes him tick and why he chose Pecan Grove for his base of operations."

"There are a few things I've wondered about too," Zeke said slowly. "I thought it was just because I'm young and stupid that I didn't get how he was making so much money. But I invested some money with him too, so if something is wrong, I want to know. And then there's that list..." He muttered the last part.

"How about we meet up next week, okay Zeke? If we put our heads together, maybe we can sort it all out."

He had settled into the musty little cabin near the muddy little "lake." Alabama didn't know what a proper lake should look like — that's one thing he'd never be able to leave: Minnesota's clear, blue water! Another thing he couldn't abide about Alabama was the bugs! Maybe it was just that the cabin had sat neglected for years, but every corner and crevice had spider webs filled with piles of bug carcasses. He'd have to clean — not his favorite thing.

But first things first. What was old George "Ray" up to by now? A 20-minute walk through the woods would land him on the grounds of "Ray's" new/old mansion.

Ruby could tell Sarah Jane was head over heels in love with Ray Jacobs. Although Sarah Jane never said anything directly, her whole demeanor had changed. She was still friendly to all the customers, especially the men, but -- Ruby struggled to find words for the difference — it was more of a 'sisterly' friendly, not the former 'sultry' friendly. And whenever Ray stopped in, her already sunshiny outlook became positively dazzling.

Ruby hoped with all her heart that her young friend wasn't in for another fall. If Ray dumped her, she might never recover. She had been pretty devastated after her last break-up, and that relationship hadn't lasted as long as this one. Not that it appeared likely to happen. Ruby figured she was just a worrier and if there wasn't anything to worry about, she had to go and make something up. If she was determined to worry, she probably should focus on Zeke. Still no regular job, still no sign of a return to school. He seemed content to make a bit of money here and there designing web sites, doing some graphic designs and filling in with odd jobs. She wondered if he was trying to be like Ray — no sign of a real job *there* either! The only thing that had improved in six months was the company Zeke was keeping. She *was* glad he had taken up with Jase Griffiths and that church group. The fellas he played volleyball with were a cut above the pool hall crew, that was for sure!

———

"I wish I could help you, Chief," Ray apologized. "I didn't realize when they had that writeup in the paper that he was from Minnesota. I thought they said he was going home to Oklahoma for burial?"

"Yes," Chief Jones replied, "he was living in Oklahoma before he joined the Army, and before that his family spent some years in Texas. We only recently figured out his Minnesota connections. It just seems like a coincidence that you moved here from Minnesota and then this guy no one knows is killed in our park, and he's from Minnesota too."

"I suppose," Ray paused, "but Minnesota is a big state. I only knew a few people at the university where I was in school and even then, I did a lot of classwork online. I worked as a companion for an elderly man and couldn't get out much."

"Yes, I heard that. It was probably too much to hope that you would know Mr. Simonson, but I *will* need a detailed account of your movements on the last day of the Heritage Festival. Just to be on the safe side."

"That's an easy one, Chief. I filled in for Will Stewart's barbershop quartet. We put on several demonstrations at the festival grounds which kept me busy 'most all day. Then the evening was the competition — we won! did you hear? Afterward we all hopped in Will's van and went out for a bite to eat and a celebration. I think you'll find I was with someone from 10:00 am until Will dropped me back at Bella's after midnight."

"Ah, yes. I had forgotten you were in the barbershop competition. Congratulations on the win — just stop by the station and sign a report, will you please?" Chief knew Bella's archaic policy - if a renter came in after 10, there was no exit again without an alarm sounding.

So Ray Jacobs was pretty well cleared as a suspect in Wayne Simonson's death, Chief thought as he drove away. But he certainly seemed nervous when he saw the police at the door. I wonder what else he's hiding?

Interesting that old George was into church going! And not just one service, but two every Sunday. Unfortunately, he had an office at his home and there wasn't any other predictable time when the house was empty. At first he thought he'd be able to search any time "Ray" went out with his girlfriend, but this afternoon he noticed that the girl and an old lady were moving in. If it were just the girl that would be one thing, but the old lady wouldn't be going along on their dates! He had noticed the tree growing close to an upstairs terrace. Even though he had gained weight since getting off the meth, he figured he could climb that tree and gain access to the house. He would be ready to search tomorrow morning. If he stayed upstairs the old lady was unlikely to hear him checking out the bedrooms and getting the lay of the house. There had to be something in that house that would point him to the money.

Pastor Kent was starting his new series this week on how to access God's blessings. He had specifically invited Ray to attend and Ray was glad to oblige. He hoped that Jase Griffiths would be busy in another part of the church. Somehow Jase's honest eyes made him squirm.

Ray was particularly interested when Kent attempted to answer the question of how to tell if your motivations were in line with God's will. "In James we read that 'we have not because we ask to use it on our own lusts.' So if we are asking wrongly, we won't be blessed! If you ask God for money and don't get any, you need to examine your motivations!"

Ray thought that was an interesting addition to his own thoughts on how God blesses with money. He had noticed the Lexus SUV in the parsonage drive and wondered how long the pastor had been driving it. It sure looked new to him.

"Good message," he said to the pastor after church. "Say, what kind of interesting things have you been able to do with your dividend money anyway?"

"Oh, we've been so blessed! One thing we were able to do was lease the Lexus. My wife and I wanted a newer, more reliable car to drive around town. And this next check we're going to use for a down payment on a boat. I want to take the boys fishing in something nicer than that old outboard we've been using."

Ray wanted to ask about the Pastor's motivation, but held back. He wondered if God needed any help keeping Pastor Kirkland from making money just to use on his own lusts. Ray could certainly make sure that Kent's investments failed.

———

Elise and Jase had something to say about the message as well, but privately at home that night. "It's just so hard to respect someone who is so transparently greedy!" Jase exclaimed.

"I know. I wonder if he even listens to himself when he preaches stuff like that!" Elise added. "But God is still in control, dear. We can't let it get to us."

"No we can't. I still wonder, though, if anyone else in the church sees what we see in Kent's personality."

"Say, Mama, let's get coffee at McDonald's this morning," Sarah Jane proposed. "You've got dinner in the oven, don't you?"

Church mornings were a bit of a sore spot for Sarah Jane and Ray. Sarah Jane couldn't understand why Ray felt the need to attend two churches every week. She had thought his habits might change when she and Cora moved in and there was dinner waiting at home, but he had made it clear that he wouldn't be ready for Sunday dinner until 1:00 to give him time to socialize with the Baptists!

"Good idea, honey," Cora replied. "We've got plenty of time."

When they were settled in the back booth, Sarah asked, "So, what's it feel like not to work at the drugstore anymore, Mama? You'd been there about as long as I can remember!"

"Relief, mainly," Cora replied. "It was a good job that had outlasted its time, I guess. Although I do feel a little out of touch living off Main Street and not seeing people all day!"

"Yeah, I think that would be the hard part. I'm still at the cafe most days so I still see townsfolk all the time. For me, I like the quiet at Ray's house. Do you still like him now that you're working for him, Mama?" Sarah Jane asked a bit anxiously.

"Oh, he's smooth and sophisticated and he's sure sweet on you. I like that best. You deserve a man who thinks you're as wonderful as I know you are." Cora enthused. "He does have his persnickety ways though. I mean that no smoking in the house rule! I could sure do without that. And the other day he accused me of going through his precious papers, as if I cared about his work stuff!"

"Funny. He asked me if I moved his papers when I cleaned his office, too. I assured him I had only dusted the top of his desk, but never opened a single drawer. After all, he locks the file cabinet, doesn't he? I suppose he has all kinds of private information on his clients and their finances in there."

"I wonder what made him think we were snooping?" Cora mused. "But I've been wanting to thank you for helping me get the job with Ray, honey. I recognize that sometimes I've been too hard on you. But I've always had your best interests at heart. I hope you know that."

"Mama, you gave up a lot to give me life. Anything I've done for you pales in comparison! But we'd better get on back now. We have a hungry man to feed!"

Kristen approached Ray after the church service. "Do you *have* a *moment* to *talk*? *Perhaps* we can *step* aside *here*?"

Ray agreed, although with some apprehension.

"I just *wanted* to *apologize* for my *reaction* when you *bought* the Lile *house*. I'm *afraid* I was terribly *jealous* and *upset* at *first*. But you *really* helped me with *investing* my *inheritance* and you *made* me *think*. I *visited* a women's *shelter* the other *day*. I've decided I'm *going* to go *back to school* and take some *social* work classes — I'm going to *open* a shelter *someday*!" She paused. "I don't think *anyone* takes me *seriously* though. I guess in the past I haven't been *exactly* motivated….at *least* not with the *right* kind of *motivation. This time I'm really going to do it!*"

Ray's first reaction was to dismiss Kristen's declaration as more pie in the sky. But he suddenly had the realization that this was exactly what others had done to Kristen and that she'd probably always been treated as inconsequential. And her last statement was said with a vehemence uncommon to the usual Kristen. "I believe you will, Kristen. And I believe you will be successful!" And Ray found he DID believe it! But he wondered where he had stashed Kristen's money, and whether she'd ever realize her goal without it.

———

He's realized that most mornings he could count on Ray being downtown at the Garden Cafe or on the golf course. The old lady went to the grocery store or for a gossip session at McDonald's. It was easy to spend an uninterrupted hour in Ray's house, but he still didn't get the information he really needed. It took just a moment's work to pick the locks on the file cabinets where he'd found paper files on each of the clients who had invested with Ray's company. From his first reading it didn't seem that the investment accounts totally matched up with the deposit amounts. However, he needed more time to find out where the extra money went. He wondered how to get everyone out of the house for an extended period... the answer was probably on the computer and that would take time. He knew enough about computers from those classes the rehab center had required he attend, but he wasn't very fast.

Chapter Twenty-nine

The Home and Garden Tour was always the week after Labor Day. Tourists came for the Labor Day activities in Jackson and stayed for Pecan Grove's Home and Garden Tour. The town council had tried various dates thinking that perhaps a time when children were out of school would be better for attracting crowds. As it turned out, however, the crowds attracted to garden tours were not the ones that had children of school age (no duh) so the second full week in September had become the regularly scheduled date for the annual event.

Zeke and Ray had made their final preparations for the ghost story re-enactment. They rented a fog machine and planned that as the hanging was taking place, the fog would partially obscure the scene. Then, as a howling wind blew the fog away, there would be a ghostly image made of gossamer gauze hanging from the rope to replace the flesh and blood scene. The narrator's voice through the fog would conclude the chilling account of the "hole that could never be filled." They were excited about their plans and eagerly awaited the reaction of the crowds.

At first he couldn't figure out what they were working on down by the river. It looked like they were planning to hang someone! He watched from his vantage point on the hill as a group of men did the same thing over and over. Were they putting on a play of some sort? Then he realized the man acting as the condemned man was none other than his enemy George Ray! Perhaps he could get him well and truly hung! Tonight he'd have to risk going to that fisherman's bar and to chat with the locals. Maybe he'd find someone who could tell him what was going on in town.

Zeke and Jase finally connected over lunch at the Garden Cafe. It wasn't the ideal spot for investigating, with both Ruby and Sarah Jane meandering by, but they were both strapped for time with the preparations for the Home and Garden tour in full swing. Jase had to hurry home to be with the kids so Elise could make it to the historical society where she was volunteering to help decorate. He and the boys had some extra lawn mowing as well with everyone wanting their yards perfect for the influx of tourists. Zeke had one last dress rehearsal out at Ray's now that all the rental equipment had arrived.

"I had some time to get on the computer the other night," Zeke began, "and it appears our friend's Facebook account wasn't activated until the week he rented a room in town! That made me wonder where he'd been before and why he's so active online now if he wasn't before." Zeke felt his loyalties were divided. On the one hand he didn't want to lose his friendship with Ray, although he was burning with curiosity about Ray's business and that list that had him as a liability to Ruby. On the other hand, he had been learning a lot from Jase and his new friends at the Bible church, so he wanted to please the pastor too.

"Hmmm. I noticed that too, but didn't pay it much attention. I just thought he was new to Facebook like me. How do you follow up on something like that? I talked with Bob who has been keeping an eye out while working at the house. He had been a mite suspicious, but after working there he now thinks everything is on the up and up."

Zeke noticed Ruby coming their way. "Hey Grandmaw! Can I get a refill on my coke?"

"Sure, sonnyboy. What's got you two so serious today?" Ruby tried to be casual, but inside she was burning with curiosity.

"I was asking Zeke for help with a computer problem, but it seems he's going to have to show me on my laptop because I don't get it." Jase laughed ruefully. "I'm afraid the technical gene skipped my family."

"I'll have more time to help you after the Tour next weekend," Zeke offered brightly for Ruby's benefit.

When she left the two men collaborated a bit more. "Thing is," said Zeke, "we just don't have much information about him. If you ask him directly about where he went to school, he jokes about the number of schools he was in as a foster child and never really tells you. If you ask about his birthday, he says no one really knows so he celebrates on Christmas. He says he has no relatives, but talks about a grandma who died. He's slippery as an eel, but so much fun to be around you forget why you wanted to know!"

So the house Ray had bought was an historic house and he was out to be respectable! Well, well, what do ya know? And there's gonna be a tour, eh? Ending on a Saturday night with a ghost story? That must be what the hanging was about. What could be more perfect?

Armed with information gleaned through a night of drinking at the Fishhook, he understood the scene at the riverbank. Now he would use it to his advantage. Ray would survive the first five performances. No one would look for a problem by the last one. While all attention was focused on the action at the river maybe he would scoop up Ray's computer and be gone. Better yet, with Ray out of the picture, no one would even realize anything was missing until much later. And to his mind, Ray deserved hanging.

In the meantime he had one more Sunday morning while they were all at church to try and crack the computer code and get the info he needed.

Chapter Thirty

"The Home and Garden Tour of Historic Pecan Grove: A Glimpse of A Splendid Past" was the grand title on the official brochure. Inside visitors could find the schedule of events for the celebration and other pertinent information. Several guided horse-drawn wagon tours were available (at a nice profit for the town), a map highlighted the walking tour, or visitors could hire a knowledgeable guide to ride along in a private vehicle. Each home on the tour was featured with a picture and a short blurb about the house as well as the title of the skit that would be performed there.

Ray and Sarah Jane had had to defer their idea of a grand ball at the close of the tour because the brochures were already at the printer. Instead they planned a private catered party for all those Grovers who had volunteered in any way during the tour. Cora was in her element getting ready for the guests; about 100 people were expected. Ray had hired a catering crew, but Cora planned to serve several of her special dishes in addition to the basic fare. She was also entrusted with planning the set up and directing the hired staff. The party was scheduled for Saturday and would start about 8:00 pm following the last tour and skit at the Lile house.

It was clear from the first that the Lile house was destined to be the star of this year's event. Those signing up for guided tours were lined up waiting for the one that would take them to Ray's house first. Those assigned to carriages that would go to other houses first were disgruntled and fussing that they wanted to be the first in decades to see inside the mansion. After the first round of skits on Thursday afternoon, there was little talk in town about anything other than Skeetoe's ghost.

Ray exulted in the attention. He thrived on anything dramatic and the renovated house and riveting skit certainly fit the bill! Sarah Jane did her part as the sickly and grieving wife watching from the upper balcony with her nurse and screaming at appropriate times. Reverend Findlay was no stranger to eloquence and his narration was done in a carrying voice with great effect. And the dramatic ending had everyone talking! It was without a doubt the best skit *ever* in the Pecan Grove Home and Garden Tour.

By Saturday afternoon the townsfolk were ready for the excitement to be over. The weeks of preparation and weekend of constant activity were beginning to take their toll. To his dismay Ray had caught a terrible cold. He limped through the performance Saturday afternoon, but by 5:00 it was clear that his voice could not handle another show, especially if he was to greet his invited guests later. Zeke had recruited Mike Sheffield to help with the backstage crew and suggested that he was about the only one tall enough to substitute for Ray. With a flurry of last minute arrangements Mike was coached on all he needed to know in order to take Ray's place. Taller even than Ray, he had been in on the plans and knew the part well enough.

The skit started with an overflow crowd in attendance. A group of ragtag Confederate soldiers approached across the lawn led by Dr. Rasmussen limping along with a cane. They were accompanied by Rob Porter dressed in judicial robes and carrying a gavel. As they approached the house, they called out for Bill Skeetoe to come out.

They produced papers that formally accused Bill of the crime of desertion. Bill loudly protested his innocence, citing his wife's illness as a mitigating factor, but all for naught. Right on the porch of his own home they declared him guilty and sentenced him to hang by the neck until dead!

The soldiers seized Bill and tied his hands behind his back to the cries and screams of his sick wife who was watching from the upper veranda. As they dragged him to the river bank, she collapsed in agony.

The crowd followed the procession down to the creek behind the house where there was a large oak tree. Zeke and another man were hidden on a platform built in the tree. Others manned the fog and wind machines concealed in the undergrowth. As the crew of Confederate soldiers threw a rope over a branch of the tree, the men up above lowered the black rope to be hooked to the harness Bill wore. As the crowd watched in horror, the rope was placed around Bill's neck and he was lifted from the ground almost high enough to hang. Colonel Eccles (played by Doc Rasmussen) noticed that Bill's feet were still touching the ground and he began to dig out under his feet using his cane.

At this point in the skit, fog began to creep over the scene. Suddenly, there was a shout from the men in the tree: "The rope broke! Hold him up! Hold him up!!!" Somehow the rope connected to the safety harness had broken and "Bill Skeetoe" was nearly hung again.

Quickly Doc removed the rope from Mike's neck and examined him. It appeared that his exceptional height had saved his life just as Bill Skeetoe's height had nearly saved him. The other soldiers hustled the crowd of tourists back up the trail to the house. Someone called 911 and soon the scene was secured by Chief Jones and his men.

"Man, I thought I was a goner! When that rope tightened against my neck and I couldn't breathe. Man! And then Doc starts digging under my feet! Whoa! I never want to do anything like that again!" Mike was traumatized - and rightly so.

"But what happened up there, Zeke?" asked Doc. "How did you know we needed to hold him up?"

"It was the tension. Suddenly there was a sorta pop sound and then there was no tension on the rope harness!"

"Yeah, I heard that too," chimed in John Cameron. "There was a second when we just looked at each other. Then Zeke started hollering."

"Ray and I talked about how important that rope was to the whole thing looking realistic. I checked it after every performance. We had a backup if it ever showed signs of wear. I swear it was in perfect working order after the afternoon performance." Zeke immediately jumped to conclusions and was excitedly trying to communicate his suspicions. "Someone must've sabotaged the equipment! Someone nearly hung Mike!"

Sarah Jane and Cora had insisted Ray go up to the third floor guest room to get some rest before the party. He had trouble relaxing, knowing the skit was going on without him. He could vaguely hear the sounds of the tourists arriving, then he heard Sarah Jane's anguished scream from the balcony and he heard the excited crowd move off toward the river. He had finally started to drift off when the sound of police sirens coming down his driveway propelled him out of bed and down the back stairs.

He nearly tore the back door off as he raced through the house and down the path. Pushing his way through the crowd of tourists, he came upon a shaken group of cast members surrounded by

Chief Jones and his men. "What happened?" he croaked. "What happened?"

The aftermath of the Garden Tour was perhaps even more memorable than the tour itself, as successful as that had been. Chief Jones had insisted that all who were present at the Lile house be kept on the grounds until they could be interviewed. To Cora's dismay, the fancy catered party became a free-for-all for tourists and townsfolk alike as they impatiently waited to be interviewed. Finally, around midnight, Jimmy Fletcher started taking down names and contact information from those who had been deemed less likely to have been involved.

An exhausted group, Ray, Sarah Jane, Cora and those involved in the skit, were gathered in the library when Chief Jones and his reporter came in. "Herschel, you know none of us had any to do with this," began Rob. "It was just a terrible accident!"

"Now Rob, you know I have to follow procedures. The youngsters here," he indicated Zeke, John and Mike, "insist they checked the equipment after the afternoon skit. Yet there are definitely signs that the rope had been frayed - possibly on purpose. That safety rope was nearly worn clear through before it broke. It would have been hard for the guys to miss that kind of damage. If it was done deliberately, and I can't see any other way for it to have happened… that would be attempted murder. If so, it looks as if Ray could have been the target, and had he been the one in the harness, he would likely be dead of a broken neck right now."

The group was silent. Although the thought had been out there, no one had voiced the word 'murder' until now. Who harbored that kind of hate? The killing in the city park took on a new, more menacing form as the idea of a serial killer took shape in their minds.

"Mike, my officer will be taking you home tonight -- You're still living with your folks, right? and he'll stay outside the house overnight as well. Ray, I'll have two men posted here. One to patrol around the house, one to guard the crime scene. We're going to want to take a closer look in the light of day. I know you've all given statements to my officers, but I will be back to talk to each of you individually. I want you to think about anything that was at all unusual tonight before the skit. "And," the chief looked directly at Ray, then Mike, "I want you two in particular, to think about who your enemies are!"

Ray spent a restless night. Several times he got up and looked outside to make sure the police patrol was still in place. By morning, the sleepless night and his stuffed up sinuses combined to give him a splitting headache and a very bad mood. He sat on the back veranda brooding as he watched the police comb the path and the woods. He was curt to Cora when she brought him chicken soup at noon. He snapped at a reporter who had crossed the crime scene tape.

He thought over the events in Minnesota that led to his months in prison. He had enrolled in school in good faith, but found there wasn't much there to his liking. Too many rules; too much serious study. He had taken a job working as a companion for old Ralph Schmidt, thinking there might be something of value in the old house that he could appropriate for his own purposes. Ralph was a gentle fellow who told him how his son had started using drugs and become abusive. Ralph had kicked him out and never heard from him again. He said George was more of a son to him than his own flesh and blood. When he died, George found that Ralph had left him everything he had - a total of $500,000. George had had no idea Ralph was worth that much.

He'd pretty much blown that money, but the job gave him an idea. He decided to be a companion to an elderly, wealthy man who had no relatives. He searched for the right position and after a couple months, he was hired by Vernon McCarthy, a crusty old stockbroker with a large home in St. Paul. George's natural charm had won the old man over and he taught George the ins and outs of trading on Wall Street. George was good at it and before long, he was making money for himself. Vernon was proud that he finally had someone who "cared for him and his business." When he died a few months later, he left George $500,000, some stocks and bonds, and the rest to charity.

If he had stopped there….but why stop when you're on a roll? No gambler ever did that and, ultimately, George was a gambler. So he began to work as a companion for Harry Jorgenson. Harry was generous and gregarious but had Alzheimer's Disease. He kept forgetting that he had given George money or valuable possessions, so when his lawyer said his money was nearly gone, Harry accused George of taking it. The charges of embezzlement and elder abuse stuck and George was sent to prison. Never mind that he paid back all the money Harry had given him, they still said he had used undue influence on Harry and sent him away for a few months. Yeah, he had used his influence on Harry, but isn't that what everyone did? If he treated Harry nicer than anyone else and Harry rewarded him, why was that wrong? But after that incident, he couldn't wait to leave Minnesota and George Ray behind.

It was clear that someone had followed him here. He wondered who. Harry's lawyer? No, he had heard that Harry died while he was still in prison. Vernon's money was free and clear, right? What about Ralph's son? He was just a screwed up addict, wasn't he? But that scenario made the most sense. If he could abuse an old man, his father even, killing Weasel wouldn't be much of a stretch. And killing got easier the more you did it, he had heard.

What was the son's name? Aaron? No, not a Bible name. Allan? Eric? He thought Allan sounded right. The old man never called him Al, always Allan. Yeah, Allan Schmidt, that was it. Didn't Weasel try to warn him once that Al Schmidt was trouble? Ray hadn't listened. He figured Allan couldn't care that much or he would have mended fences with his dad long before he died. The big question now was, if it *was* Allen, was he acting alone? Or did he have a drug gang helping him?

How could Ray let the authorities know of his suspicions without having them look too closely into his own background? His good standing in Pecan Grove was based on a pack of lies: he had never finished Bible School, he had never enrolled in any Trading College, there was no grandma to inherit from. He was just an ex-con who had served time for misappropriation of funds! Even his name was fictitious.

Finally Sarah Jane ventured out to talk to him. "Ray, sweetie," she began timidly, "I'm scared. Can we talk?"

"Oh, Sarah Jane, I'm worried too."

"I can't stop thinking it might have been *you* who was supposed to die last night. I don't want to ever think of losing you, Ray!"

"Ye-es, Chief made it clear that he isn't buying the accident theory. I don't know what's going on here. I mean, I know buying this house made some people in town jealous, but I hate that I'm even thinking Kari or Kristen could have been involved. And the guy in the park. The other day Chief Jones told me they had traced him to Minnesota! That makes it look like I'm right in the middle of *everything*."

"Oh, Ray! Everything was going so well. I had such high hopes for the future."

"Sarah Jane, whatever is happening is not your fault. I've decided one thing today. If something bad happens, I want you taken care of. I'm calling Rob in the morning to make some arrangements."

"But I don't want *things!* I want *you!*" Sarah Jane burst into tears and threw herself into his arms.

"Oh Lordy, what have I done?" Ray thought as he tried to comfort Sarah Jane.

Chapter Thirty-one

First thing Monday morning, Ray followed through by calling Rob as soon as he could. Rob, just finishing a round of golf, was glad to stop by on his way to the office.

Ray settled the lawyer in a comfortable side chair and locked the door. "I don't want to be interrupted or overheard," he stated firmly. "I'm worried that something bad is going down and I'm going to be in the middle of it. I'm not sure why, although I intend to find out. But in case I'm too late and the police are too late, I want Sarah Jane taken care of. Is there a way I can give her this house? I bought it with cash so there is no mortgage and no lien. The house is fully insured and I paid for five years ahead. I'll leave money with you to pay the taxes for at least those five years. If nothing happens, fine. But at least she'll have a place to live. She can turn it into a bed and breakfast if she wants. She and her mother will be taken care of as best I can."

"Well, if your mind is made up — and I can see it is — it's a fairly simple process. You'll just need to file a quitclaim deed and I can get that ready for you yet today. If you can come to my office tomorrow morning, I'll have it ready for your signature and my secretary can be the witness. We can also set up a standard will to distribute the rest of your possessions as well."

"Perfect, Rob. I appreciate your willingness and expertise here."

"Please, Ray, call me anytime. Saturday night was a terrifying time and I'll do whatever I can to make things easier for you."

"Rob, what do *you* think happened Saturday night? It really bothers me that I wasn't there, but I guess if I had been there, I might not be here!"

"Ray, I just don't know! We were all excited because it was the last performance. You know, hamming it up for the crowd and whooping and hollering like the Confederate mob might have done. Everything was just as usual. 'Course no one can match you for getting the crowd worked up, but young Mike wasn't doing too bad. I could tell he was a little nervous about the hanging, but that made it seem realistic, you know. And then whammo! It was too real."

———

Herschel Jones was also in foul humor. As if it weren't frustrating enough to have a murder unsolved on his watch, now the whole town was in an uproar over the near hanging of young Mike Sheffield. He felt sure the two events were connected in some way and that it had to hinge on Ray Jacobs. But he had learned nothing — *nothing* — about the man, either from his dealings here or from the obstructionist police force in Minnesota. Well, there was nothing like careful police work for bringing the truth to light. Talk, talk, talk. He had to talk to *everyone* associated with Mr. Jacobs.

He was met at the door of the Lile mansion by Cora Windham. "Hello, Cora," he greeted her. "What are you doing here today?"

"Why Chief, I thought you would have heard. I took on the job as chef and housekeeper here. Sarah Jane and I live in the apartment behind the kitchen."

"I'm losing my touch, Cora. I missed that entirely. Whoever is supposed to fill me in on town gossip is going to get a talking to!"

Cora laughed. "It's a step up from that dinky rental, isn't it? Do you want to talk to Ray?"

"Yes, but I have a few questions for you, too, Cora. Can we sit down and talk?"

"Ok, we'll just step into the drawing room here. Can I get you some coffee?"

"I think I'm already over-caffeinated this morning, but thanks. Now, you remember I asked you to think about anything unusual that happened Saturday or at any time since you've been here. Has anything at all come to mind?"

"Oh, things have been in such a tizzy with the last of the renovations and the Garden Tour and cooking for the party and everything. I was *so* upset when all that work was just gobbled up by a mass of strangers. I'm not even sure what *is* normal yet....but the one thing I wondered about was the last house tour. You know how there would normally be some people going to the skit and some staying to tour the house? Well, while the skit was going on outside, there was a very small group, only five I think, touring inside. I was busy in the kitchen getting ready for the private party, but I remember Jeannie getting upset with the one gentleman. There were two couples, I think, and one single man, and he kept straying from the group. I heard her admonishing, saying, 'Sir, stay in the appointed rooms,' and 'stay with the group, sir'." I'm not sure what he was doing, but when they came down from upstairs he ducked out the front door instead of finishing up in the library like the rest. Then all the hullabaloo broke loose down at the river....well! That's all I know."

"What was Ray doing while the tour was going through the house? I know he was sick, so he wasn't at the river. Just where was he with the house open to tourists?"

"I was so busy getting ready I never really saw him. But he had taken all his private stuff; computer, personal toiletries and some clothes, up to the west wing where the nursery used to be. He had put a decent bed up there and made it into a guest suite. He said he'd just stay up there during the Home and Garden Tour. I expect that's where he was…"

"Thank you Cora. Is Ray in? Can I just see him in here?" Chief made a note to talk to Jeannie March as well.

———~~———

When Ray came in, Chief was shocked by the change in the man. He looked haggard and unkempt; a startling contrast to the impeccably dressed man he had questioned in August.

Ray immediately apologized. "I've had such a horrid cold! Haven't felt up to shaving and all that. And I haven't slept more than an hour at a time since Saturday night."

"I heard you were sick. Probably a lucky thing in the long run. Have you thought about anyone who would want you dead, Ray? Further examination of that rope showed it had *definitely* been tampered with. You would be the obvious target since you were scheduled to play the part of Bill Skeetoe."

Ray looked uneasy. "I've thought about little else, Chief Jones. I think it had to be a prank. You know, kids not realizing how dangerous their little game could be. I just can't see why anyone would be targeting me!" He knew he didn't dare to tell the chief about Allan Schmidt - that would expose his fake name and the whole house of cards he had built so carefully would fall.

Chief looked skeptical. "I suppose that could be….but I doubt it. I will not have two unsolved mysteries on my watch, and I don't want you to be the second victim here either. Has anything else happened out of the ordinary here?"

"I really can't say. Ever since I moved in there have been remodelers and decorators coming and going all day long. It was an ambitious project to get the house ready for the Tour. Then

Sarah Jane and her mama moved in just under a month ago. What's normal anyway?"

"Okay. I know you gave your statement to my officers, but let's just go over a typical day for you." Nearly an hour later the Chief was ready to call it quits for now. "So, one last time. The people investing with you were all happy with the results? No one lost a pile of money in some risky stock? No threatening phone calls?"

Ray half chuckled, "Not yet. I suppose it could happen one day, but thankfully, not yet."

———

He didn't know how he had managed to bungle that perfect opportunity to remove Ray from the scene. And the nosy old tour guide kept her beady little eyes so focused on him that there was no way to sneak into the private rooms. He'd had to take the risky step of sneaking into the house the next night while the occupants were sleeping. Luckily, they were all so exhausted after the police questioning they slept soundly. He had to find the numbers and information he needed to drain Ray's accounts! The old oak tree next to one of the unoccupied second floor bedrooms was almost as good as the front door. It had the advantage of being so close to the woods not even the police patrol caught a glimpse of him coming or going.

Last night he had finally been able to access the password protected areas of the computer and as he had hoped, Ray had been squirrelling millions of dollars away somewhere. He must have some offshore accounts. Where, oh where, had he hidden the account numbers? Surely the man wasn't so egotistical as to think he would be able to keep them in his memory alone!

———

Zeke had been deep in thought about the Saturday night incident. When Chief Jones came by to see him he was ready with his theory. "The way I figure it, Chief, is that whoever tampered with that rope was familiar with how we had it hooked up. If someone had just happened along and decided to mess with it, they wouldn't have known just which part of the rope was going to take the weight and break. It was frayed *right* where it would cross over the branch so *any* weight was sure to finish the break. That means either it was someone on my technical crew or someone who was watching us pretty closely. And furthermore, I figure they had to be gunning for Ray. Mike was just that much taller than Ray that it didn't work on him."

Chief just let him talk. "So do you have any suspicions, Zeke?"

"I've been thinking over each guy on my team and can't come up with a reason for any of them to do a thing like that! Ray was treating us real well, buying fancy lunches and stuff. We were all kind of pumped about going to that private party because we're not usually the kind of people that get invited to fancy parties!

"But one thing bothers me. Mike had an argument with Brandon at one of our last practices. Brandon has a mean mouth and he was ragging on Toby for being slow. You know, teasing, but with a nasty tone. Mike defended Toby and laid into Brandon and the two of them got into it for a bit. You don't suppose…"

"We'll look into it, Zeke. Tell me how it came about that Mike played the part of Bill Skeetoe. Had he ever practiced for the part before?"

"No, he and I joked about that once. Neither of us wanted to be out front acting like that. Ray *loves* the attention, but we agreed we were backstage kind of people. So when Ray's voice was just a croak by the end of the afternoon skit, we knew we had to do something. Mike is about the only one tall enough. We purposely recruited short people for the soldiers to make Ray look taller! Mike could see that the only way to keep the show going was if he acted the part, so he agreed."

"Did you ever see anything that would make you think someone had been prowling about the site?"

"Not really. But once or twice I thought I smelled marijuana smoke. Could have been from anywhere, though. I thought there might have been a fisherman up the creek a ways, although the smell seemed to come more from the woods. We would occasionally see someone fishing in the creek thereabouts."

"Ever the same person?" Chief was instantly alert.

"Never paid much mind, I guess," Zeke said slowly.

"I'll have them search the creek banks carefully for any sign of someone coming and going along there."

———

Chief caught Sarah Jane as she was leaving the Garden Cafe. "Kind of surprised to see you at work today, Sarah Jane. Mind if we talk for a spell?"

"Oh, Chief Jones, I just couldn't stay home and brood anymore. I'm worried and it makes me jumpy. Ray is worried and it makes him grumpy. Trust me, it's not a good combination!"

"I can just imagine. What can you tell me, Sarah Jane? Has anything else happened since you've been living up at the Lile house? Anything that may have been suspicious?"

"It's just the three of us most of the time. Bob Huggens has been working on the grounds with his crew, but I can't bring myself to think he would ever hurt a fly. Leroy and MaryEllen were coming and going quite a bit, but they finished up the inside stuff a week ago or more. Ray really hasn't acted any differently. Except that one day when he thought either Mama or I had been looking through his papers. We hadn't touched them, but he was pretty upset. I suppose he has to keep private data on his clients.

But he keeps the file cabinets locked. Neither Mama nor I would have any idea what to do with financial information anyway."

"Thank you, Sarah Jane. I'll let you get on home now."

———

Ray felt a small portion of his burden lifted after he signed the papers with Rob. But he knew he still had a long way to go to clear up the mess in Pecan Grove. Always before, Ray had blamed any problems he had on other people, circumstances, or the government. He felt that if he had been treated fairly in life, if his mom hadn't been an addict, if the government had released his papers to the adoption agency instead of the foster home service, if... His time in Pecan Grove had served to teach him that it only took one person to mess up his life, and that person was George Jacob Ray. Could he still be successful here? People liked him, trusted him and were grateful to him. He just couldn't help himself: he saw an opportunity to get money and, legal or not, he went for it.

He knew he had a lot of work to do to clear up all his — and his investors — finances before they would stand scrutiny so he spent long hours closeted in his office poring over his options. He felt like he was in a race against time and that some unknown presence was breathing down his neck.

His time of moody reflection had brought clarity about Weasel's killing too. He had thought that Weasel had probably tangled with some rough element when making a false ID and he had come to Ray for help. He had felt guilty because he was too busy that Saturday to find Weasel and help him. Now he figured that the opposite was true. Weasel had come to warn Ray of imminent trouble, probably that Ralph's son was on his track, and he had paid the ultimate price for his loyalty. Ray wondered what Weasel would have told him to do — save himself first? stay and face up to whatever comes? or try to fix everything?

Chapter Thirty-two

oug Swinney and Logan Powell had been best buds since the day Logan's family had moved into the old farmhouse a quarter mile down the dirt road from the Swinneys. Doug was a year ahead of Logan in school, but they both loved outdoor sports such as hunting, fishing and even trapping. Come fall, nearly every afternoon they would jump off the bus, dump their books and grab their guns to hunt rabbits for a few hours before sunset. This beautiful September day was no exception.

"Hey Logan! Let's head over to that wild area beyond the old gravel pit. It's open to hunting, and we can scout for deer while we're hunting bunnies."

"Great plan! I'll meet you behind your barn. If we go 'cross the fields it's only a half mile or so."

The boys were engrossed in following a deer trail winding through the rugged terrain when they came upon an area of crushed and broken undergrowth. "Whoa. Do you think a wild hog came through here?" wondered Logan.

Doug was a bit ahead of him. "Naw, look here. Someone dumped a car in here!"

"Man! It's not even old and rusty. I wonder why someone would dump a good car in a sinkhole?"

The boys thoroughly examined the car, but since there were no keys, no license and nothing else in it they lost interest. "We'd better be heading back," Doug said. "Our mamas will skin us if we're not back for supper."

That evening they both eagerly told their families over dinner about the car they found down in the woods. And that is how, after three months of nothing, Chief Jones got *two* calls in one evening about an abandoned car in the wilderness off Old Quarry Road.

———

Of course, thought Chief Jones, his bad luck was holding steady. The car had been wiped clean of prints other than the ones the boys had left. He figured he could spend endless man hours having his men crawling around on their hands and knees and maybe eventually finding where the keys and any other identifying papers had been thrown. More likely they'd never be found. Trouble was, his department had already spent more money on these investigations than had been budgeted. With the election nearing, the mayor was pressuring him to solve his cases, but was reluctant to allot the additional funds necessary to do a decent job. Yeah, he could call for a citizen posse, but then any additional clues would be trampled to smithereens. Perhaps....

Bob Huggens took the call from his friend Herschel Jones Thursday morning. He was amazed at the tale of a late-model Toyota abandoned in the woods. "Ya thinkin' this is tied to one of your little myst'ries?" he asked.

"Bob, you know I don't believe in coincidences and there have been too many of them in town these last few months. I'm convinced that if we can trace this car, we'll find it ties either to Wayne Simonson's killing or the near hanging at the Lile place.

Hopefully, both. So, you got any hounds that could tell me if Mr. Simonson was ever in this car?"

"Wa'al shore. Old Lucy'll pick up a scent even if it *is* three months old."

Bob and Lucy met the chief on Old Quarry Road about an hour later. He had also brought Lucy's son Lucas, and Sam's boy Oliver to work him. "Lukey and Oliver need some practice too," he told Chief Jones.

Chief brought out a ziplock evidence bag containing a bandana that had been tied around Weasel's head. Bob let the dogs take a good sniff; then gave them the command to search. Lucy hesitated as she sniffed the air. Then she headed directly toward the sinkhole where the car was resting.

Lucas, on the other hand, began to snuffle through the underbrush poking his nose into piles of leaves here and there. Oliver figured he'd probably gotten distracted by deer scent or some other animal. About a hundred yards deeper into the thick growth than where the car had been found, Lucas started digging. Oliver stopped him and he sat whining while Oliver put on gloves and carefully removed the top layers of leaves and debris from the area. He was surprised when he found a wallet. Praising Lukey effusively, he made his way back toward the group gathered around the vehicle.

"So, Bob, does Lucy's response indicate that Wayne was in this car?" Chief was asking.

"I'd say it's pretty much a given, Herschel. She's never been one for false alerts." He turned to Oliver.

"So, young Lucas led you on a wild goose chase, or deer chase, eh Oliver? We're gonna have to work with that boy."

"Wouldn't say that, Bob. Lookee what our boy alerted to," he said as he produced an evidence bag with the wallet.

"Well, well, well," Chief was practically purring. "How in the dickens did he do that? Maybe our luck is turning."

Cora had caught Ray's cold. Miserably feverish and stuffed up, she couldn't do much more than shuffle from her bed to the recliner in front of the TV. Even that was too much effort most of the time. But her nicotine addiction wouldn't let her skip too many smokes. She was sorely tempted to disregard Ray's no smoking in the house rule.

Sarah Jane tiptoed in to check on her mother. "Ray and I are thinking about getting out of the house for a bit tonight now that he's feeling better. Will you be okay by yourself, Mama?"

"I'm not sure," Cora whined. "What will I eat? I'm not up to cooking anything."

"How about that nice chicken soup you made for Ray when he was sick? It made such a big batch I put some in the freezer. I'll warm it up and bring it to you before we go, okay?"

"That would be nice, dear. Where are you going?"

"Chief Jones doesn't want us to leave the county, so we thought we'd try that new supper club that opened on the road to Mobile. We checked and it's barely this side of the county line."

"Will you be late? I'm a little nervous out here alone with all that's going on in town."

"Promise. Just dinner and home."

After Ray and Sarah Jane left, Cora propped herself up in bed and tried to read a magazine, but she kept imagining she could hear someone walking around upstairs. She tried playing a game on the iPad Ray had given her for her birthday, thinking the game sounds would block out any noises that could fuel her imagination. But now she needed a smoke. She supposed she'd have to wrap up and step out on the back porch. Oh, how she hated that rule!

Cora pulled on her quilted robe and old slippers. Thank goodness there was a comfortable rocking chair just outside the back door. The nights were getting cooler, but the September twilight was almost pretty. If only she felt a little better.

―――

He watched from his favorite vantage point as the Mustang pulled out of the driveway. Too bad they weren't taking the old lady with them. He had heard her coughing last night so he knew she was likely to stay in her room. Tonight would be a good chance to explore the upstairs before it got too dark. He wanted to look behind all the pictures to rule out any hidden safe.. Yesterday he had seen a wrecker going by with the blue Toyota. He had cleaned it thoroughly, but what if... No, he couldn't think of that. He just needed to finish his search and get out of town!

If he didn't find those numbers by this weekend he might have to kidnap the girl. From what he could see Ray was crazy about her. He'd probably give up the numbers for her safety. Kidnapping was risky though. He would rather work behind the scenes.

―――

The car had been hauled out of the sinkhole with great fanfare. The evidence techs, such as they were in a small town like Pecan Grove, had gone over it carefully. Chief knew he was dealing with an experienced criminal when they found the VIN obliterated. His mind kicked into high gear... there was something that might help... it was niggling at the back of his brain. What was it? Something they knew because of their interviews? Something about the car, he was sure of that.

The wallet yielded one smudged partial print that didn't match Wayne's. It wasn't even enough of a print that they could send it in for analysis. It might be of use if they ever caught up with the guy though.

Chief settled down to go over everything in the file once again. Something was niggling his brain about a car. What evidence could they have found about a car? Wait a minute - wasn't there something about a car dealership? "Jimmy! Get me that pen from the car dealership in Iowa!" That had to be the clue that was so elusive.

By the time Jimmy dug up the pen from the evidence room, it was too late to call the dealership. And Chief had come up with a few more people he wanted to check back with. Tomorrow would be a busy day!

He didn't know how long Ray and his girl would be out. They had been sticking too close to the house all week. He almost laughed out loud when he thought about the security measures Ray had taken. Guess he didn't know that when he was using, burglary had supported his meth habit. The window locks were especially ineffective. And the old lady usually had the TV or radio blaring while she cooked.

He hadn't found anything behind the upstairs pictures, but he had found a pile of cash strapped to the back of a dresser drawer. He left it there for now since there was no sense raising suspicions. As he went to leave out the bedroom window he smelled cigarette smoke. Look at that, coughing up a storm, but the old lady was still out there having a smoke. Made him want to light up too. Hey, maybe she was giving him a chance. If he locked her out he could search in peace. No, Ray and the girl might come home anytime.

He'd better not take the chance. But when would the old lady go back inside so he could leave?

———✧———

The new supper club was called the Buccaneer and decorated in a pirate theme. The waiters wore bandanas and eye patches, the waitresses wore short skirts and lace-up vests. Sarah Jane and Ray were thrilled to find that they featured a band on Friday nights with a small dance floor. It was *so* nice to get away from reminders of the past harrowing week and just enjoy each other's company.

Sarah Jane relaxed as Ray held her close on the dance floor. His lips, close to her ear, crooned the words to the old love song the band was playing. As the set came to a close, Ray looked deep in her eyes and said, "Sarah Jane, I've never said this to anyone before, but I love you! Every word I sang was true, I *do* cherish you."

With tears in her eyes, Sarah Jane replied, "Ray, I think I fell in love the first day you walked into the Garden Cafe. And every day since has just caused me to love you more."

The rest of the evening was magical, the dinner delightful, the dancing divine. Soon Ray and Sarah Jane were laughing and talking as if the previous week had never happened. They began to show off on the dance floor to the entertainment of the other diners. Totally enthralled with each other, they forgot the passage of time and their promise to be home early.

It was nearly midnight when Sarah Jane heard a woman cough behind her and the sound instantly transported her to her mother's bedside. "Ray!" she gasped. "We forgot about Mama!"

Laughing, he grabbed her hand. "Let's go, Cinderella! Your carriage awaits."

"But my handsome prince is coming with me," she giggled.

Chapter Thirty-three

Saturday morning found Herschel Jones back at his desk early. He finally had some direction in these cases and he was impatient to get started. By the time 8:00 rolled around, he figured if people weren't up yet, they needed to be. He called Will Stewart.

"Will, Herschel Jones here. Hope I'm not calling too early."

"Hey, Chief. Naw, you know me, I have to work on my sermon on Saturday. I've been up awhile already."

"If I'd realized that, I would have called earlier. Anyway, I want to run a few things by you — test your memory. Tell me about the events on that last day of the Heritage Festival."

"Aw man, that was three months ago," Will groaned. "Sometimes I can't remember what happened yesterday."

"Start with getting over to the festival grounds and work through your day. It'll come back."

"Well, when the barbershop quartets sing it's always a full day. The festival grounds are so packed that we've taken to all riding in one car to ease the parking. I took my van so we had room for our equipment too. I picked up the two guys who live farther away first and then stopped by Bella's and got Ray."

"So he was still living at Bella's?" Interrupted the Chief.

"Yeah, he moved right after the festival. I remember he talked about it during the day. Anyway, that was about 9:15 am. We were scheduled to sing at the pavilion at ten, at the food court at noon, and on the midway at two. After that we had a break before the competition at six, but we were supposed to mill around keeping interest up for the show in the evening."

"How did Ray Jacobs act that day? Was he secretive? Did he stay with the group? Did he seem nervous? Did he leave for any amount of time?"

"Hmmm. Do you know Ray very well, Herschel? Because Ray never shows what he's really thinking. He is fun, intelligent, a good conversationalist, but I would be hard pressed to think of a situation that caused him to be serious or reflective. It's not that I don't think he feels deeply, he is just a master at concealing his emotions. I've always figured it was a result of being raised in foster homes. You know, the lack of a secure home life damaged him emotionally or something. But to answer more directly, Ray seemed the same as always to me. I think he was with one of us all day until supper when Sarah Jane came over. He was watching for her to show up all afternoon. Now that's one person who seems to have penetrated Ray's veneer."

"And after the contest? Who did Ray leave with?"

"We all went out to celebrate. Ray rarely drinks alcohol and I never do, so I drove Ray and Sarah Jane and the other guys. At the restaurant we met up with the wives. We stayed out pretty late and it was a good thing I drove too, because Ray had a couple beers and he was feeling them. I dropped Sarah Jane at her mother's, then drove Ray to Bella's."

By the time the Chief was off the phone with Will, it was late enough that he hoped to get an answer at the car lot.

"Jefferson County Auto Sales," the pleasant voice answered after the first ring. "How can I help you?"

"Good morning. This is the chief of Police in Pecan Grove, Alabama. May I speak to the owner or a manager, please?"

"Oh my!" the woman gasped. "I hope there's no trouble, Chief. I'm the owner, Ruth Peterson."

"Wonderful! We have reason to believe that a car we recovered here may have been purchased from your lot. It was abandoned and we are looking into some suspicious circumstances surrounding the man we think bought this car. Now, is there any way we can figure out who was working the lot and may have sold a pale blue Toyota Camry, about 85,000 miles on the odometer, somewhere around mid-June?"

"Let me pull up the employee log. But why don't you talk to my dad? He sold me the business so he could retire and do what he wants. It seems what he wants to do is sell cars, not run a business," she laughed. "He knows every car we've ever had on the lot. If he didn't sell it, chances are he'll know who did."

Chief pondered his good luck while he waited for Ms. Peterson's father. "Hello, Lars Peterson here!" boomed a friendly voice. "Ruth says you're looking for the skinny on a blue Camry? I remember that car — unusual color for a Toyota. Sold it early in the summer as I recollect."

"That would fit our time frame down here, Mr. Peterson. Did you sell it personally? Or can you tell me who did?"

"Oh, it was me. Fella came in late one afternoon. One of those biker looking dudes with a bandana twisted 'round his head and a few too many tattoos. He was driving a dinged up red Jeep and he wanted to trade for something less obvious, is what he said. The Toyota was the closest we had to what he wanted."

"Did you happen to get his name?" Chief interrupted.

"Yeah, and I even remember it. We joked because I'm Peterson and he was Simon-son." he laughed. "You know, like Simon Peter in the Bible?"

Herschel Jones rarely attended church. He did *not* know. But he murmured, "Oh sure."

"Funny thing is," and Lars' voice became less confident, "there was a fella come in right soon after he left. Now that alone is unusual. We might see two customers a day, but not real close together like. This second fella — he homes in on that Jeep and wants to know all about it. I told him I just took it on trade and hadn't had the mechanic check it for sale yet. But he looked it over right careful-like while asking me a bunch of questions about who traded it in, why, and what the fella bought. It made me uneasy, I tell you. I was pretty evasive after the first couple questions and told him I couldn't remember much of anything. Pretty soon he left without ever looking at another car."

"Strange, but it fits with the little we know," Chief said. "What kind of car was the second guy driving?"

"A gray Chevy Malibu," came the quick reply.

After thanking him profusely, Chief Jones hung up. Wow, had he hit the jackpot with that call. Now he knew for sure that someone followed Wayne--and it wasn't Ray.

Cora had stayed awake waiting for Sarah Jane to get home. She had been hearing noises all night, and when she was on the porch she was sure she heard a window being closed upstairs. Returning to her apartment she wedged a chair under the door and sat in her recliner covered with a blanket and holding a butcher knife in her hand.

Finally, after midnight, she heard the car doors slam and laughing voices approach the house. When Sarah Jane entered the kitchen, glowing with love and laughter, she found a disheveled Cora coming out from her bedroom holding a knife.

"Mama! Whatever are you doing with that knife?" Sarah Jane gasped.

"Where have you been so long? I kept hearing noises -- I was scared to death!" Cora croaked out.

"Oh, Mama, I'm so sorry. We were having so much fun we forgot the time. Mama, Ray said he loves me!"

"I'm sorry to be such a baby and you so happy. We'll talk in the morning. I'm just so glad you're home and safe."

Sarah Jane woke the next morning to the sound of Ray stomping from room to room upstairs. Then she heard Cora's deep cough from the next bedroom. "Oh no, trouble on two fronts," she thought. She knew that when Cora's cold settled into her chest like that they would be making a trip to urgent care, and on weekends, the only one open was in Jackson. If only Mama weren't so stubborn they could have seen Dr. Swanson at his office in town yesterday. But Ray worried her even more. She wondered what had him so upset.

Quickly showering and throwing on jeans and a tee shirt, she was barely ready when she heard Ray knock on the apartment door. "Good morning sweetie," she greeted him. "What's happening so early this morning?"

"I wish I knew. Could Cora have gone upstairs last night dusting picture frames? Every picture is slightly askew!"

Sarah Jane paled. Instantly the worried look she had worn for the past week returned. "Mama was waiting for us to get home last night. She was so frightened. She said she had been hearing noises all night. She'd been sitting in her chair with a butcher knife since 8:00 pm!"

"So I haven't been imagining my papers messed up and my drawers disordered. Someone *has* been in here. More than once and he's getting bolder."

"We have to call the police, Ray!" Sarah Jane cried. "Maybe they'll send the patrol officer out again."

"Yes," Ray said slowly. "I think I will do just that."

The two women were just leaving in Sarah Jane's car to take Cora to urgent care when a police car pulled into the drive. The officer who stepped out wasn't someone Sarah Jane had ever seen before and he looked about sixteen. But at least someone had come.

Ray greeted the young officer at the door. After hearing Ray's story and taking copious notes as they toured the house, the officer said, "I'm sorry I don't have the authority to order a patrol here. Let me call the station."

After being on his phone for what seemed forever to Ray, the youngster told him, "They say there is still a patrol car coming by every hour. They promised to ask the Chief if he'll authorize a foot patrol as well. I suggest you check all your doors and if possible, change the locks. Or you could move to a hotel until all this is settled…."

"No thanks," Ray answered shortly. "I'm not leaving so whoever it is can rob me blind."

Unfortunately, the Chief was too preoccupied with his investigation into Weasel's stalker to answer calls from his newest patrolman. The request that was submitted for foot patrols at the Lile place went unheeded. The lengthy report that was turned in about Ray's suspicions of an intruder was likewise ignored. By the time Chief Jones returned to the station from following up on possible sightings of the gray Malibu he was already late for his grandson's birthday party. He figured anything else could wait.

———

That night, Cora slept better with prescriptions for antibiotics, cough medicine with codeine, and an inhaler. The house was quiet, although Ray slept lightly, alert to the creaks and groans as the old house settled.

"Mama. Wake up. Mama, Ray and I would really like to get out for church this morning. Are you going to be okay here alone?" Sarah Jane was dressed and ready to go.

"Ok, just go." Cora mumbled. "I'm going to sleep some more. But hurry home."

———

As soon as the Mustang pulled out of the driveway, he was up the tree. He had had an idea yesterday and, if he was right, it would all be settled today. There was a pair of paintings that had bothered him since he first saw them. Obviously hand painted, they didn't seem to match the decor of the old house. He wanted to look at them again, maybe pry off their backing.

He went immediately to the library and took down the first picture, which depicted a vase with a topiary rose bush. Around the edges was an uneven tile border design. As he brought the painting close to work on it his vision shifted and he thought he saw numbers instead of the tile pattern. Was he hallucinating? He looked closer and everything was normal. When he squinted to look once more, he again caught numbers hidden in the tiles. This had to be it! It was like those magic eye posters he had seen as a kid. The good-for-nothing snake had had the account numbers hidden in plain sight all along!

He attempted to write the numbers down as he deciphered them but he kept losing the pattern. He didn't have time to squint and get all those numbers right so he took the paintings and set them by his window escape. Now to destroy Ray, once and for all. First, he tiptoed down the stairs and carefully positioned a match under each outside door. When the door was opened again, there would be a spark. Creeping down to the basement he found the fittings for the new furnace and loosened the connection. He heard the satisfying hiss of gas as he quickly scurried up the stairs. Just to be certain, he blew out the pilot light on the gas fireplace insert as he passed the parlor.

As he passed Ray's bedroom door on his way to the window, he remembered the cash behind the dresser drawer. No sense leaving that behind, he thought. But when he pulled out the drawer, the money was gone. He searched frantically knowing there wasn't much time, knowing Ray could come home to his doom at any minute.

Cora woke craving a cigarette. Too weak, sleepy and drugged to make her way outside, she decided smoking in the house just one time wouldn't kill anyone!

Chapter Thirty-four

After the service Ray and Sarah Jane visited with friends for a few moments outside the church. Gradually they became aware of the scream of sirens. "I wonder if there's been another accident on the highway," someone commented. Then they heard the distinctive wail of the fire engines. "Whoa, must be something big," another friend said.

As they visited, first one, then another police car screamed past, headed in the direction of their house. Ray looked at Sarah Jane. Some unspoken communication passed between them and they spoke almost in unison, "We'd better hurry home and check on Mama/Cora!"

They raced for the car and Ray drove as fast as he could toward the Lile house. Sarah Jane was hanging on for dear life while urging him to hurry. Now they could see flames ahead and their dread intensified. "Oh please, not the house!" Sarah Jane murmured.

The scene that met their eyes as they rounded the last curve in the drive was appalling. Fully engulfed in flames, the Lile house was in ruins. For an instant shock overwhelmed them and the only sound was Sarah Jane's horrified whisper of "Mama!" Then she tore from the car and ran toward the house screaming, "Mama, Mama! My mama's in there!" The policemen stopped her just as Ray caught up with her.

"You can't go closer, ma'am. It's too dangerous. If your mama didn't get out, well…" his voice trailed off.

Sobbing, Sarah Jane clung to Ray. Ray patted her automatically but his mind was racing. He knew it could have been them inside that inferno. Indeed, he was sure it was *supposed* to have been him at least. He realized that his enemy would be satisfied with nothing less than Ray's destruction. He couldn't continue to put people in danger like this. It was his actions that had precipitated Weasel's murder. Mike had nearly been hung. He had surely caused Sarah Jane to lose her mother. Would Sarah Jane be next? Would he?

With sick fascination, nearly the entire town gathered to watch the destruction of one of the landmarks of historic Pecan Grove. Church services were abandoned as the town flocked to whatever vantage point was allowed. Rumors passed through the crowd that Cora Windham had died in the fire. Will Stewart stood at a distance with one arm around his wife, the other around his daughter.

"Oh, Will, the memories! My entire childhood up in flames! I thought I had come to share your view that it was just a house, but oh, it hurts to see this!" Kari was sobbing.

Kristen stood stoically on his other side. "How are you doing, dear one," he asked her.

"Dad, I feel *so* bad for *Ray* and *Sarah Jane*. They've lost everything - even Sarah Jane's mama! I-I thought a *house* could make me *happy*, but how *quickly* that can be *gone*. I've been *such* a *fool*! These last few *months* have *shown* me how *wrong* I was. Dad, I've *recommitted* to put *God* first in my life! Not Kristen." The last was murmured in a near whisper.

Will stood, awed at the enormity of the events of the day. Silently he prayed for those affected by the horrendous destruction, and found himself thanking a God who could bring a bit of good out of a mess of evil.

Ray would forever after think of that horrible day in terms of the contrasts: the heat of the fire at his back and the cold hatred for whoever did this; the softness of Sarah Jane's body against him and the hardness of his resolve to protect her; the sweetness of her love and the bitterness of knowing he would hurt her. He could never remember how they arrived at Pecan Grove's one hotel. He didn't remember who booked a room for him. He only remembered feeling a dreadful numbness as someone led Sarah Jane to a room, insisting that she get some rest.

—⁓—

The unreality of the events of the week made Chief Jones all the more determined to get to the bottom of the curse that was shaking Pecan Grove to its core. As the firefighters battled the blaze, he concentrated on talking to the bystanders.

"What can you tell me about this morning?" was his standard opening question. *Everyone* who lived within a mile reported hearing a muffled explosion. Some thought it was gunfire, some thought it was a car backfiring, and those who lived within a half mile often said they thought there was an earthquake because it seemed like the ground shifted. One elderly lady added that she saw Ray and Sarah Jane headed for church before it happened. She couldn't get out of her house much anymore, but she liked to keep an eye on who went to church on Sundays!

—⁓—

From the amount of debris scattered across the area and the ferocity of the blaze, it was apparent that the fire was preceded by an explosion. The comments of the bystanders confirmed that.

Chief knew that there would have to be arson investigators called. There was no way he would accept *this* as accidental!

For Sarah Jane the scene was etched in her mind as the end of the world - at least the end of the world as she knew it. Mama was gone, Ray seemed to withdraw, she had no home, no family, no hope. She wasn't sure how she got there, but she found herself in a hotel room with Dr. Swanson bending over her. He gave her a sedative and told her things would look brighter in the morning. She doubted that.

Late in the day, the Chief got around to calling on Ray at the hotel. He had plenty of suspicions regarding the man following Wayne Simonson, regarding the near hanging, and regarding Ray himself! He was convinced Ray knew more than he was saying and wondered again what he had to hide.

He found the younger man sitting in the lobby of the hotel. He seemed shell-shocked. Still grimy and smelling of fire, it was as if he hadn't moved since his arrival. "What's really going on Ray?" Chief asked gently.

"Sarah Jane," was all Ray could choke out. "Sarah Jane. Cora is dead, right? What will this do to Sarah Jane?"

"Try to pull yourself together, Ray. It's important that you help us out here. Sarah Jane will be best protected if we find out who is terrorizing you and this town. *What* do you know? *Who* do you suspect? You must have *some* idea!"

"Anything I think of is too far fetched. Why Cora? Why Mike? Why that Simonson guy? Why ME?"

"The site is too hot yet, but perhaps by tomorrow we'll be able to get a team in to examine the remains and see if we can figure out what exactly happened out there today. But somehow, it all connects to you, Ray. Something in your life is triggering this rash of violence. You *must* know something. Please, help us before someone else gets hurt!" Chief wondered how to get through to him, get through to the knowledge he must have, knowledge he may have repressed or that he refused to express.

Chief Jones had his men guarding the scene of the fire overnight. Roads accessing the area were blocked off and all who wished to pass were forced to register their identities and destination with the officers. He had called on the county sheriff to provide extra manpower to search the property and surrounding woods for debris from the explosion or other evidence.

By mid-morning Monday there were firefighters and arson investigators combing the property surrounding what had once been the magnificent Lile mansion. There was little evidence of the life that had been inside the building when it exploded, just grisly findings of a hand, a portion of a leg, bits of bloodied clothing. The young investigator in charge of the human remains was aware of the seriousness of his task and was collecting and labeling each part meticulously. By mid afternoon, he had enough puzzling evidence to cause him to interrupt the crusty chief investigator.

"Sir," he said politely, "there's something here I'd like for you to look at."

"What is it?" the Fire Marshall barked.

"Well, it's about the body parts, sir. They don't seem to match up."

"What the devil do you mean, don't match up? Of course they don't match up. They're fragments!"

"No, sir, I mean, yes, I know that. But it seems there are two left thumbs, sir. And one foot that looks like a male foot. Didn't you say there was *one female* on site, sir?"

The Fire Marshall hurried over to see. "Well, son of a biscuit," he muttered. "Trouble upon trouble."

Sarah Jane awakened in late morning to a feeling of dread. Her brain was still fuzzy from the sedative, her eyes felt like sandpaper ground over them with each blink, and her throat ached with the residue of salty tears. Her first thought was of Ray, and then she remembered her mother.

She gradually became aware of a figure at her bedside. "It's just me, Sarah Jane. Elise Griffiths."

"What? Why? Where is Ray?"

"The doctor thought you needed someone to sit with you. Some of us are taking turns. What can I get you?"

"Bathroom. Water. Ray." Sarah Jane's voice was little more than a croak.

"First things first," said Elise gently.

After Sarah Jane showered and dressed in some clothing the women had scrounged up, Elise went to see if she could discover Ray's whereabouts. But no one had seen him since shortly after he talked with the Chief of Police in the lobby the night before.

Elise insisted that Sarah Jane should have something to eat. "I don't think you've eaten since yesterday morning, honey. You need to take some nourishment. There are still some hard days coming."

"I need to know where Ray is!" Sarah Jane repeated.

"I'm sure he's dealing with the aftermath of the disaster, Sarah Jane. There's a lot to do and I'm sure there are a lot of questions that only Ray can answer. Would you like me to call Reverend Findley for you?"

"Yes, yes, I suppose you must. There's no doubt that Mama's dead? There's no hope?"

"I'm afraid not. Jase said there was nothing left after the fire burned down. Barely a brick left stacked on a brick."

Chapter Thirty-five

~

B ut Ray didn't return. The Chief came by looking to talk with him again but no one had seen him. Calls to his cell went unanswered. Sarah Jane was frantic and Chief Jones was worried.

"What if whoever blew up his house took him? What if they killed him? What if they're torturing him for information? You've got to find him!" Sarah Jane was nearly screaming in her anxiety.

"Don't panic yet, Sarah Jane. I'm going to check his room and perhaps we'll find out where he went."

After Chief finally got the hotel attendant to open the door to Ray's room, the search was short. The bed had not been slept in. Ray's wallet was on the dresser, with his credit cards and driver's license inside. There was no sign of a struggle. Only his cell phone and car keys were missing.

"I'm aware that he's in danger, Sarah Jane. We'll do all in our power to find him. Unfortunately, we're stretched thin on manpower right now."

"Perhaps it's time for the community to start a search, Herschel." Ruby had come to take over for Elise in staying with Sarah Jane.

"I guess you're right, Ruby. That young man got involved in something bigger than himself, I'm afraid. I'll call Will Stewart. He knows how to get these things organized."

"Maybe Bob and his hounds can help as well," Ruby suggested.

Within an hour citizens began gathering at the city park. Will had a county plat map and was dividing the volunteers into teams and assigning them each a section to search. They had strict instructions not to disturb anything that was remotely suspicious, but to call in to 'command central' as they called it. They were also instructed that sunset was 7:00 pm, so they should be leaving their sections by then. They didn't want anyone else lost.

There was no consoling Sarah Jane. She had a moment of hope when they reported Ray's Mustang had been found on a back road near the river and a police patrol responded. That hope was dashed when the Mustang was searched and found to have been stripped of any papers or belongings and wiped of fingerprints. The keys were found carelessly tossed near the back tires. Sarah Jane was sure that Ray had been kidnapped and perhaps thrown in the river.

Bob and his hounds were called out again, but the dogs seemed confused.. They kept running back and forth between the car and the nearby boat landing. Bob waded down the river with Lucy for a half-mile or more, thinking all the way. Bob had come to like and trust Ray, and wondered what would be gained by bringing him back to town. He figured Ray was either dead and floating to the Gulf, or he was trying to escape from someone who was trying to kill him. He figured that in the first case, there was nothing to be gained, and in the second - well, Ray deserved a chance, didn't he?

Most people thought they could cover their tracks by going through water, but Bob knew Lucy could follow Ray's scent all the way down the river to the Gulf of Mexico with no trouble. Around a bend in the river, he made his decision. He fussed with Lucy until she began to howl. Then he returned and reported that Lucy had lost the scent and it was useless for him to continue searching.

———

At the Lile place, the Fire Marshall had his hands full. His crew had found the cause of the blast to be a leaking connection to the new gas furnace. Leroy Roberts was called in for questioning. "When was that furnace installed? Who did the installation? Was it tested? Was there any way the connection could have worked loose?"

Leroy was sweating by the time the Marshall was done with him. But apparently he had given all the right answers because finally the Marshall grunted and said, "I already figured it couldn't be the installation or the house would have exploded in July, not September. I'm leaning toward the extra body being the arsonist. The arsonist who didn't get out in time."

———

One thing that was working in favor of Chief Jones and his crew was that the sensational nature of the explosion and the fact that it was the third time something catastrophic happened in sleepy little Pecan Grove had caused the entire country to sit up and take notice. They were promised no delay this time when they sent a print from the thumb they had found in to the state crime lab for comparison.

———

The citizen search resumed the next morning. This time it was the crew working the section of woods on the far side of the creek from the Lile property who called in a suspicious finding. It wasn't Ray, but at the top of the hill they'd found a trampled down spot. They almost didn't pay the spot any attention, but one of the guys, a little taller than the rest, noticed that he could see part of the Lile house from where he stood. He ventured to climb the tree and from there he had the perfect vantage point for watching anything that happened on the Lile property, even more so if you had binoculars! Looking closer the group saw a couple roaches from marijuana joints tossed carelessly into the brush. When the sheriff's deputy came for a proper investigation, he recognized the distinctive heel print that had been circulated earlier in the summer. Looking a bit further afield he noticed the faint path through the woods which led to a derelict hunting cabin deep in the overgrown underbrush near the lake.

The deputy had to work his way out to the road before he had cell service, but when he called in he was still so excited he could hardly talk. "Ch-chief! I found — I mean *we* found — well, *they* found…"

"Just spit it out, spit it out!" the Chief barked impatiently.

"It's a cabin sir. I-I mean it passes for a cabin. Really just a shack. A guy, well someone anyway, has been living here. I mean there."

To Chief Jones it seemed like forever before he got a coherent report from the deputy, but when he did he wasted no time in pulling his technicians off the explosion investigation and sending them to meet the sheriff's deputy. As the crow flies, it wasn't far from the house. By road, it took them 45 minutes to find the track where the deputy waited.

The days passed in a blur for Sarah Jane. Each day was a repetition of the one before with no news of Ray. She was certain that he was dead. She tried to get the police to drag the river, but had no energy to pursue it. What did it matter anyway? If he was dead, he was dead.

The memorial service for Cora was held on Friday. The church ladies did a great job of organizing it when it became apparent that Sarah Jane was incapable of making decisions. Reverend Findley preached his heart out, addressing Sarah Jane particularly, "We have to trust God. When we lose a loved one, we need to trust God that they are resting in heaven, held in His embrace forever. He is a loving God and will not abandon his own, even in death." Sarah Jane paid no heed. She felt that God had abandoned her, even before her death.

———

Chief Jones was careful to keep Sarah Jane informed of all they found, although he was afraid her depression would only worsen as she learned the truth. "There is no doubt that there was an intruder in the house when it exploded, Sarah Jane. The fingerprints match those found at the hunting cabin too, and also with a partial print we found on Wayne Simonson's wallet." Chief wondered at the blank expression on Sarah Jane's face. Was she even capable of comprehending?

He continued anyway. "When the analysis was complete, this man was found to be a low level gang member from St. Paul, Minnesota, Allan Schmidt. He left Minnesota about the same time as Mr. Simonson and our investigation indicates that he followed Mr. Simonson all the way here. We are looking into what the connection might be between these two men and Ray Jacobs, but we are convinced there is one.

"Are you understanding me, Sarah Jane?"

"Yes," she answered dully. "Two thugs from Minnesota got into a fight and one died. You think Ray was a third thug — but you're wrong!" In defending Ray, Sarah Jane came to life. "Ray was not a thug. Ray was good and kind and God-fearing. If they were after him, it wasn't because he was *involved* with them!"

Chapter Thirty-six

The endless days turned into a week, then two. Ruby and some of Sarah Jane's friends helped her rent a room at Bella's "for the time being." They knew Bella would look after her. Sarah Jane returned to her hostess job, albeit a shadow of her former exuberant self. At the Garden Cafe she heard rumors about Ray. People were saying he was a thief or a con artist; that he had skipped town with loads of money; that he was a cheap operator. Sarah Jane learned to ignore the innuendo that swirled around her. She only hoped to keep her job until she could leave town.

"Ruby, I'm going to leave this place as soon as I have the money." she said repeatedly. "There's nothing for me here, that's for sure."

"But, honey-child, where will you go?"

"Doesn't matter. Ray and I used to play a game, "Where in the World am I?" Ray made every place seem wonderful and exciting. I'll never forget Ray, you know. But in a different place, maybe I won't see his face at every corner."

One Saturday morning Daryl and Lisa Marshall came into the cafe. Daryl caught Sarah Jane and drew her aside before she seated them. "I'm on your side, Sarah Jane," he said. "Ray must have been killed by those thugs. Maybe he knew something about them and they had to silence him. Ray was good to me and to my family.

Moreover, he was good *for* me, he helped me get my confidence back. I just can't believe what people are saying about him."

Kristen Stewart was, surprisingly, another bright spot. "Sarah Jane, I apologize for all the nasty things I've ever said to you. I hope you can forgive me. I know years ago I lied about you to cover my embarrassment about Drew breaking up with me. I can't believe how shallow I allowed my life to become. Ray believed in me and for that I will be forever grateful. I would like to be your friend."

Sarah Jane was shocked. But she gave Kristen a hug and murmured that she hoped things would be better for them both in the future. She wasn't sure about this forgiveness thing and she didn't mention that she hoped to be long gone from Pecan Grove before they could ever be friends.

After a month had passed with no word about Ray, Dr. Swanson called the Securities and Exchange Commission. He finally reached someone who would listen to his problem. "I invested a large sum of money with a man here in Pecan Grove, Alabama. He has gone missing and may be dead. I want to know the status of my investment. Unfortunately, his office and all his records burned to the ground. I'm sure there are a number of other people in the area who are wondering also." Eventually, it was agreed that the situation merited an investigation.

By Thanksgiving it was official. There was no stock broker who was bonded and insured by the name of Ray Jacobs. Further investigation showed that stocks traded in Alabama followed the pattern set by a George Ray who had been active in Minnesota.

Adding to the scandal, the news was uncovered that George Ray had been imprisoned for misappropriation of funds. In short, he had stolen from a vulnerable adult.

This information made everything fall into place for Herschel Jones. He had been convinced that in Allan Schmidt they had their man, albeit a dead man. What he could never figure out was the connection between Allan Schmidt, Wayne Simonson and Ray Jacobs. After realizing that he had been wrong to believe *anything* Ray told him, he put in another call to Minnesota, but this time he called the St. Paul newspaper.

The newspaper searched their archives and immediately sent the Chief the report of George Ray's trial. They had also traced George Ray's employment history at the time of his arrest and discovered that Allan Schmidt was the son of a man George had worked for. They found out that Schmidt was furious when he realized George had been the recipient of his father's estate and had ranted to his friends that he'd "kill the bastard."

A bonus was a small article which said the only character reference for George Ray was his foster brother, John Wayne Simonson. Finally!

"Can you believe that all this mayhem was perpetrated by a man who was determined to get revenge?" Herschel commented to Jimmy. "I know Ray was involved in some questionable business up there and that he was definitely conning his customers here, but it appears the transaction that caused Allan Schmidt so much animosity was deemed to be perfectly legal."

As the news of a major financial scandal came out, the newspapers descended on Pecan Grove yet again. An investigative team from Mobile managed to ferret out the information that Ray

Jacobs, also known as George Ray, had invested only a fraction of the money that had been entrusted to him. Most of his investors would face financial ruin. They had lost all, or nearly all, of the money they had given him.

The newspaper listed the names of several people who had invested money with Ray. They began a highly popular series of articles interviewing each investor highlighting what the loss meant.

Most of the investors complained bitterly about Ray Jacobs. Comments such as "He claimed that God would bless me! I think he meant 'God would bless *him!*'" and "That was our children's college fund. We entrusted him to invest $20,000 but come to find out he only invested $2,000!"

Doc Rasmussen said, "I should have checked out the broker as carefully as I checked out the stock. However, the fraction of my money that *did* get invested is doing very well. If he had invested it all, he would be very wealthy and so would I!"

Among the victims were a few that refused to place the blame on Ray. "How can I blame his greed," said Pastor Stewart, "when it was *my* greed that led me to entrust Ray with money before I checked his credentials."

Daryl was loyal to a fault. "Ray Jacobs was the best thing that ever happened to me and my family. The money I invested is performing well. Oh, not as well as what Ray quoted, but a nice, steady return. Moreover, Ray gave me my confidence and my family back."

Kristen Stewart refused an interview, saying, "I'm too busy with classes and getting on with my life to waste time being bitter." Then she shrugged and added, "It doesn't matter anyway. Grandfather got the money through gambling, and I lost it the same way."

The entire town was incensed when the paper ran Dr. Swanson's story. They realized he would not be able to build his clinic without the money he'd lost. Some of the business owners in town started a fund to restore the money for the clinic, figuring it would be in their best interest. A clinic would attract new residents and new businesses.

Kent Kirkland became so bitter and angry it began to affect his preaching. He seemed desperate to replace the money he had invested and talked about suing Sarah Jane, the government, the SEC and whatever else he could think of. Jase wondered just how deeply in debt Ray had left the pastor.

With the findings by the Securities and Exchange Commission, the investigation was officially taken out of Chief Jones' jurisdiction. Although he hadn't technically solved anything, he was praised for doggedly assembling evidence that assisted the Federal investigation. The mayor had won the election, but Herschel doubted that he would stay on as chief for the complete term. The stress of this past year had made him realize he wanted to relax and enjoy his grandchildren before it was too late. He'd wait until the new detective they had hired settled in, then he would retire. He was just glad it wasn't his job to trace all the money that had disappeared from Pecan Grove.

Bob Huggens' pecan trees had produced an amazing harvest. He hinted to Mae that maybe they could afford a vacation to someplace warm. He credited his harvest to that early spring prayer in his orchard. But in his heart, he still wondered. Was Ray dead? or had Bob let a criminal escape when he called off the hounds? If so, Bob wondered if God could really have blessed his crop or did he somehow call up a darker spirit with that prayer?

———

Sarah Jane just kept her head down and continued going about her business as quietly as possible. She was surprised to see Rob Porter waiting for her as she trudged up the walk to Bella's one afternoon in December. "Good news, Sarah Jane!" he greeted her enthusiastically. "The insurance company has agreed to pay in full for the Lile house."

"Whatever. I suppose the investors will be fighting over that now," she murmured as she tried to brush past him.

"Don't tell me Ray never told you?"

"Told me what?" she replied with a small spark of interest.

"That he had signed the house over to your name. It was insured for its full value plus all the contents. You'll be quite a rich young lady."

"When?" she asked suspiciously. "I'm just trying to hang on until I can save enough money to get out of town."

"It should be completed in just a couple weeks. They said they're processing the check now." Rob patted her shoulder. "I understand a little of what you're going through. I lost my wife and kids in a bitter divorce. Everyone believed her lies about me. Now when I meet our former friends they look at me like I'm some sort of monster. But, just so you know, I miss Ray something fierce. He was so much fun! Life seems flat without him around cracking jokes all the time."

Sarah Jane began to cry, the first tears she had allowed to fall in a month or more. "Thank you, Rob. Thank you for everything."

As he turned to leave, Sarah Jane was struck with a thought. "Wait Rob — what happens to the land the house was on?"

"Well, that's yours as well, Sarah Jane. Do you want to sell it?"

"I've been thinking it would be nice to have a memorial where Mama died. Maybe I could donate the lot for a park? Maybe the Lile-Windham Memorial Garden?"

"That would be great! I'll get on it right away if you'd like."

———～～———

Just a few more weeks, Sarah Jane thought. And she almost smiled.

Chapter Thirty-seven

It was the uncertainty that was killing her, thought Sarah Jane. She could handle the fact that her mother had died, although the manner of her death was still a shock. In some ways Sarah Jane felt the freedom of having a lifelong burden lifted. She missed her mom the way she would miss a toothache - a pain that was always there. She had had enough failed love affairs to know her usually ebullient personality could bounce back from rejection in a short period of time. It was not knowing what had happened to Ray. That was the reality she couldn't deal with. That and the fact that Ray had become part and parcel of who she was. She ached deep in her bones for Ray.

It had taken longer than Rob expected, but finally the day came when she would be able to leave Pecan Grove. With Ray, she had thought she could either leave or stay and be happy. Now, without him, there was nothing here for her anymore. Especially since many in town looked at her as if she might know where Ray (and their money) had gone. Especially since most of those already thought she was just scum. Well, her bags were packed, she had said her goodbyes, she was working her last shift at the cafe and then she would be gone. She was going to cash the check for the insurance on the house and drive Ray's Mustang off into the sunset and never look back. She found it hard to believe it had only been a year since Ray had first walked into the Garden Cafe.

As Sarah Jane left the cafe for the final time, she was met in the parking lot by a strange old man. Bald as a billiard ball with a bristly gray goatee and thick glasses, he hobbled quite quickly with the aid of a cane. "Miss!" he called out in a husky old man's voice. "Miss! Are you called Sarah Jane?"

"Ye-es," she answered hesitantly.

"I've been asked to give Sarah Jane Windham this envelope. You fit the description. Here." He thrust a manilla envelope into her hand and turned, hobbling briskly away. She noticed that there was a taxi from Mobile waiting for him, and in a cloud of dust he was gone.

"Strange,'" she thought, turning the envelope over before slitting it open. "I almost felt I was looking into Ray's eyes there for a moment."

In the envelope was one item. The key to a safe deposit box at the Grove City Bank.

Well, that fit with her plan. She was planning to stop at the bank to cash her check anyway. She could find out what was going on with the mystery box at the same time.

The bank manager ushered her into a private room. "This room will be locked while you are here. Just press the buzzer when you are finished and there will be someone to open the door. Remember, it's 2:45 pm and we close at 4:00 sharp." his tone was impersonal although she had known him since she was a child.

Sarah found her hand shaking as she turned the key to open the box. The first thing she saw was an envelope with her name written in Ray's familiar scrawl. Her eyes prickled with tears at the sight. "How like Ray to send a message in this mysterious way," she thought.

The letter she unfolded started out: "If you are reading this, I am not dead." And Sarah Jane began to cry. Ray was alive! But why would he leave her when she needed him most? The letter continued: "I tried to go straight for you but my past caught up with me. Just know this, Sarah Jane, I love you. I know I will always love you; you will always be the only one for me. Take some time to decide, but if you decide you can still love me, open the package. Yours forever, Ray."

By now the tears were streaming down Sarah Jane's face. As she thought of Ray's dear face, his irrepressible grin, his charming dimples, his expressive eyes, she thought she didn't really need time to decide. But alongside her memories of his laugh, the easy camaraderie they shared and his kisses, came unbidden the question: But can I trust Ray? Would he change? Could she help him change?

What finally made the decision for her was thinking about the tender, compassionate and strangely vulnerable Ray that showed up when they were alone together. Yes, she loved Ray. She would always love Ray. She didn't care if what the townsfolk were saying was true - that he was a con artist and a fake - she knew the real Ray and she loved him with all her heart and soul. She opened the package.

As she read through the contents her face changed from tears to wonderment. Could she? Would she? Should she? The last thing in the box was a small brown envelope. When she opened it, a beautiful diamond solitaire with a tag that read "Be Mine," slid into her hand. As she slipped the ring on her finger, any remaining doubts fled away. With the hint of a smile teasing the corners of her mouth, Sarah Jane left the bank, left Pecan Grove, and, carefully following the instructions Ray had left for her, Sarah Jane Windham disappeared.

Epilogue: One year later

R uby Carter was walking through downtown Pecan Grove on her way to work. She waved at young Jimmy Fletcher; she had heard he was taking his duties much more seriously these days. She thought he was shaping up to be a very good police officer. She could hear Mark Griffiths' whistling accompanied by the rhythmic thump of the newspapers on the porches. She supposed Mark would be giving the route over to his brother Matt soon. But for now, everything in Pecan Grove was as it should be.

Ruby's brisk pace slowed a bit as she reflected on the many changes their town had seen over the past two years. It had been a difficult and unsettling time, but, for the most part, the town was stronger for it. Kristen Stewart was a case in point. When she realized the greater part of her inheritance was gone for good, she hardly blinked. Her new resolve to help battered women only got stronger. She began raising money by speaking at various venues. Who would have guessed her lilting manner of speaking combined with her deep southern drawl would make her a mesmerizing public speaker? Or perhaps it was the passion that went into her speeches. At any rate, she was able to purchase Bella's Bed and Board for a women's shelter. She called it 'Bella's Place'.

Bella herself had never recovered from Ray's duplicity. She felt that she should have been able to tell he was up to no good. She had that reputation for being able to sniff out evil, after all! She was only too glad to list her home with Daryl and move to a condo in New Orleans close to her children.

Ruby arrived at her new place of employment. She had accepted the offer to be one of the housemothers at Bella's Place. It wasn't so hard on her knees as Kristen had installed an elevator in place of the back stairs. Plus, she offered generous insurance benefits. Ruby was enjoying the change and she had someone to fuss over now that Zeke had moved out. All was not sweetness and light with Kristen — she still struggled with loving African Americans the same as others, but Ruby admired the way she was determined to overcome her upbringing.

Zeke himself, now that was another major change. It seemed that overnight Zeke had transferred his loyalty from Ray to Jase Griffiths. Jase was a much more worthy role model in Ruby's opinion. And, oh, the change in that boy! He had worked it out with the technical school to complete his few remaining credits online and then taken a job as web artist with the new health clinic. Recently, he and Mike Sheffield had rented an apartment together. Ruby couldn't be more proud.

Kristen greeted Ruby as she came into the office. "Oh, *good!* We have *such* a busy *day!*" She listed several things going on that Ruby would be responsible for, then added, "and I *almost* forgot. Elise Griffiths is bringing her little *boys* over to *play* with Tara's *kids* this afternoon so *Tara* can go for an *interview.*"

When Kent had become so bitter over the money he'd lost, Jase had talked to Chuck, telling him, "I'm pretty sure he still owed on the RV. I know the lease contract on that Lexus came with some pretty heavy penalties if he tried to cancel it. I just wish I had been able to find a reason to sound a warning about Ray before all this came down. I didn't want to slander the man without clear reason though."

"You were smarter than 'most everybody else in town. I tell you, I was this close." Chuck held his finger and thumb about a quarter inch apart, "to investing a hefty sum with Ray myself. But, maybe I ought to suggest the church board call in an accounting firm to see just what kind of damage his investment has done to our pastor's finances. Perhaps the church can help him get on track again."

"You're doing WHAT?!" Kent had nearly screamed when the board chairman told him about the upcoming audit. "I can't believe you don't trust your own pastor! I can't believe you're undermining God's appointed prophet for this church!"

However, when the accounting firm was finished they found that not only was he still in debt for the RV and behind in lease payments for the Lexus, but also most of the furnishings of his house had been purchased on a maxed-out credit card. When they moved on to the church's financial records, they realized that the pastor was skimming from the offerings to try to stay afloat. The Grove Gazette had a heyday when he was dismissed and Jase Griffiths took over as head pastor.

<hr>

When Elise came by the women's shelter, she and Ruby had a few minutes to talk. They saw each other more frequently now since Ruby and Zeke had started attending Bethel Bible Church. Ruby mothered Elise and her kids just like she did the women at the shelter. "Has Megan thought any more about where she wants to go for college?" Ruby asked.

"I think she's pretty settled on Pensacola Christian. It's not too far away and has a great nursing program."

"That's wonderful! Maybe she'll be able to get a job at the new clinic when it opens!"

"Isn't it amazing how the community pulled together to get the clinic built after Dr. Swanson lost all the money he had raised?" Elise was pensive. "I think it's a good thing for the town to be invested in the clinic. This way it's "The Grove Clinic," and it could have been "Swanson's Swanky Sickroom" or something!"

"I was thinking just this morning about all the changes that took place as a result of Ray's treachery," Ruby replied, just as Kristen came into the room. "He encouraged people to pray for God's blessing and they expected that would mean money. But I think God *did* bless people in much more lasting and rewarding ways!"

"That is *so* true, Ruby!" Kristen joined the conversation. "But I always wonder what happened to Sarah Jane. In a way, she invested more than anyone else: she gave Ray her heart!"

"And how are you doing with everything that Ray's sojourn here cost you, Kristen?" Elise asked.

"You know, I always believed that as the last in the Lile lineage it was up to me to preserve the way of life my mom and grandma had grown up with. When Ray relieved me of my excess money and the house burned, I realized I was free from that burden, too. For that I will always be grateful to Ray. But I feel sorry for him — and Sarah Jane too. They never came to know the peace of God and the peace with God that I feel now."

"I'm not sure I'm as forgiving of Ray as all that," Ruby replied. "But I do pray that as Sarah Jane traveled she was able to find peace and love in a different setting. She certainly never found that in Pecan Grove."

Acknowledgements

I have enjoyed this initial foray into the world of writing. There have been many who have encouraged and supported this effort, but special thanks are due to several people.

First of all, I would like to thank my husband, Rich, for his constant encouragement, support and endless plot development discussions. Thanks also to our adult children for their willingness to read and critique my fledgling attempts and also for their contribution to the anecdotes in this book. You guys are the best!

My sisters, Julie Phend and Jan Oldenburg, both authors in their own right, donated their valuable time and energy in editing this manuscript. I couldn't have, and wouldn't have, done it without their help and encouragement!

And always, I thank God for any ability He has given me. I pray that He will be glorified through this book.